KILLER OF KINGS

Kiru Taye

First Published in Great Britain in 2020 by
LOVE AFRICA PRESS
103 Reaver House, 12 East Street, Epsom KT17 1HX
www.loveafricapress.com

Available in eBook and paperback

KILLER OF KINGS

YADILI SERIES

DEDICATION

To Nma Bekee,
When I think of badass women I know, you are one of them. In my next life, I choose you as my sister again. Love you.

ACKNOWLEDGEMENTS

I want to give a special mention to Oluwakemi. You made this story happen. Thank you.

And thank you to Edits by Modus for your help.

PART ONE

ONE

THE TARGET stepped out of the car. The door was held open by one of the bodyguards while the other stood by the front door of the white two-storey mansion.

The glow from the floor-level spotlights accentuated the deep lines on the man's umber-hued face, making him appear older than in the photograph. His gaze swept along the driveway as if he sensed something out of place.

Back pressed against the rough wall, Xandra remained frozen where the shadows swallowed her in the alcove between the brick perimeter fence and the hibiscus hedge. She wore nothing that would reflect the light—dark clothes, a hood over her head and a mask shielding her face. The morning was wet, cold, and dark, dawn still a few hours away. Her gaze stayed on him as she mentally confirmed he was the man she wanted.

Dimi Yahya. Forty-nine years old. Six feet tall. Eighty-five kilos. Grey hair grew at the sides of his neatly cut, short dark hair. His facial hair was shaved off, although a shadow showed on his chin. He dressed in an expensive, opaque, fitted suit that would've been made especially for him and his polished shoes shone under the streetlamp.

From this distance, his eye colour wasn't visible, but it would be brown—she'd seen it in the photograph sent over with his file.

Yahya walked down the narrow path.

Xandra waited. The car door obscured her line of fire.

The bodyguard shut it, giving her an opening.

She squeezed the trigger of the FN Five-seveN with a smooth, even pressure.

Fat drops of rain splattered on the pavement masking the *p-taff p-taff* of the suppressed gunshots. The man slumped against the side of the car with a dull thud, hit twice in the sternum in rapid succession.

The bodyguard by the front door let out a low curse as he spotted his colleague falling and ran towards Yahya, hand reaching inside his jacket.

Xandra squeezed out another couple of rounds of low-powered, subsonic 5.7mm bullets. The copper-enclosed lead tore through the skin of his back and neck. He collapsed forward, hitting the ground with a muted *thunk*, arm outstretched toward his boss.

Yahya froze in a crouch behind the car, eyes sweeping the area as he pulled out his handgun and held it ready to shoot. "Who are you? Be a man. Show yourself!"

Melting out of the darkness, Xandra took a measured step forward.

Yahya's eyes widened as soon as he saw her. It seemed he recognised her. That would be impossible considering she was covered from head to toes.

He understood her purpose, though—his death—and straightened confidently, the rain plastering wet clothes to his body.

"I'll pay you double—no—triple whatever he's paying you to kill me," he offered.

Her response was to squeeze the trigger of the FN Five-seveN in her hand and put a bullet through Yahya. He collapsed to his knees, a hole in his chest, right of his breastbone. She fired another shot into his head, right between the eyes just to be sure. In this job, there was no room for mistakes.

The expended cartridges clinked on the stones and rolled into a forming puddle shimmering with dull orange light.

He fell back onto the paved driveway, his mouth slackened as he expelled his last breath. Perhaps from surprise that she hadn't accepted his bribe. Maybe one of his men would have taken the money, and he would've done the same.

However, her survival so far depended on fulfilling the terms of a contract once accepted. In a cutthroat and ruthless business, agreements were binding. There to be honoured and delivered.

Any person on her hit-list was as good as dead. She had never reneged on a contract before.

Wouldn't start now. Not for money. Not for anything.

She took the time to observe the area. It was still early for anyone to be out and about in the quiet, neighbourhood of detached houses surrounded by high fences on a cul-de-sac. No lights or movement flickered in any of the nearby windows. Even if someone was out there, they would only see an unidentifiable person in a dark outfit in the rain.

Yahya's mansion stood on a secluded corner. The tall hedges and wall surrounding the house meant no one would see the dead men on the ground. No one would have heard the gunshots. Not with the subsonic ammunition, a suppressor, and the added benefit of the splattering raindrops.

Not seeing anyone else, she squatted and picked the cartridges. She checked the FN's magazine. Fourteen left. Checking was part of her routine for staying alive. She always had to know how many bullets she had available. Even the spares.

Losing count was only an invitation to death.

She pocketed the cold, wet items, unscrewed the suppressor and placed it inside the pocket of her hooded top.

Squatting, she heaved Yahya's body over her shoulder. Then she jogged up the stairs into the already opened front door. The hallway light was on, but she flicked it off. Having studied the blueprint for the house, she knew exactly where to go.

Inside the office, she strode to a Rembrandt painting hung on the wall. She lowered Yahya, glad to be rid of the eighty-five-kilogram deadweight. Searching the side, she found a switch and clicked it. The painting slid along a rail and revealed a safe. Propping Yahya to stand in front of her, she held his head up with her left hand. Once the retinal scanner beeped, she placed his right hand on the palm reader. Another beeping sound and the safe door popped open. An internal white light displayed the content—bundles of cash, passports, and a small black flash drive.

Yahya's body slid to the floor as she reached into the safe. Pushing the bundles of cash aside, she took the flash drive and slipped it into her pocket. It barely seemed enough reason to have a man killed. But the contract had been specific. Kill Yahya and retrieve a flash drive from his safe.

She wasn't here to analyse the reasons why one man should live, or another should die.

Neither did she care about the contents of the flash drive.

Job done. She headed outside, but not to the front entrance.

She strode down the hall to the large kitchen. In the dark, she still made out spotless surfaces and expensive gadgets as she unlocked the side door. Slipping out quietly, she hurried across the garden, staying on the winding, stone path, avoiding the blue, glimmering pool. A small gate stood at the back wall. The men had already disarmed the alarm, so it didn't go off as she shifted the lock and pulled the metal panel open.

Back on the pavement, her gaze swept the area again for signs of exposure, but there were no people or cars in sight, no footsteps to be heard. The rain had slowed to a drizzle.

With a steady pace and ensuring her heart rate was slow, she walked two streets down to where she parked her car, making sure she wasn't followed. Inside it, she pressed the button for the ignition, checked the mirrors and pulled out onto the road. A half-moon sat in the dark sky as she drove the two hours to her apartment in Jokogi. Halfway there, she stopped at a lay-by and changed the fake number plates of the car over before removing her mask and pushing the hood down from her head.

The sky was tinting grey of dawn as she rolled up the drive of her two-level Bauhaus style house and clicked the remote to open the garage door electronically. She drove in and waited for the garage door to close before getting out of the car. The space was large enough for two vehicles and painted white. There was no place for an intruder to hide.

Punching the code for the door, she unlocked it, strode into the house, and made sure the panel shut behind her. She went through each room, checking that none of the intruder alert seals she'd put in place had been dislodged.

The windows were designed to allow sunlight in but remained obscured from the outside as well as being bulletproof. She had invested in solar energy which meant she didn't have to depend on the national grid for steady electricity supply. Once satisfied no one had gotten in or was currently lurking anywhere in the house, she strode into the bedroom.

Pulling the flash drive out of her pocket, she slipped it into a white, opaque plastic pill bottle, stuffed cotton wool around it and sealed it. To anyone else, it looked like an ordinary bottle of painkillers. She strode into the bathroom and put it among the other items in the cabinet above the sink. In there, it looked even more unremarkable.

Perhaps that's what Yahya should have done instead of hiding it inside a high-tech safe. Technologies designed by humans were hackable by other humans. She used gadgets because they made life more comfortable, but she always had a backup.

Stripping down, she stepped into the shower cubicle. Under the warm spray, an image of Yahya slumped on the paving stone returned. His brown eyes seemed filled with accusation.

Her chest tightened, making it difficult to breathe for a few seconds. She turned off the faucet before stepping out. With a white towel slung around her chest, she reached into the discarded black trousers and pulled out her phone. Leaning on the counter, she drew in a long breath and typed out a short, encrypted note.

Need to confess.

The constriction in her chest eased when she pressed the send button. She tossed the phone on the counter and went about tidying up. She picked the clothes she'd taken off and walked across to the laundry room. Then she loaded the machine, continuing the routine that restored her life to normalcy after a kill.

Grabbing a water bottle from the fridge in the kitchen, she returned to the bedroom just as her phone beeped. Her heart rate sped up as she hurried to retrieve the gadget from the bathroom counter. She read the message.

Arufin. 10 pm.

Closing her eyes, she exhaled in relief even as a spike of adrenaline rushed through her. She had over twelve hours to kill. Time to catch up on sleep. She wouldn't get much of it tonight if everything went to plan.

TWO

'YOU HAVEN'T lived until you've been to Arufin.'

The actual quote was 'You haven't lived until you've lived in Lori Osa.' But the phrase could be applied to the club.

Lori Osa was an overcrowded megacity that accommodated the spectrum of humanity from the richest to the poorest.

One of the best things to have sprouted out of the largest city in the region was Club Arufin. Like the name, the place was for misfits and renegades. But most of all, it was a pleasure club. Whatever you desired could be acquired at Arufin—sex, drinks, drugs, even rock 'n' roll. It had it all. For the right price, of course.

It had been a while since Xandra had been here.

In her line of work, she could never trust anyone enough to fully relax in their company.

Here, she was anonymous. It didn't mean she could drop her guard. But she'd found an equilibrium that provided what she needed and still maintained a level of caution.

Outside the charcoal-walled, brick building, she didn't wait to queue in the line snaking around the block. Instead, she strode to the discreet side entrance tucked in an alleyway and tapped on the black door. A burly man opened it three seconds later and waved her in when she raised the black card with Arufin embossed in gold across the top. Her host had couriered the card over when she'd sent the request to meet up.

She walked into the dimly lit foyer where a man in a grey shirt sat behind the glass screen.

"Good evening. Welcome to Arufin. Card, please."

She placed the card on a small electronic machine. It beeped as the man watched the screen before he nodded.

"Please take the lift to the top floor and go to the blue room. You'll need to swipe the card on the panel to gain entrance." The man smiled as he looked up at her.

"Thank you," she replied before heading to the private lift.

The floor beneath her sneakers vibrated from the bass thumping in the club. She looked longingly at the doors leading to the main arena. Sometimes she yearned for the freedom that would allow her to get lost in the crowd of revellers. Unfortunately, she couldn't afford such an indulgence.

Shaking her head, she pressed the button to call the boxcar. Her host had a few rules if she wanted his company.

First. Anonymity. Going into the dance hall would mean others would be aware of her presence. The fewer people who knew her whereabouts, the better.

Second. No alcohol. He'd refuse to play if she had one drop of liquor. Water was the only drink permitted while she was upstairs with him.

Both rules worked fine for her. Intoxicants dulled the senses and slowed reflexes. Also, entering the building undetected aside from security, provided anonymity.

At the top floor, she stepped out of the metal box into the well-lit hallway. The place looked like a luxury hotel—expensive silver brocade wallpaper, the plush grey carpets and the crystal chandeliers.

Striding to the door with the word 'Blue' written in gold cursive on a black plaque, she inserted the card into the slot, and the lock clicked open. Pushing the slab, she entered the studio.

This was the most basic and functional of the rooms at Arufin. She'd seen the other suites before she'd chosen this one. Named 'Blue' for the colour of the walls and coordinated furniture. There was a large titanium grey metal frame bed with a thick mattress covered in cerulean sheets at one corner. A small table and matching armchair stood next to it.

At the other end, a swing, nylon straps and metal chains hung from a hook in the white ceiling.

A navy wooden St Andrew's cross leaned on a wall. Similar coloured shelving units with rows of drawers beneath stood further down.

On the shelves were a range of floggers, whips, canes and paddles. In the drawers would be ropes, ties, cuffs, collars, clamps, plugs and other items. She'd seen them before.

She took her jacket off and hung it in the wardrobe, patting the inside pocket as routine to make sure the FN Five-seveN pistol and suppressor were in place. Being without her weapons of choice made her feel naked more than taking her clothes off did.

It couldn't be helped in this situation. The rules meant being totally bare for what would come next.

In any case, the process of stripping down was therapeutic, clearing her mind and stripping away any lingering concerns.

Stepping back, she toed off her shoes and spread the socks on top, lining them up at the bottom of the closet. Methodically, she undid the steel cufflinks, which doubled as poisoned darts when uncapped. Unbuttoned the stylish tunic with slits at the sides for smooth movement and weighted hems for concealing weapons. Then she placed the links in the top drawer and hung the shirt in the closet. Finally, she removed the chemise, trousers and panties.

Naked, she walked over to the box in a corner and sat on the narrow wooden bench. A sound outside the room made her straighten, body tensed and alert.

She'd done this several times. Still, a part of her worried about being found out. About being weak and open to attack.

A few seconds later, the door to the suite opened. A man walked in wearing a long black priest robe with the stiff white collar. The black leather boots beneath indicated this wasn't a real priest before she saw his face.

He was at least ten years older than her. Thick dark hair on his head, a dash of grey interspersed the neatly trimmed stubble on his chin. His weathered skin indicated a man who enjoyed the outdoors. With robust, asymmetrical features and a tall, rigid frame, he commanded attention in any space he occupied.

Some of the tension left her body, muscles relaxed.

He was Osagie Peters. Businessman. Powerful. Dangerous.

She was Xandra Gowon. Assassin. Powerful. Dangerous.

They were a match. Not in the way people might expect.

Their arrangement was contractual. Theatrical, almost. A play of sorts.

He provided what she needed and, conversely, she served him, only within these walls. Silently, he approached the other side of the latticed screen and sat in the chair.

They'd played this game a few times before. Anticipation made her hands tremble. Being in a vulnerable situation and displaying herself to him made her breathless, considering he was a ruthless man. He could have a weapon hidden beneath the flowing robe.

Their first meeting had been in Arufin. She'd come looking for something to take the edge off the weight threatening to crush her.

A week earlier, she'd executed a job involving a politician, his wife and their bodyguard.

Afterwards, she'd become restless.

As a child growing up in an orphanage where the nuns flogged the badly behaved children, she had learned to associate the atonement of wrongdoing with the pain of corporal punishment.

Then Tiye Himba had bought her and had trained her to become a killing machine.

However, none of the training had been able to scrub the Catholic guilt from her mind when she'd undertaken her first kill. Unable to visit a priest to confess her sins and seek penance, she'd resorted to self-flagellation.

Until she'd killed a woman for the first time. The self-reproach hadn't reduced the guilt.

She'd ended up at Arufin with a man who took her to one of the rooms. He'd tried to tie her up without her consent. She'd hit him, almost killed him before security arrived with Osagie.

Instead of throwing her out, Osagie had taken her to his office and spoken to her. He'd explained he could help her. Since then, she visited Arufin only to see him.

Osagie had once asked her to work for him. She'd turned him down. Her loyalty was to the Himba clan.

However, Don Himba wouldn't be happy if he found out about Xandra's twisted cravings.

Hence the need for the discrete visits to Osagie and the implicit level of trust required between them. They had a lot to lose if anything went wrong.

"In the name of Arufin, I will hear your confession, child," Osagie said in a smooth, deep voice.

Head bowed forward in contrition, Xandra said the words of penitence. "Bless me, father, for I have sinned. It's been three months since my last confession."

One childhood confession replayed in her mind.

The other kids had delighted in making fun of her and calling her ugly names. Every time she'd complained to the nuns, they hadn't done anything to stop it. One day she had taken matters into her hands. When a kid called her a freak, she jabbed him in the throat. A nun had dragged her to the confession box and made her testify to the priest.

She'd learned valuable lessons from the event.

Firstly, people respected strength more than weakness. The kids never picked on her again because they knew she would hit back and wasn't afraid of the punishment.

Secondly, never get attached to anyone or anything. The nuns sold her to Himba and sent her away from the only home she'd known.

Mostly, repentance was cleansing.

These days, she wouldn't consider revealing sins to a stranger. Priest or not. She would have to kill the person afterwards.

Now, this staged performance provided the same mental purification without the hazards.

"What are your sins, child?" Osagie asked the question she had come to expect from him as part of this routine.

"I used rude words many times." This was the easiest to confess, a remnant from childhood when you had to admit after using colourful language. She always started with the easy sins and ended with the most difficult.

"I lust after men and women." She never confessed this sin in the past tense as it was a part of her. Something that no amount of contrition would ever wipe out.

"I've killed fifteen people in five years." Including the three men, she'd killed this morning.

Delivering death was her job, what she'd been trained for. While other teenagers were in high school, she had spent the time in a military facility being taught a hundred and one ways to take lives. This was another sin she couldn't escape. Another part of who she was.

After she left the military facility into the employment of Don Himba, she'd been excited about being able to utilise the skills that she'd learned. She hadn't given thought to the people she'd be ordered to execute. She'd been eager to show loyalty and to belong to a group with a defined purpose.

Soon, she found out that even in a group of gangsters, she was still considered a freak and an outsider, first, as a woman in a man's world. Then as an assassin. The men feared her. They knew if the boss ordered a hit on them, she wouldn't hesitate to pull the trigger.

"I feel anger when I think about the orphanage." Her back muscles tightened, and her jaw ached. This was the big one. The big sin. The infested cancer eating her up inside. If she ever went back to the orphanage, she would put bullet holes through the skulls of the mother-nuns.

What else should she feel? They had sold her to Don Himba, who moulded her into a monster.

"Say your act of contrition," Osagie said in a firm yet soothing voice, drawing her out of her messed up thoughts.

"I'm sorry for my sins. Please help me to do my penance and to do better," Xandra said, injecting remorse into the words.

"I absolve you of your sins. Go and stand before the cross to begin your penance."

She counted out five heartbeats before walking over to the St Andrew's cross. Facing the wall, she listened for him.

Fabric rustled as he took the robe off first and then the t-shirt underneath.

She stretched hands and legs across the bars as wide as she could go while keeping balance and gripped the wooden frame.

As part of their agreement, she wouldn't be restrained physically. She could never give anyone that level of control over her body. Not even Osagie.

Still, she offered her body in this manner.

This wasn't romantic. Nor was it supposed to be.

Sex was a minor side, and sometimes it didn't happen during the session.

Once she left here, he didn't contact her and vice versa until they both wanted to book a new meeting. Usually, she was the one requesting to see him.

His boots thudded against the bare floor as he strode over to the rack. He was a striking man with tattoo artworks all over his arms, chest and back. His narrow hips and long legs were in black trousers. He reached for one of the thin, black rubber canes on the rack, weighing it in his hand and running his palm along its length as he checked it. He flicked it through the air, and it made a swishing sound that promised an intense sting.

Satisfied, he strode over to stand behind her. His warmth settled on her skin just as his breath fanned her ear and nape. "For your penance, you will receive thirty strokes of the cane."

Two strokes for every person she'd killed. Just what she needed. Pulse racing, she closed her eyes.

"Yes, sir," she replied in a breathless voice.

THREE

SWISH.
THWACK.
Sting.
Flinch.
Grunt.
Breathe.
Repeat.

This was how it started. The steady rhythm of the strikes made Xandra anticipate each one, yet unprepared for its impact on her body. Soon her back flamed and the burn detonated all over nerve-endings.

Halfway through, she struggled to keep count of each hit, brain now consumed by hurt. Mind kicked into 'fight' or 'flight' mode, adrenaline flooding her veins. Fingers dug into the wooden frame as her grip tightened. Otherwise, she'd lash out at the man behind her.

He was confessor. Punisher.

She deserved every blow. Every hurt. For the sins she'd committed. For the lives she'd taken.

Please stop. I won't do it again.

Gritting her teeth, she fought against the pleading cry threatening to escape. A promise to stop would be an outright lie. The day she stopped being a hitwoman would be the day she died. Taking the punishment was the only way to absolve her crimes.

The grunts turned heavier. Knees weakened, she clutched the cross with painful digits, determined not to crumple onto the cold floor. Defeat wasn't for her.

Lungs constricted, she struggled to breathe, only managing shallow inhales and exhales. Dizziness made her body sway at each impact. Just when black spots hovered on the periphery of her eyesight, the strikes stopped.

Leaning against the cross, she tried to catch a breath, to get her balance back.

Osagie stood beside her, raising her right arm over his shoulders so he could support her.

"I'm okay." Her voice sounded alien as she struggled and tried to pull away. She never liked showing weakness.

In the two years since she'd been meeting up with him, he offered aftercare each time.

She always rejected it. She was suspicious of any form of affection.

In the context of what they had; he felt the need to complete the cycle—from confessor to punisher to comforter to lover. He could wear all those hats if she let him.

But she didn't want their 'relationship' to become more than it was.

She didn't care who else he played with when she wasn't here. She didn't care if he had a harem of 'lovers' at his beck and call.

All she cared about? That he was available when she needed him.

Osagie didn't let go. "No, you're not okay. Thirty was more than you've ever taken before. You're going to let me take care of you. Or this is the last time I do this with you."

Turning her head, she looked at his face. His lips were stretched in a taut line. His eyes were blocks of glinting granite. He wasn't going to negotiate this. If she didn't allow him to take care of her, this would be the last time.

Narrowing her eyes, she flexed her arm, shaking him off. He let go but didn't back away.

They glared at each other, both trying to assert dominance over the other and take control of the situation.

Locking her knees, she balled hands into fists. Her body became weak as the initial surge of adrenaline waned. She was using the last of it just to stand upright. Her pulse sped up, the beats whooshing as her anger rose.

"What the fuck, Osagie? This isn't our deal," she said through gritted teeth.

He crossed his arms over his chest and raised one dark eyebrow. "Our deal states that while we're both in here, I'm in control and you do what I say."

"Yes, but the rules also say I only do the things that are within my limits, damn it."

His eyes turned cold and hard. "I was just trying to help you over to the bed so you could rest and I could apply some salve to your back. How is that beyond your limit?"

He was correct. She hadn't explicitly named 'aftercare' in the hard limits. "But you've never insisted before."

"Because you've never been this—" He paused as if searching for the right word. "—exhausted before."

He said, "exhausted."

But she heard, "weak, vulnerable, powerless." Her spine stiffened, her chin rising.

"Blue," she said, ending their session there and then with the simple safe word.

Something flickered in his gaze that she didn't recognise. He nodded and stepped away, turning his back as he strode to where his navy-blue shirt hung over a chair. He slid his arms in, buttoned and tucked it in before facing her, hands shoved into the pockets of his black trousers.

"You know, one day, someone is going to strip control from you totally. You won't be able to do anything without his permission."

She suppressed the desire to laugh in derision at his words. To refute them. She should ask him why he hadn't attempted to assert his authority over her.

If any man could've tried, it was him. He had enough men in this building to attempt to overpower her. He could try sedating her with drugs. He had the resources, and it wasn't beyond him to do something like that.

But he hadn't. So, what was the point of someone else trying? She would kill anyone who attempted to force her. She would never give up control for anyone.

"And, no, I'm not that man," he said as if reading her mind. One corner of his lips curved up in a half-smile. But the look in his eyes was a mix of frustration and understanding. "Take care of yourself, Xandra."

Without waiting for a response, he strode to the door.

"Osag—" her voice sounded shaky. Coughing, she cleared the lump that had suddenly formed in her throat. "Osagie, do I need to barricade the door when you leave? Do I need to have weapons ready when I walk out of the room?"

He jerked his head to the side so he could look her in the eyes. "Although our agreement is over, our truce still remains. You can visit Arufin anytime you want. My men won't harm you in any way unless, of course, you're trying to harm me."

He smiled as he spoke, his meaning clear—If she ever threatened him or his business, he wouldn't hesitate to order her execution.

"Thank you," she said, feeling a little release of tension in her shoulders. She hadn't been relegated to 'rival' status as it had been before.

He nodded, turned the lock and opened the door. Then he was gone, the slab of wood slamming behind him.

Her knees buckled, and she slumped to the hard, cold floor, head bowing from exhaustion. She stayed there for a few minutes and concentrated on gulping in air and regaining some equilibrium.

No matter how much she tried to shake it, a knot wound her belly tight about not seeing Osagie again in a personal capacity. They'd had a satisfactory arrangement. Not in a conventional sense. Still, it had worked. Why did he have to ask for something she couldn't give him?

She dragged her body to a standing position and walked to the closet. Methodically, she put the clothes on and grimaced. Her back still burned from the cane lashes, aggravated when the cotton grazed the sore skin.

She puffed out a sigh. If Osagie had stayed, the session would have progressed to sex.

The last time, she'd been bent over the bed, him behind her, fucking her. Their moans and groans had filled the air along with the musky scent of sex and sweat, the sting of it on her sensitive skin intensifying the experience.

Her pussy clenched and she moaned, scrubbing a hand over her face. She could undress and pleasure herself with her hand or use the shower. But she didn't want to stay here any longer than necessary, in case Osagie changed his mind about maintaining the truce.

Her phone buzzed as she tied the laces of her fancy sneakers. She pulled it out from the pocket of her tunic, entered the encryption code to unlock it.

There was a message from Zoe Himba: *Zoe's. 1 pm. Bring the parcel.*

Xandra sent a reply: *Got it.*

Messages sent between them were encrypted to prevent anyone else intercepting them. Still, Zoe didn't want anyone linking any of Xandra's activities to Don Tiye Himba. So, they kept contact simple.

Checking the room one last time, she headed for the door. Her hand was hidden in the pocket of the tunic, covering the gun in case she had to use it. She would aim and shoot through the fabric if necessary.

She opened the door a crack, listened for sounds. Nothing. A peek into the hallway showed that it was empty. She walked to the lift. The ride down was without event. Music still thumped from the main club floor. The reception desk lay empty.

"Good night," the guard at the exit said.

She nodded in response, exited the building and glanced at her watch, five minutes past three o'clock in the morning.

The partial moon was obstructed by a dark cloud, and most of the earlier revellers were either inside the club or had gone home. Stragglers remained in the streets, staggering drunkenly or chatting noisily with their friends. A few streets down, a car with steamed windows rocked in place.

Xandra could imagine the fun the people in there were having, reminding her of what she'd missed with Osagie tonight. The only regret of her life—she couldn't have intimate relationships the way other people did.

Sighing, she strode to her car, checked it for any trackers or explosive devices and got inside. She left the window open on the drive home, grateful for the chilly air on her face chasing the tiredness away. Five hours later, she repeated the usual security routine before stripping, taking a shower and crawling into bed. She managed to set the alarm on the phone before sleeping.

***

Zoe's was an African fusion restaurant in a neighbourhood of designer boutiques and tea shops. It had flower boxes of orange tulips, dark wooden tables and cushioned seats set up outside on the terrace overlooking the river.

Two Himba crew members, Vanni and Bruno, sat at a table, smoking cigarettes and playing a draughts board game. They acknowledged Xandra in greetings and chatted briefly.

Inside, Zoe met her with a warm, tight hug that lingered longer than it should. Zoe was the 'handler' or 'intermediary' for want of a better word. She negotiated the contracts with the clients and loaded them onto the server.

"How are you doing, Xan? We don't see you around anymore unless Papa summons you."

Smiling coquettishly, she batted her thick, black lashes.

Shrugging, Xandra extracted herself. "You know how it is. How are you doing?"

"Waiting for you to sweep me off my feet." She winked.

Xan chuckled at the joke. "Abeg. Your father will use me for cooking pepper soup if I ever looked at you that way."

Zoe had never hidden her attraction to Xandra, and they'd once shared a brief kiss.

However, while Xan desired the pleasures of a willing adult, she didn't want the complications or the bad blood associated with a failed relationship with her boss's daughter.

"Oh, come off it." Zoe waved one hand in dismissal as she arranged the centrepieces on the tables unnecessarily. "I can convince Papa that the two of us will make a formidable team."

Zoe was the daughter of Don Himba and, at twenty-nine, one of his capos. When she'd left university with a law degree, her mother had wanted her to settle down and marry a *nice young man*. Instead, she'd gone to work for her father. Whoever married her would become the future Don. That was pretty much guaranteed. A few men had their eyes on her, although she remained single.

"And you think the men will accept a woman in charge of them?" Xan asked the obvious question.

If there was anyone in the Himba family that Xandra could trust, it would be Zoe. But the other woman's first loyalty was to her father and the business.

"If it were just you..." Zoe shrugged. "But you and me? No one can touch us. Think about it." She waved her hand towards the stairs and smiled. "Go on up. Papa is waiting."

Xan returned the smile. "I'll think about it. It's good to see you again, Zoe."

"Same here."

FOUR

TWO WEEKS later, Xandra left home before dawn, travelling east to Bakili. A six-hour drive across the glittering River Niger, bustling midsized towns, emerald green rain forests, and rolling acres of farmed land.

Of course, a road trip across the country would not be complete without the usual police or military personnel at checkpoints asking for monetary tips. She handed out a few of those to avoid any delays.

However, restlessness plagued her. A couple of rest stops to stretch her legs and use the bathroom didn't help.

All because of the new kill contract.

Xan was primary, and she got the first refusal. Not that she had ever refused a contract.

She took on the job and executed it without questions.

But, on seeing the dossier of the latest target, her scalp had prickled with disquiet.

So, she'd gone digging for more information. She'd hacked into Zoe's computer and found out the hit had been ordered by Ralph Nweke.

More searching provided details about the man. Mr Nweke was the Commissioner for Justice and State Attorney General in Bakili. Why would someone charged with upholding the laws want someone killed? Granted, many corrupt government officials allowed the cartels to flourish.

The target was probably involved in criminal activities.

She shoved away misgivings, putting them down to the termination of the agreement with Osagie. She wasn't one to obsess or mourn the loss of anything. Still, she hadn't expected it to end abruptly.

She arrived at Bakili city, driving past the famous roundabout with its glittering water fountain towards the hotel she'd booked.

As she pulled into the hotel parking spot, a dark cloud of foreboding hovered over her. Eyes closed, she sucked in a deep, calming breath.

She was Xandra and afraid of nothing.

"Welcome, Madam." A man in a sky-blue t-shirt, black trousers and black leather boots greeted as she walked to the entrance. "My name is Thomas."

"Thank you, Thomas," she injected a twang to skew her usual speech pattern and make it sound more local. She needed to be incognito and didn't want to stand out.

Same reason she wore a long, fringed wig, contact lens and makeup to change her facial features.

In her skirt suit, she looked like an everyday businesswoman.

"Can I take your luggage?" He indicated the black hard-cover carry-on case on wheels.

"It's okay. I'll take it in." She dragged the bag up the ramp.

"Okay, ma." He clicked a button on the wall, and the doors slid apart.

"Thank you." She strode into the foyer and approached the receptionist desk.

After checking in, she went up to the room, ordered lunch and studied the map of the ranch she needed to get to. The terrain was mainly plains on the edge of a mountain with a river running through it.

Then she unpacked the toiletries and clothes before pulling out the smaller damage-proof case and opening it.

One of the advantages of driving instead of flying commercial was that she got to take her kit. Otherwise, she would have to find local dealers to buy weapons, which meant getting more people involved.

She checked the content of the pack. Along with her weapon of choice the FN Five-seveN, she'd come with a sniper rifle, currently dismantled, and C-4 plastic charges. She wasn't a fan of using explosives for a job and only applied it as a last resort.

A knock sounded on the door.

She closed the case, picked up the pistol and walked noiselessly to the door. Checking the peephole, she saw a man dressed in a bellhop outfit with a silver tray laden with dishes. She stepped aside and asked in a heavy accent, "Who is it?"

"Room service," he replied. There was nothing in his voice that indicated agitation or stress.

She tucked the gun into the nearest drawer and pulled out her purse, taking the cash tip in readiness. No reason for him to hang in the suite while she fished the money out. Then she opened the door.

"I brought your lunch," the bellman said, holding up the tray.

"Place it on the table." She stood there, holding the door as he walked past. He lowered the tray and headed back to the entrance.

"Thank you." He took the notes and walked out. She shut the door.

The smell of the Ofada rice with assorted meat sauce made her mouth water. Dismissing work for a few minutes, she tucked into the food and malt drink. Not always able to soak up the cultures of the regions she visited, she made sure to enjoy the cuisines.

After eating, she dropped the tray in the hallway outside the suite, locked the weapons case and stowed her cash bundle in the safe. Then she headed out with a small rucksack containing the handgun, a bottle of water and fruit bars.

Her car was matte grey and absorbed light instead of reflecting it. The last thing she wanted during surveillance was to have a brightly coloured vehicle that would attract attention.

It took two hours to drive out to the location, a ranch in the middle of nowhere.

She was a city girl. She loved the buzz, the noise, the hustle and bustle of the concrete jungle. Out here, there was nothing. Just miles and miles of scrubland interspersed by a few trees. Mountains and valleys and plains. What did people do with themselves?

A wooden arch proclaimed Njoku Farm and Ranch. Nailed to the post on the left side was a sign saying, 'help wanted.'

She drove under the archway and followed the wide, winding dirt road for half a mile. Then turned right and went off-road for a mile until she spotted a copse of trees and headed toward the canopy. It was the only shelter she'd seen for a while, and she wanted somewhere secluded to park the vehicle.

The trees provided shade for a hot afternoon as she got out and surveyed the area. A river wound its way past. It didn't look deep, but it was extensive, perhaps a quarter of a mile across.

In the other direction, the main house would be more than two miles to the west of where she stood, according to the map she'd studied.

With the long-range binoculars, she saw the cattle on the east field. She returned to the car and pulled out the rucksack, placing it across her shoulders. Then she walked to the tree and climbed.

She needed the elevation to see past the shrubbery and any trees in the way.

She'd learned rock and tree climbing as part of completing the assault course in military training along with everything else.

At a sturdy branch, she sat across it, legs dangling, and leaned against the trunk. Pulling out the binoculars, her gaze swept across the plains below.

Beyond the grazing cattle, she found pigs in a pen and horses grazing in a paddock. Further down were barn structures. The main house had a rustic look in an early 19th-century colonial style.

She zoomed in on two men who stood inside a paddock with a single, big white horse.

The horse appeared agitated. One man stood by the side and looked like he was stroking the horse and talking to it, while the other strapped on a saddle. The horse reared up, and the man with the reins continued soothing it until it calmed.

The interplay between the men and the animal they were trying to control fascinated her.

Suddenly, the man with the reins mounted the horse. But the stallion didn't comply. It raised its head and bucked, kicking out with its hind legs continually until the man on top fell. Luckily, the second man pulled him free, so the animal didn't hit him in the process.

A smile curved Xandra's lips. She didn't feel any sympathy for the men. Instead, she had an affinity with the horse.

The animal was untameable. Unbreakable. Like her.

She managed to get a look at the two men and pulled out the tablet to compare the image of the target. Neither of them looked like the man she was hunting.

Something caught the corner of her eye, and she swivelled in its direction.

A blue truck with the ranch logo on the side drove up the dirt road headed into the ranch. From the hidden perch in the tree, she saw it clearly, dust clouds in its wake. The driver was not visible. But she followed its trail until it pulled up in front of the house.

The driver hopped out and shut the door of the vehicle.

Xandra's pulse rate kicked up a notch. She glanced at the photo—a long-range shot and not the best—of the target again.

The new arrival appeared to be the same person in the image. The only way to be definite would be to get closer to him.

Tricky, since this wasn't a busy city where she could walk past him on the street. There were very few hiding places close to the house. Otherwise, she would have done the trek down there.

Her mind flicked to the 'help wanted' sign at the entrance to the ranch. She didn't know what kind of service they needed. Probably a farm or ranch hand.

She knew little about working on a ranch but could ride a horse. She was a quick study too. How hard could it be?

Mind made up, she climbed down the tree and headed to the car.

If she was going to play the part of a ranch hand, then she needed to look the part.

She drove to the city, visited a clothes shop, bought t-shirts, jeans and work boots. In her room, she created a fake resume, although she doubted the necessity of one for what would amount to manual labour.

The next morning after breakfast, she packed her things and checked out of the hotel.

Travel case in the boot, she drove the two hours to the ranch.

Her senses heightened as she went under the archway onto the dirt road, adrenaline spiking.

An adrenaline rush during a kill situation was par the course. However, the surveillance process itself never engendered the same emotions flowing through her right now.

She would get to talk to the target and possibly work with him for a few days.

Gravel crunched under the tyres as she stopped in front of the stone-built house. A light-skinned young woman in a pink t-shirt and blue jeans came around the corner. She had a pretty, oval face and long brunette hair tied in a ponytail.

From the dossier, the target had a younger sister in her mid-twenties whose description matched the girl who'd just stopped by the veranda.

Xandra stepped out of the vehicle and shut the door.

"How can I help you?" the girl asked in a soft voice.

Smiling, Xan took a couple of steps in her direction. "I'm here for the job."

She squinted, her forehead creasing into a frown before her brown eyes went wide. "Oh, you mean the farmworker job?"

"Yes, that job," Xan replied, stepping up and extending her hand. "My name is Allie." Alexandra was her given name. When she'd gone to the military camp, she'd become Xandra. However, in situations when she needed anonymity and a pseudonym, she adopted a variation of her full name.

"It's nice to meet you. I'm Ginika, although my friends call me Gigi." The corners of her lips curled up, and they shook hands. "Sorry if I seemed confused. You don't look like a farmer."

Smart lady.

Xandra had never worked with animals or crops. Her clothes were practically out of the packaging. Best to stick to the truth—as close to the truth as possible—and hope it worked.

Still smiling, she met Ginika's brown eyes with a steady gaze. "You're right. I'm not a farmer. But I'm good with my hands, work hard and can do whatever needs to be done."

"Okay. My brother is the one you need to see. He's inside on the phone now. Come in, and I'll get you a drink while you wait for him." She stepped onto the veranda, looked over her shoulder with a warm smile. "Welcome to Njoku Ranch, Allie."

This was the first time Xandra had been unknowingly invited into the target's home.

Her observation instincts kicked in as she walked through, checking out the layout, recording exits as well as objects.

The interior was open and welcoming, with archways leading to the living area, high ceilings and dark wooden beams, furniture arranged to showcase a family home. The decorations were modern, but the house retained some of its rustic charms. Steps with intricately designed tiles stood at the end of the hall, leading to the next level up.

Ginika led her through an arch under the stairs into a beautiful, large kitchen with a range cooker, terracotta floor tiles, honey-coloured walls, cherry wood cabinets and a matching rectangular table with eight chairs.

"Please, sit." She pointed to one of the chairs as she opened a door. "What would you like to drink?"

"Water, please," Xan said, pulling out one of the wooden chairs and settling into it sideways.

"Sure." She flashed white teeth and opened the door to a large fridge which, on the face of it, seemed to be the only high-tech gadget in the rustically modern house.

The friendly welcome and the homely environment sent a twinge across Xandra's chest. She resisted rubbing a palm on it.

She had never received this kind of warm reception from the family of her mark. When she entered their homes, she usually tampered with the locks or, as in Yahya's case, entered while the door was already opened.

Her skin prickled.

She should warn Ginika about inviting a stranger, a killer, into her home so readily.

In the cities, people tried to be aware of whom they allowed onto their premises. Perhaps crime wasn't as rampant out here in the countryside.

This begged the question. If these people were so innocent, why did someone want one of them dead?

Why did the question spring into her head? She had never bothered with it before. Now it did, she wanted answers. She would get them when she met the target face-to-face.

Ginika came back with a bottle of water and poured some into a glass with ice cubes.

"Thank you," Xan said.

"You're welcome." She tugged a chair and sat on the other side of the table. "Your accent. You are not local."

For a moment, Xandra wondered if she'd been discovered already. "No, I'm not from the Bakili region. I came here to enrol at the university for a part-time course. But I also need a job which is why I'm here."

"Wonderful. That's my alma mater. You'll love it there. If you need me to show you around."

"That's nice. Thank you. So, what do you do? Do you work in the area?"

She remembered the distance between the ranch and the nearest town. It wasn't an easy daily commute.

Ginika shrugged and brushed loose strands of hair back from her face. "I haven't been able to find a job. I would like to travel and see the world. But for now, I have to stay and help my brother with the ranch."

An ache bloomed in Xandra's throat. She has no real friends. None she could have chats like this. Yet, she understood the constraints in the other woman's life. Felt a connection to someone she'd only just met.

This necessity to sacrifice themselves for a more significant cause—family in Ginika's case and the Himba cartel in Xandra's—connected them.

"If it's really what you want to do, then you should just go. Life's too short." Not to mention that Xandra would deprive her of her brother. The twinge in her chest returned.

Ginika gave an uncertain smile. "You think so?"

"I do."

Steady footsteps echoed in the corridor behind Xandra. The hairs on her nape stood erect. Usually, she didn't sit with her back to the door. She'd been relaxed in Ginika's presence and had lowered her guard.

While the other woman was harmless, this new arrival was an unknown.

Xandra's first instinct was to reach for the gun. She lifted a hand to pat her chest.

Damn. No hidden panels in this outfit. Unarmed, she was dressed like a farmhand, not an assassin.

Pulse accelerating, she twisted in the seat.

A tall man strode into the kitchen. He wore brown boots and blue-washed jeans, the muscles of his broad shoulders and chest filled out the light blue chambray shirt. His thick black hair was cut in a taper-fade, while dark bristles on his chin and thick brows framed caramel skin, scrutinising eyes as black as night, and full sensuous lips.

Recognition punched Xandra in the gut and her breath hitched.

He was the man in the dossier. Ebuka Njoku. Owner of Njoku Ranch and Farms.

Her target.

"Gigi, I didn't know you had a guest," he said in a deep commanding voice.

Feeling light-headed, a sizzle went down Xandra's spine. Heat washed over her skin. The space in the kitchen seemed constricted, the air sucked out.

His piercing gaze unsettled her. Like he could see more than she projected. Like she was the prey.

It seemed she'd temporarily forgotten how to inhale and had to force the action.

Suddenly not wanting him standing over her, she straightened and shook out her shoulders. She wasn't afraid of him. She was nobody's prey.

Ginika waved her hand in Xan's direction as she stood too. "Ebuka, this is Allie. She's here for the farm job."

"Nice to meet you, Allie, but have you worked on a ranch before?" He looked her over as if he didn't believe she was suitable for the job. His direct approach matched his sister's.

Back ramrod straight, Xandra held her breath, wondering if she passed the examination. Wanting his approval for more than one reason. She didn't want to leave. Not now. Not until she found out more about this man.

"No," she replied. "As I said to your sister, I can do whatever job you want me to do. I'm great with woodwork, and I don't mind getting my hands dirty."

He put his hands on his hips, exuding confidence and power. "Ranch work is back-breaking and has to be done no matter the weather outside. Are you sure you can cope with it?"

Xandra was petite, fit and toned. Anyone who mistook her appearance for weakness did so at their peril.

She stepped forward, extending her hand and met his gaze. "Why don't you give me a trial, and if you're not satisfied, you don't have to hire me."

He nodded, reaching out. "I'll give you twenty-four hours to prove yourself."

That was more than enough time to learn what she needed to do her job.

"Deal," she said, accepting his firm callused hand.

An electric shock spiked up her arm. His eyes widened, indicating he felt it too. He didn't pull away. Something unspoken passed between them and the rest of the room seemed to fade.

The man took her breath away. She understood physical attraction. But this?

Xandra should assess all the ways she could take his life. He was her mark.

Instead, she pictured him on top of her, stretching her as he filled her up, their sweat-slicked bodies sliding over each other in sync. Her nipples hardened, and her insides clenched.

Damn.

FIVE

FOR A MOMENT, Ebuka stood stunned as he shook Allie's hand. His heartbeats raced, tingles shooting up his arm.

What in Hell?

She had a firm grip, something he hadn't expected from someone who appeared small and refined at first glance.

However, this close to her, their eyes were almost at the same level.

She was tall, considering she was in low-heeled boots. Her leanness masked her height when she'd been sitting, making her appear small and delicate.

The direct and calculating way she stared at him would have made any other man shift uncomfortably.

Heat flashed through Ebuka. Fighting not to show any outward sign of being ruffled, he withdrew his hand. The tingly sensation meant nothing.

Yet, something about her unsettled him.

She wasn't from around here. And she wasn't the rural sort.

She looked the part if a fashion magazine had done a photo-shoot of what a farmer would look like, black polo shirt on skinny denim trousers. She was just too impeccable. There wasn't even a scuff on her shiny knee-high leather boots. At least they were flat-heeled.

Sleek brown hair in a low bun and a long fringe almost covered her tawny oval face, high cheekbones, button nose and round glossy lips.

Why did she want a job on a farm? She didn't look like the usual applicants who were from the surrounding small towns. And if the car outside was hers, then she was used to earning more than a labourer's wage.

Still, her kohl-lined amber eyes shone with steely determination. She was willing to prove him wrong.

No time like the present.

"Your trial can start immediately. One of the fences is broken, and some of the cattle got out. The other men are busy, so we're going to round them up and mend the fence." He didn't wait for her response and headed to the door.

"Yes, boss," Allie replied.

He detected sarcasm in her voice and turned with an eyebrow raised. "What was that?"

"Just acknowledging your instructions." She had an innocent expression as if she hadn't done anything wrong.

Ebuka frowned. "Don't call me 'boss'. It makes me sound like a gangster."

Across the room, Gigi broke into giggles. "Oh, you're so paranoid. Anyway, you're kind of bossy. Would you rather she addressed you as 'Sir'?"

"Of course not," he griped.

One look in Allie's direction, and it looked like she was suppressing laughter. When did this stranger become a co-conspirator with his sister?

He didn't like the ease with which Gigi had taken to Allie.

Their little portion of the world was secluded. He wasn't usually suspicious of strangers.

However, the past two years had been tough on the ranch. He'd shielded his sister from the problems and didn't want to worry her. The problems were his responsibility.

Perhaps he shouldn't take out his stress on Allie too. She couldn't be that much older than his sister.

Sucking a deep breath, he held and exhaled it slowly. "Look, my name is Ebuka, so you can use it. No sir or boss or any other title."

"Got it." Allie nodded.

"Good. See you later, Gigi," he said.

"See you," she replied and headed through the archway into the hall.

Ebuka went for the kitchen door, leading outside to the terrace. The sun was high in the sky, and the air was heavy with humidity. It would likely rain later, so the sooner they rounded up the loose cattle, the better.

Allie stayed behind him by a couple of steps. She didn't say anything as they strode across to the storage barn which housed all the equipment, gravel crunching beneath their boots.

"So where are you from?" he asked to distract from the prickly sensations on his nape. He took the toolbox from the shelf, checking it contained what he needed.

"Jokogi," she replied.

"Big city," he said, almost triumphantly. His instincts had been correct.

She was a city dweller. Ebuka was a simple farmer.

He remembered someone else who preferred the glamorous city lights to the mundane country life. His muscles tensed. He wasn't going there.

"It is." She shrugged as if it didn't matter.

He moved the box to one of the All-Terrain Vehicles and secured it. "What are you doing out here? This must be different from what you're used to."

She shoved her hands into the back jeans' pockets. "I'm here for a university program."

Her pushed-back shoulders, furrowed brows and alert gaze said she could handle whatever life threw at her. They'd soon find out since a storm was on the way.

"Can you drive the ATV?" he asked.

"Sure." She nodded, swung her legs across it and started the engine without hesitation.

"Good. You take that. I'm going to saddle up Chocho and meet you outside the paddock."

He met her gaze, and she nodded in response.

He became aware of the strength of his heartbeats and his fingers tingled with the need to touch her.

What was going on with him? Not only was it inappropriate, but he didn't know much about her. Maybe he'd been without a woman for too long. He needed to get back on the saddle, go into town and find a willing woman, instead of ogling potential employees.

Back stiffened, Ebuka walked out of the barn and focused on saddling up.

The ATV was handy for carrying equipment and for covering distances quickly on the range. But he preferred to move cattle with a horse since it was less noisy and more comfortable to handle in certain situations.

When he came out to the paddock, Allie waited with the idling ATV.

"Follow me. Keep behind me at all times and make sure you don't spook the animals," he ordered and kicked the horse into a gallop.

It didn't take long to find the break in the fence. Discovering the straggling cattle proved harder. It took a while to reach and direct them toward the grassland. He worried they would go wild and stampede.

To be fair to Allie, she did as instructed and didn't spook the animals. The ATV buzzed like a motorised mosquito as she gently coaxed the cattle toward home.

Once the animals settled in the field, he got off the horse and tied the reins to a post. Allie climbed off the ATV and started on fixing the fence.

For a few seconds, he stood there watching her use the pliers to loop, twist and secure the wires. She looked like someone comfortable with working with her hands. She wasn't even wearing the available protective gloves.

Yet the hand Ebuka had shaken earlier had no calluses. The two things didn't match.

She was a ball of contradictions he couldn't figure out. And he hated not knowing who or what she was.

Striding up to the toolbox, he picked up a hammer and grabbed a fallen post, knocking it back into the earth before cutting off a length of galvanised wire.

They worked together in silence. It wasn't awkward. Repairs almost completed; the sky darkened.

"You can head back to the house. I'll finish off here." He glanced at her, twisting another loop of wire.

"No. If we both do it, then we'll be done sooner." She didn't meet his gaze and carried on working.

Ebuka gasped in surprise because she hadn't taken the option of getting inside and avoiding the wet. He couldn't think of any woman who would choose to stay in the rain. Ginika would have returned home as soon as the weather deteriorated.

Still, he smiled and went back to work.

They were on the last post when Heaven opened, and a downpour of stinging cold rain hit them.

Allie didn't complain as the hard shower pelted their skins through the fabrics.

Done, she packed the box and returned it to the ATV.

"The rain doesn't look like it will let up anytime soon and the ATV is dangerous to handle in this weather, especially to drive all the way back to the house," he yelled to be heard in the howling wind.

"What else can we do?" she asked, hunched over, hands in jeans pockets.

"There's a clay hut not far from here. We use it when we have to work long days, and there isn't enough light to return to the house."

"Sounds good to me." She straddled the ATV. "Lead the way."

Ebuka nodded and climbed onto Chocho. The horse had a pleasant disposition so shouldn't be a problem to handle. He turned to Allie.

"Be careful on the ATV. Just go slow. I don't want you breaking your neck on your first day here."

She flashed a grin full of white teeth. "Yes...I'll go slowly."

It sounded as if she'd intended to say "Yes, boss" again before changing her mind.

He hid the blooming smile by turning away as he nudged the horse forward.

In the rain, it took longer than usual to reach the cabin.

Ebuka kept glancing over his shoulder to make sure Allie was still following. The light on the ATV didn't penetrate the sleet, and he couldn't hear the buzz sometimes.

He was soaked by the time they eventually got there. Allie parked the ATV in the shed as he settled Chocho into a stall and used the sweat scraper to get most of the wetness off while Allie piled the hay. Then he turned on the generator, ensuring they would have electricity.

He headed for the porch and climbed the step. "You're going to have to take your clothes off out here. Ginika will kill me if we drip water all over the clay floor inside. It only got resealed recently."

He said the words in a matter of fact tone as he sat on the stone stairs to pull boots off.

"Okay," Allie said and mirrored his actions.

His pulse raced at the possibility of seeing her without clothes.

What was wrong with him today?

Shaking his head, he ignored his hardening dick. He turned his back to her and unbuttoned the soaked shirt, dropping it on the floor before undoing his fly. He tried to maintain nonchalance as he peeled the drenched denim down, making sure he couldn't see Allie.

Keeping the boxer-briefs on, he opened the door, switched on the overhead lamp and walked into the main room. He kindled the firewood under the stone tripod used for cooking. The fire sparked and crackled. Although the rain had been cold, the temperature inside the cabin remained mild. The heat from the fire would help to dry the clothes quickly.

He lifted his head and froze to the spot.

Allie stood in the living area, wearing a white chemise and panties.

Air left his lungs. His lips parted, and the chill fled his body.

The sodden clothes revealed more than they hid—slender breasts, bullet-tipped nipples, tight lean muscles, flat belly, curvy hips and long legs. Wet hair held in a band plastered around her face. Her expression had no shame or embarrassment.

He'd never met a woman this brazen and unashamed of her near-nakedness.

Her tongue traced the upper lip, enticing him.

His gaze tracked its pink progress and his mouth moistened. What would she taste like?

"Where do you want me to put these?" She held the soaked clothes.

Her question jarred him into action. Cheeks heated, he grabbed an old wooden chair.

"You can hang them over this," he said in a gruff voice, shaken by the way she affected him. He was in trouble if he couldn't control his libido. They had another twelve hours before daybreak.

He went to the small bathroom cupboard, pulled out two grey towels, walked back and tossed one at her. "Cover your body."

SIX

A SMILE curved Xandra's lips as she grabbed the towel Ebuka chucked at her.

Okay. This was new.

Xandra was used to men who took what they wanted, when they wanted it, usually by any means necessary.

So, to see Ebuka fighting the apparent attraction between them was surprising and kind of amusing.

He'd gone back to wearing a stony, keep-away-from-me expression. But the bulge stretching his damp briefs proved there was more going on with him that just wariness of her. The notion of chastity and piety were not alien to her after being raised in a nunnery-orphanage. However, those things had no place in her life now.

Having fun with watching his unease at their predicament, she didn't cover up immediately.

Instead, she used the towel to dry her body in a slow, seductive manner.

His gaze followed the movement as if enraptured.

As soon as she'd confirmed his identity earlier this morning, she should have returned to her car, grabbed her weapon, gone back into the house and shot him. That would have been messy because there was a witness. Ginika.

Still, she could have left the ranch and ambushed him as he drove out or she could have come back later at night and completed the assignment.

However, instinct told her there was more to this situation. Ebuka and Ginika did not look like the unscrupulous people in her circles. They looked innocent.

If Ebuka was innocent, why was he on Xandra's hit list? Curiosity meant she wanted to find the answer.

In any case, pretending to be someone else that was freeing. Liberating. Probably the same with actors or actresses. Living as someone else, away from the constraints of their ordinary lives. Away from the expectations.

She had come to Njoku Ranch for a specific job.

Still, the minute she'd crossed the threshold into their house, her chest had tightened, and adrenaline had rushed through her body.

The friendly reception from Ginika had awakened a different side of Xandra. A side she hadn't realised she possessed, considerate and sympathetic. And then the other woman had teased her brother about his grouchiness, and Xandra had felt included for the first time in her life. She'd felt like she belonged with the two of them. Like she could have a fun and carefree life, with them.

Being Xandra was a heavy cross she carried, and for the past few hours, she'd been able to put it down and rest.

Not that she wanted to discard the cross totally. She would pick it up again. It was hers to carry forever.

For now, she would make the best of being someone else. Someone who could live in the moment. Someone who could be considerate and sympathetic, fun and carefree.

Not much else she could do, anyway. A storm raged outside, and she was stuck in the hut with Ebuka.

His quiet and reserved demeanour was deceiving.

She'd seen something in his eyes when they'd shaken hands. Latent power waiting to be unleashed. The kind she craved.

Her breath caught as she watched him.

He wrapped a towel over his hips, abdominal and bicep muscles rippling. He was broad and sturdy. Caramel skin wrapped around sinews sculpted through hard outdoor work on the farm and a V-trail of short dark hairs disappeared below the towel.

A thrill raced down her spine, and her pussy throbbed. She yearned to feel those muscles pressing against her, pinning her down. To explore this lust between them because that was what it had to be. She hadn't had sex for four months. The kind of work she did didn't mesh with her cravings, so she always waited for the encounters with Osagie to finally let go.

She hadn't achieved release from the last meeting with Osagie. And she wasn't sure if she could find someone who would play the role he'd done so well.

She wouldn't let this temporary opportunity with Ebuka slip by. No reason she couldn't fuck him now and kill him later. One had nothing to do with the other.

Ebuka strode across the room, snatched the towel from her hand and looped it around her chest. "I told you to cover up."

His fingers grazed her skin.

Her clit throbbed, her pulse racing.

His scent intoxicated her—the smell of man and the outdoors on a rainy day.

Unable or somewhat unwilling to censure herself, she leaned forward and pressed her lips to his firm ones.

He jerked back. "What do you think you're doing?"

His thunderous expression couldn't mask the layer of heated lust that sparkled in his dark eyes.

Gaze fixed on his mouth, she stroked her tongue around hers, relishing the brief contact. "I couldn't resist. You taste good."

He narrowed his eyes. "Who the hell are you? Did Nweke send you to set me up? Is there a video camera in here?"

Shit! Her chest tightened. His words were close to the truth. She forced a smile to stay on her face. "What are you talking about?"

Ignoring her question, his gaze swept the large space, and he moved the furniture around as if searching for hidden recording equipment. After a while, he huffed and walked to the small kitchen at the other end. He filled a kettle with water and set it on the stone tripod to boil. Then he opened a cupboard and took out some cans and sachets of food.

Xandra wanted to help, but he looked like he needed to be alone. Good idea to give him some breathing space since he was jumpy about Commissioner Nweke. He couldn't find out she knew Nweke or that she had links to the man.

She washed her hands in the sink and then focused on spreading out the damp clothes on the wooden chairs. With the towel around her body, she removed the chemise and panties.

The heat from the fire warmed the room. The world outside seemed distant except for the pitter-patter of rain on the thatched roof, lightning flashes and thunder cracks.

The cabin was built from clay, stone and wood and had a studio feel. A reclaimed wooden three-seater acted like a divider, separating the sitting area at the front from the kitchenette at the back.

Wooden shuttered windows were on opposing sidewalls.

She picked up one of the cushions covered in pastel fabric. "Is this Ginika's handwork?"

Ebuka glanced up as he poured hot water into two mugs with teabags.

"Yes. She wanted to make the workers comfortable when they had to spend the night in here." A smile curled his lips, the fondness he had for his sister evident in his tone.

"Make the workers comfortable? What's that about?" She huffed, surprised. The people she knew would never go the extra length for their workers. Paying them was enough.

"Do you want sugar and milk in your tea?" he asked, seemingly ignoring her question. Or perhaps thinking about it.

"No milk. I'm lactose intolerant," she volunteered, not sure why she gave the information freely. "Two cubes of sugar, please."

He picked the white cubes out of the blue box and popped them into a mug. Then he stirred and handed over the steaming cup. "Food should be ready soon."

"I can help." She moved to stand.

"There's no need." He shook his head. "You worked really hard out there today, and I appreciate it. So just relax. I'm not always going to be this generous."

He walked back toward the kitchen.

Smiling, she turned to the side to watch him. "Does that mean I've got the job?"

He glanced sideways with a smile on his face that made her heart skip a beat. "Yes, you've got the job."

"Great. Thank you." She blew into the tea before taking a sip. It tasted good, surprisingly.

"About your question. Every member of staff is like family, and we treat them as such. I believe if we take care of our people, they, in turn, will take care of the farm and do their jobs well, which makes for a successful business. It's a win-win for everyone."

Speechless, Xandra rubbed a hand over her breastbone to ease the tightness in her chest.

Was this guy for real, or was he just giving her the spiel?

To be fair, he and his sister had been charming and accommodating since her arrival. No boss she knew would stand over a hot stove cooking while his employee sat on a chair drinking tea that he had made.

Ebuka was an enigma she wanted to unravel. The reason she hadn't put a bullet through him, yet. Also, she wanted to fuck him.

"When we get back to the house, mention your milk allergy to Ginika, so she makes sure the menus cater for your dietary requirement," his voice roused her from her thoughts.

He was serious about the whole taking-care-of-staff business. No one else bothered about her dietary requirement, except Zoe. But Zoe wanted to get into her knickers. So that didn't count.

"Do you feed your staff as well?" she asked.

"Yes. The ranch is isolated, and the area is rural. People can't pop out to buy lunch as you do in towns or cities. During the busy seasons, they spend nights on the premises too. So, we provide all the meals here."

"Makes sense."

"I'll also introduce you to the other employees," he continued. "Mama Ebele is the housekeeper and cooks the meals. Hector, Obiano and Adiele are full-time. The other staff are either part-time or seasonal."

He moved around the space like he owned it. Of course, the ranch was his. But it was more than that.

He had the air of a man with a purpose. A man in control of his universe. A man who cared about his people, who called them family.

He fascinated her.

And the smell of the food made her mouth water.

"Was there someone else doing my job before?" she asked, wanting to keep him talking, so she could understand his link with Commissioner Nweke.

"No." He paused from stirring whatever was in the pan. "We're expanding. I've been fighting for years to get permission from the officials to extend the ranch. We finally got the license so now the plans can go ahead."

"Sounds good. So why did it take so long to get the permit?"

He shrugged, transferred the pot onto the counter and started scooping the food into ceramic plates.

She sat straight as he brought the plates and cutleries over and placed them on the low table.

"Local rice. Thanks," she said as she lifted a fork and took a bite. The flavours of palm oil, smoked fish, tomatoes and spices exploded on her tongue. "Yummy ... How do you store food here considering there is no refrigerator?"

"The clay larder is designed to stay cool all year for the yams and cocoyams. Then we have dried grains and spices, canned vegetables. The meat and fish are dried, so, they last longer."

He settled on the settee. There wasn't anywhere else to sit aside from the floor or the chairs covered in wet clothes.

Their bodies didn't touch. Shame.

"You seem to have this all worked out."

They were similar in that aspect. She liked to plan for all eventualities.

Then again, sitting here, in a cabin in the middle of nowhere, eating a meal prepared by the man she was sent to kill was not in her original plan.

She was flexible, adaptable to any situation, a skill key to her survival.

However, she'd never stopped to ask why a target was chosen like she was doing now.

Why did Nweke want Ebuka dead?

Still unable to answer the niggling question, she carried on eating. Glad to have some food in her stomach. Although she'd learned to survive prolonged periods without food, the work today had sapped a lot of energy. "This is pretty good."

"Thank you." He sounded surprised.

Done with the food, she volunteered to wash up, and he let her. She even made tea for him with hot water from the aluminium kettle and dried milk from the tin.

They sat quietly, sipping the tea. There was no TV or anything for entertainment. Not that she expected such in the remote hut. She'd left her phone and gadgets in the car.

After a while, he placed his mug on the table and rubbed his left shoulder, rotating his arm.

She put her cup down. "Is something wrong?"

"It's nothing. I sometimes get twinges in my shoulder blade. I think the cold rain just aggravated it."

"Here, let me help." She wiggled her fingers as well as eyebrows. "I'm good with my hands."

He stared at her and shook his head. "It'll be fine."

"Come on. I promise it'll be good." She stood and walked over to stand on the side of the sofa, leaning over him.

Sighing, he leaned forward, surrendering his back.

She rubbed her palms together to warm them and placed both hands on his back. The muscles twitched as he sucked in a breath.

She smiled and kept rubbing until she found the knot of muscles. She kneaded, working the knot in an outer arch.

His body relaxed, and he sighed. "You're right. This feels good."

"I told you so," she muttered silently and continued massaging until all the tight muscles loosened.

He groaned, his whole body going pliant.

She carried on rubbing the rest of his back for a few more minutes.

He didn't stop her, although it was apparent that she had moved on from the original spot. Her fingers trailed to his hips.

He swivelled suddenly and grabbed her hands.

Her breath hitched. She hadn't been expecting him to move that quickly.

"What is this game you're playing?" he asked in a husky voice.

His expression made her heart hammer against her ribs.

She swallowed to clear the lump in her throat. "It's not a game. I want you, and I think you want me too. We're adults— "

"You're my employee, and what you're implying is inappropriate." He glared, still holding her hands.

She could escape his hold. She didn't, liking the way he restrained her.

"Have you never done anything inappropriate? Never been with an employee? It isn't illegal."

Granted, she was used to interacting with gangsters, people who had no qualms about breaking the laws. So, it was strange to be around someone who baulked at doing something pleasurable and legal.

"It might not be illegal. But it's immoral. I've never been involved with one of my workers. Being with you is equivalent to taking advantage of you. That's wrong. I don't want you to feel that your job safety depends on sexual favours to me."

His honesty unravelled her. Her stomach dropped.

His sincerity was visible in his dark eyes. He was a good man, principled, compassionate, even to a stranger because he didn't really know her.

The man she would have to kill was trying to protect her.

What now? She stood still, unsure of what to say. She'd never been this conflicted in her life. She shouldn't care, had never bothered before.

He released her hands, turned away.

"No," she said, moving to stand in front of him. "Would it make you feel better if I resigned? I'm no longer your employee."

"What? No."

"I need you more than I want the job. I can get another job. But there's only one you. Please."

Not that she needed the farmworker job anyway.

Her hands shook, and for the first time in her adult life, desperation clawed at her skin. She hadn't begged anyone for anything since she left the orphanage.

He stared into her eyes, searching, probing.

She wanted to avert her gaze, to avoid appearing vulnerable. But didn't move.

Did he see the pain she had bottled up for years? Did he see the little girl who begged the nuns not to take her away from the only home she had known? Did he see the cold-hearted woman who could kill without flinching?

"It's just the two of us here for the next few hours. I promise I'll leave in the morning if you want me to go." A shame because she wanted him for more than one night.

"No. You don't have to leave."

He closed his eyes briefly and puffed out a breath. Lifting his eyelids, he grabbed her hand and tugged.

Breath whooshed out as she landed on his hard body. Damn. He was strong.

Her pulse rate skyrocketed.

He clamped her arms-to-sides and lifted until she straddled his lap.

"You are going to be trouble," he said, his expression more lustful than disapproving.

She just smiled in response. He was right. She was trouble for him in more ways than one.

He rolled his eyes upwards and shook his head. "Okay. If we do this, we do it my way. It's just sex, and it's just for tonight."

A fluttering sensation settled in her gut.

"Deal," she said in a breathless voice.

SEVEN

THE MOMENT Allie agreed to the deal something sparked within Ebuka. A dark craving long dormant inside him. It caught and spread fire through his veins, making his grip on her arms tighten.

The bold way she'd tried to kiss him had caught him off-guard and roused his suspicions again. He'd wondered if his old friend Ralph Nweke had sent her as a rouse to settle a disagreement between them. He wasn't used to women snatching kisses from acquaintances. Then again he hadn't dated in years. Maybe he was out of touch with etiquette.

"I need you more than I want the job."

His resistance had crumbled when she'd spoken those words, accompanied by the most fragile and genuine expression he'd seen from her since her arrival.

She'd seemed to be a woman hiding her true self. But at that moment, he'd caught a glimpse of the real person behind the mask.

A person who needed him. Someone he couldn't resist.

He thrived when he took care of others—his family, his workers.

Now, for tonight, he could take care of Allie too. Give her what she needed. Himself.

Raising his left hand, he held her chin, keeping her still.

Her amber eyes darkened, the pupils blowing out. She smelled of musk. Arousal. Unable to hold back, he lowered his head, needing to taste her.

At first, there was a little tension as if she was cautious. Her heart-shaped lips were pliant, soft, giving way to his tongue, letting him slide and glide. She tasted of sweet and spice, decadent and beyond any price.

Moaning, she clung to him, grabbing his nape, demolishing any gaps between them.

The tightness in his chest loosened. He'd missed the touch and taste of a woman, missed being needed like this.

The stresses of the business, of the past few years, meant he hadn't been able to relax fully in female company.

He broke the kiss, leaning forehead against hers. Their breaths intermingled.

"Tell me what you like," he said, his voice husky with desire.

The towel around her chest loosened, revealing two petite breasts, perfect for her slender almost boyish body. She was perfect. Although he would rather have her hair short. But that was a preference. Not a deal-breaker.

He moulded one breast under his palm, pinched the taut nipple.

She gasped. "Anything you want."

Jerking, he scrutinised her face. "Are you sure?"

She nodded. "Yes. You can do whatever you want with me."

His heart raced at the possibilities. He tugged the nipple between thumb and forefinger, hard.

She let out a long moan, arched her back and presented her chest. Oh. She liked a little pain.

He repeated the action with the other nipple, and her response was the same.

She was a different person from the woman he'd met in his house earlier. That one had seemed cold and distant and strange. This woman was warm and enticing and beautiful.

Ebuka loved the skin to skin contact. Loved her responses to him. His heart thundered in anticipation.

"Anything you want."

No one had ever offered such free rein before. There'd always been boundaries and limits. Worried he would break his lovers; he'd learned to suppress his true desires.

Now like a kid taken to a toy store and told he could pick any plaything, adrenaline rushed through his veins. He could unleash his cravings, no matter how depraved.

He trailed his left hand from her chin to her nape and tangled fingers into the damp hair, gripping tight.

Allie arched her body again, lips parting.

"You make the most beautiful sounds of surrender." He placed a kiss in the hollow of her collarbone.

Another moan. Almost a whimper this time. "You make me want to give everything to you."

"Only if that's what you want." Lifting his head, he tugged her hair and leaned in to kiss her.

She relaxed in acceptance, opening, letting him in with no hesitation.

He explored her mouth, loving her taste—sweet tea, spice and Allie. Not rushing it, He tilted his head and deepened the kiss, letting it go from exploratory to intense.

He licked inside her mouth and tangled their tongues, tugging and pulling each other. Lust was a fire in his veins, heating his body, his erection hard and pulsing.

She wriggled, hips gyrating against his hardness with abandon. Groaning, he lifted his head.

"Ezigbo obele m," he said, watching for her response. A fitting pet name, considering her size and the age difference. He had at least ten years on her. She had to be in her twenties.

Her pupils widened briefly, and her eyelids drooped in deference. Interesting.

She understood the reference, although he guessed she wasn't Igbo. And she accepted his authority. Acceded his use of the phrase 'my good little' and the implied power dynamic.

She was his responsibility. Here and now.

It was a heady feeling, caught between taking what he wanted and respecting her capitulation. In a world where women were expected to submit to a man's dominance without question, he wanted submission that he had earned or had been gifted.

Demanding it was easy. Earning it was the challenge.

He wanted the challenge. Wanted to know that when she yielded, she was his. He reached between their bodies and removed the towel, dropping it.

She gasped and rocked her hips.

"Stay still," he said in a low voice.

She stilled in obedience and took shallow breaths as he slid his fingers between her labia, stroking the dewy slippery flesh.

She made a small noise that sent a thrill down his spine.

He held her nape, her body bent in compliance, keeping her still as he worked her pussy, caressing, stroking.

Pulse thumping at the base of her neck, her breathing became heavy, and she rocked her hips again.

"I told you to keep still. I'm going to tie you up."

Her body froze, and her eyes went wide. "No, you can't."

Now, they were talking. She had limits, after all.

"Are you trying to tell me what to do? Remember, I can do whatever I want." He loosened his grip, waiting to see what she would do.

Her muscles tensed, as though she would bolt. "You're going to have to make me."

She sprang off his lap and stared down, eyes sparkling with the challenge.

She wanted to see what he would do, how he would react. If he was worthy of her submission.

He hid his smile, excitement fizzing in his blood. This had turned into a game, and he was ready to play.

"Obele, come back here," he ordered.

She backed away, giggling. "Make me."

Ebuka stood, reaching out.

She swerved and bolted across the room towards the door.

Discarding his towel, he gave chase, their footsteps pounding on the hard floor. She yanked the door open, raced across the veranda and down the steps.

His heart pounded like galloping horses. Rain splattered on the thatch.

With adrenaline high and body temperature up, he didn't feel the sting of the cold rain. The grass was slippery, and he had to curl his toes with each stride to stay upright. The sky had darkened, and not much could be seen beyond the reaches of the light streaming from the front door and windows.

Allie ran in a circular motion around the perimeter of the hut, swerving each time he reached for her. Watching her naked body wet with rain heightened his arousal.

She slipped as she rounded the corner to the front of the cabin.

He took the opportunity and leapt at her, crashing into her body.

They tumbled to the ground, and he tried to pin her.

She shifted, the mud and rain making her slither.

Ebuka was larger, bulkier. He took advantage and bore down, wrestling her until he grasped her hands. He yanked them back and sat on her, trying to catch his breath.

Her head was pressed to the grass, wet hair plastered to her face. Eyes closed as she panted.

Leaning over, he spoke into her ear. "Obele, do you yield to me?"

She said nothing and didn't try to struggle.

He stroked his right hand down to the fleshy bum cheeks. He caressed slowly before bringing his hand down in hard swats.

She jerked as each smack thudded against her smooth skin. But she didn't cry out or fight.

He stopped after five and asked again. "Do you yield to me?"

"Yes, boss," she replied, her lips curled in a smile.

Somehow, he didn't mind her use of the term.

"Climb and kneel on the step." He shifted, allowing her to move.

She moved like a languid cat, getting into position, knees on the lowest rung while her body was prostrate on the rest.

She did wondrous things to him, presenting to him like this.

The rain ran down their bodies in rivulets, washing away the mud and grass.

He parted her bum cheeks, stroked his tongue down the crack to her pussy.

She moaned and bucked.

Grinning, he swatted her. "Don't move."

He returned his attention to her opening, licking, and prodding with his tongue. Her essence in his mouth was delicious. Occasionally, he would sink his teeth into her ass cheek, and she would jerk, resulting in another smack. He worked continuously until her moans turned into whimpers, and finally she begged.

"Please..."

"Obele, are you asking for something?"

"Yes. I want you inside me."

He swatted her ass hard.

"Please, boss." Her tone was more whimper than words.

"Grab hold of the top step."

She obeyed, curling her long fingers around the edge of the stone slab.

He grabbed her hips, lifting her bum to the correct angle. Seeing her unguarded and almost powerless made something clamp in his chest.

Her head remained pressed to the stone. Her bum presented to him. Damn. She was beautiful and sexy. Hot in her submission.

His body was wound tight, his dick hard enough to pound concrete.

Unable to restrain himself any longer, he gripped her hip with one hand, guided his cock to her opening with the other. With a forward press and short jerk of his hips, he was encased in her tight, slippery channel.

She moaned, eyes closed, her expression blissful. She clenched around him, gripping him snugly.

"Obele," he groaned, pausing to catch his breath, not ready for it to end. He leaned forward and pressed a kiss between her shoulder blades.

Then he pulled out and slammed in. Hell, he wasn't going to be slow. Not for this first time. This was the victory fuck. The spoils to the winner of their little tussle. This was proving he could be the man she needed.

Out here with the rain drenching them, he wanted to own her. Her body. Her heart. Her life.

A crazy thought. And considering their situation, something that would never happen.

But he could own her for tonight. Right here.

So, he fucked her, one hand gripping her nape, the other on her hip, holding her in place as he rammed in continuously.

Her moans got louder, her body writhing and her insides rippling around him.

She was close to climax.

"Your orgasm is mine. Don't come until I give you permission."

"Yes, boss." She sucked in heavy breaths, and eventually her body relaxed.

Her obedience was his undoing, pulling his release out of nowhere, nearly making him lose control.

He slammed into her, held still and reached for her clit. He couldn't wait much longer, and he wanted to reward her compliance. He leaned forward, pressing his lips against her warm skin as he stroked her.

"Obele, nye m ya."

Another tug on the hard nub and she let out a long moan and clenched in waves around him.

He pressed lips one last time to her skin before letting go and thrusting into her almost mindlessly. Heat rushed to his extremities as his balls tightened.

"Fuck, obele," he grunted as the climax ripped out of him.

His knees gave way. He slumped on top of her, rolling to the side and tugging her over him. They stayed that way until he'd caught his breath and some strength back.

"Was that good for you?" he asked, concerned he may have been too hard on her.

She smiled. Her expression filled with admiration as he stroked her back gently. "It was perfect. You were perfect."

The constriction in his chest eased. He swiped the wet hair off her face gently. "Good. We're going to stand and let the rain wash away most of the dirt. Then we're going inside to shower. Afterwards, I'm doing whatever else I want to do to you for the rest of the night."

Her eyes sparkled, and her smile widened. "Whatever you say, boss."

Chuckling, he pulled her head down and breathed against her lips. "You're right about that."

He kissed her intensely and smiled when her breath hitched.

EIGHT

BIRDS CHIRPED as Xandra peeled her eyes open. Dawn's grey light streaked through the windows. The rain had stopped.

Inside, the fire had died, the embers low and crackling.

Under her ear, Ebuka's chest rose and fell with each breath as his healthy heart pumped blood around his arteries. His warmth seeped through her skin, and she didn't want to move.

A new day meant work on the ranch. Completing her mission. Moving on. Her chest contracted.

She wasn't ready to move on. She was enjoying being Allie the farmworker a little too much.

But would it be so bad to have a few more days out here?

Most kill contracts took over one week anyway to allow time to arrive at the location, mount surveillance, plan the kill method and execute.

This was her third day on the job.

Granted, she'd done the first two things in the checklist, but she hadn't started thinking of the kill method yet.

Yesterday, she'd been consumed with proving she could work on the ranch and then focusing attention on Ebuka last night.

He'd been the centre of the universe.

Being with him had been different from anyone else.

The times with Osagie, the focus had always been to cleanse her guilt with pain before she could enjoy the pleasure that followed.

But with Ebuka, she felt no guilt. Yes, there had been some pain. But nothing on the scale she'd endured previously.

And the pleasure had been out of this world.

Ebuka had discarded the respectable farmer. In his stead had stood a man whose dark and dominant desires had pushed all her needy buttons.

The way he'd chased her and taken her outside, with the rain and dirt and grass and mud.

So primal. So freaking sexy.

The memory would be on playback for many months to come.

She was wet and clenching already just thinking about it. She shifted, and her thigh grazed his dick. He was sporting morning wood.

Sliding a palm down his abs to his groin, she calculated how long they had before they had to get up and dressed. The sun wasn't fully up.

They could fuck and then get dressed before anyone came to look for them.

She shifted until her mouth hovered over his cock. Leaning down, she swallowed the head in her mouth. The taste of man, tang and salt exploded on her tongue.

Fingers wrapped around her hair and tugged.

She looked up. Ebuka's dark eyes were glazed with sleep and lust.

"Come here," he said, the corner of his mouth curled in a smile.

Abandoning his bobbing erection, she crawled up his body.

He pulled her head down and kissed her, the taste of him and her mingling as tongues tangoed. He kissed with as much passion as he fucked, and it took her breath away.

Breaking the kiss, he said in a low voice, "It's a new day. We have to get back to the house."

She sighed, not bothering to hide her disappointment. The deal had been sex for only last night.

He was a man who kept his word, and she respected him for it.

He kissed her briefly and swatted her bum. "Move. Someone is probably on the way to check on us."

She rolled out of the sofa bed. "You're probably right."

He scrambled to his feet. "Of course, I am. Ginika will send someone out to make sure we're okay. She would worry since we didn't return last night."

He pulled dried clothes from the chair and started dressing.

She tugged her clothes on. They'd opted to sleep on the sofa bed in the lounge instead of the bunk beds provided in the bedroom. They were single units and not much room to move.

Fully clothed, she helped Ebuka fold the blankets away and put the sheets in the laundry basket. The dirty laundry would be taken to the main house for cleaning.

They'd just about straightened the place out when an ATV pulled up outside the cabin. Ebuka raised his brow in an I-told-you-so expression as he went outside to greet the man. He introduced the darker-skinned man as Hector. He was probably in his mid-forties and stood shorter than her and Ebuka.

Ebuka let her ride the ATV back to the ranch while he took Chocho.

Afterwards, Ebuka disappeared into his office, and Ginika took her to a bedroom upstairs. The male workers stayed in an annexe.

A quick shower and a meal and Xandra went out on the range, this time working with Hector. They made sure the cattle were fed, checking on them every couple of hours and then tagging and vaccinating the calves. That became her job for the next few days. She didn't see much of Ebuka except at the dinner table. He didn't spend any more time with her than he did with the men.

He was back to being a respectable businessman. It was as if their night in the cabin hadn't happened.

She shouldn't be bothered—wasn't worried. They'd agreed it would be for one night only. And despite the disguise and alter ego, she was still Xandra, here to do a job. He would be dead, whatever happened.

That was what she'd thought until Thursday afternoon. She was in the kitchen with Ginika helping to clean up. They'd just had lunch, and Xandra volunteered to hang back so she could have a chat with Ebuka's sister. This had become a routine she enjoyed.

Wanting to bump into Ebuka on the way out. To see if something would spark. If he thought about their night together.

The sound of tyres on gravel announced a new arrival. She didn't bother to check who it was as the ranch had regular visitors, whether it was the vet on a scheduled visit or delivery vans.

"Are you expecting groceries?" Xandra asked.

Ginika ordered online and had them delivered. It saved on the two-hour round-trip to the nearest town.

"No," she said as she headed out through the side entrance.

They rounded the house when Xandra saw Ebuka talking to another man. The man stood beside a low-slung sports car that looked out of place.

"Ralph," Ginika said.

Ralph Nweke. The man who had taken out a kill contract on Ebuka's life was here chatting with Ebuka as if they were acquaintances.

Xandra sucked in a breath as her heart slammed in her chest. She tried to retreat, but the man had already seen them.

"Gigi," he said as he strode towards them, Ebuka walking beside him.

"Ralph," Gigi said before he kissed her on the cheeks. "What are you doing here?"

He leaned back with a smile. "I came to make sure you will be at the party on Friday night. Your brother is being a bore as usual, but I'd love the pleasure of your company. Please say yes."

If his car looked out of place at the ranch, the man himself was an anomaly too in his flashy fitted black suit and white shirt and the black leather derby shoes. Even his haircut was designer and coiffed to perfection, and his teeth were too white.

Such a contrast to the rough and ready Ebuka who lived in t-shirts, jeans and scuffed brown boots.

Ginika glanced in Ebuka direction before turning back to Nweke with a smile. "Of course I'll be there."

"Fantastic. I look forward to seeing you there." He kissed her on the cheeks again.

"I'll walk you to your car," Ebuka said, interrupting them.

Nweke gave Xandra another quick look before heading back to his car. He shouldn't know who she was as she hadn't met him face-to-face before. It didn't seem as if he recognized her, which was good. She worried, nonetheless.

What was this party? Surely Ginika wasn't planning to go by herself. Nweke was a crooked State Attorney General and had his fingers in so many crime pies. He was the last person Gigi should be getting involved with.

Xandra didn't know why it bothered her, but it did.

Maybe she'd developed a fondness for Ginika like the feelings she had for Zoe Himba, whom she looked upon like a sister of sorts. But Zoe grew up in a crime family. She was a capo, capable of handling her business, and she could deal with the likes of Nweke.

In contrast, Ginika appeared to have led a sheltered life. She would be a lamb among wolves at that party.

She headed towards the house.

Xandra followed and stopped her by the door. "You're not serious about going to the party, are you?"

"Of course, I am. It's just a party," she said nonchalantly.

Xandra had seen what could happen at parties. Women drugged and made to perform sexual acts they would never have agreed to. Some even abducted and sold by human traffickers.

She was thinking worst-case scenario. Still a possibility.

"Do you even know what goes on at that kind of party?" she asked and placed a hand on Gigi's shoulder.

"How do you know what will happen at the party? Have you been to any of Ralph's parties?" She walked into the kitchen.

"No," Xandra bit out. "But I know his sort. He looks like a dangerous man."

She laughed. "He's the State Attorney General. He's one of the good guys."

Xandra wanted to shout that she was so wrong, but Ebuka walked in then. "You're not going to let her go to this party on her own, are you?"

He looked at her quizzically for a moment before replying. "Of course not. I'm going to the party too."

"Good. The more, the merrier," Ginika cheered and kissed her brother on the cheek. "Now, I have to go and shop for an outfit and find someone who will deliver it by tomorrow."

She disappeared under the archway leading into the hall.

Neither Ebuka nor Xandra moved. The air in the space seemed charged with something she couldn't decipher.

"Why don't you want her going to the party alone?"

Her cheeks heated as if he'd caught her doing something she shouldn't have. "I care about her and that Nweke doesn't look very honourable to me."

"He looks all suave in his expensive lawyer suit, but he's no good. Certainly not good enough for my sister. I'm going to be there to keep an eye on her."

"Good," Xandra said. "Because if you weren't going, I would've gone there myself."

His eyes darkened, and he took a step towards her. "You are fond of my sister. It seems you're trying to get close to her."

Only because she was attracted to her brother.

Why was she caught up in their domestic situation? She had a mission to complete.

"I like your sister as a friend. Perhaps as a sister. I never had one."

She didn't have a sister or friends. In the cartel world, there were no friends. Just associates and bosses and enemies.

Not to mention that for the first time in her life she was amongst people who seemed to genuinely like her. She didn't feel like a freak.

The admission made her uncomfortable. She had never admitted that to anyone before. Ebuka's mouth hung open, his body frozen to the spot.

Temptation sizzled in her veins, made her fingers itch. To move close, caress his lips and feel his warmth.

Balling them into fists, she swivelled and walked out of the kitchen before she did something that she'd promised she wouldn't do again.

NINE

FRIDAY NIGHT, Xandra went to the city with Ebuka and Ginika.

Ebuka hadn't explained why he'd invited her along, but she wasn't going to argue.

He drove them in the blue double-cab Toyota pickup that Adiele had washed and buffed so that it gleamed like a new car.

Xandra sat in the back, and Ginika sat up front, chatting excitedly about the people who would be at the party.

Ralph Nweke was a big shot around here, and the movers and shakers of Bakili would grace the event, supposedly.

The evening Commissioner Nweke came to the ranch, Ginika told Xandra about the animosity between Ebuka and Ralph. They'd been best of friends while they had been at university together. But something happened between that made the two of them fall out. She didn't know what. Both men refused to discuss it.

Xandra didn't say much on the drive. She enjoyed listening to Gigi talk with such enthusiasm about life. She had so much exuberance. So much joy.

In contrast, before she came to the ranch, the only thing that made Xandra excited was her visits to see Osagie. Those moments after her penance when she could finally enjoy the pleasure of sex had been the closest she came to joy.

Until she'd met Ginika and her brother.

The night with Ebuka had been the most bliss-filled of her life. Neither of them had spoken about it since.

Ebuka pulled into the parking lot of the hotel he had booked. He didn't want them driving back to the ranch in the middle of the night.

At the reception, they checked into individual rooms and took their luggage up.

Xandra's room was suitable for a mid-range hotel with off-white walls, a double bed against the accent wall painted in gingerbread colour, coordinating curtains, bedspreads and carpet. A small sofa and a tea table stood by the window overlooking the city. A TV screen sat on a long table opposite the bed. There was also a chair next to the table.

It didn't have the luxury of the suite she'd checked into on her first arrival in the city. Still, it was a good room. First, she washed the wig and left it to air dry. She stripped off and stepped into the shower. She'd spent most of the day repairing blockages in the water system, and it had been a hot day. However, temperatures had cooled slightly when they headed to the city.

After scrubbing her body clean and washing her short hair, she rinsed off, switched off the faucet and stepped out of the cubicle.

Dressing meticulously, she wore a blue linen dress and studded strappy stilettos.

She locked the small handgun in the safe. She'd brought it along in case there was trouble. On second thoughts, it was best not to take it. She wouldn't be able to explain to Ebuka if the scanners found it.

Dressed, she headed across to Ebuka's room. He opened the door, and her mouth dropped open.

Hot damn. The man was fine with a capital F. He looked fantastic in a white dress shirt and navy slacks, which set off his caramel skin tone. He'd trimmed his beard, and along with the new taper-fade haircut, he had swag.

She'd never seen him in anything other than jeans, chambray or t-shirts. Instead of boots, he wore brown leather brogues.

He stared at her with an odd expression before saying, "You look good," and turning away.

"Wow," Ginika said, looking her over. "You scrub up well for a farmhand."

She wore a lovely emerald silk dress that was cut off across one shoulder and draped in an asymmetrical style beyond her knees. Strappy diamante sandals and her hair styled in a loose chignon completed the classy outfit.

"She sure does," Ebuka added, still giving her that look that made her heart thud faster.

"And there I was worried you wouldn't have anything suitable to wear." She beamed a smile at Xandra, and then turned to her brother, holding up a maroon silk tie. "Come on, Ebuka. The tie will go great with your suit. Tell him, please, Allie."

"No, I don't need one. I'm just escorting two beautiful women to a party." He turned away as if he hadn't expected the words to come out as awestruck as they did.

Xandra's smile blossomed. Ebuka really liked her dress then.

"You can't let an ordinary employee like me outshine you, boss." She winked at Ginika. "But the tie will work well with your suit. Here let me help you."

She walked over to Ginika and took the tie from her.

"You look amazing," she said and pressed a kiss to the other woman's cheek.

Then she sashayed over to where Ebuka leaned against the table. "Trust me, you'll look great."

"Hmmm," was all he said, but he let her come close enough to turn the collar of his shirt up.

She was conscious of Ginika behind them, so she maintained a reasonable gap between her and Ebuka as she slid the silk around his neck.

Each breath she took filled her lungs with his scent—man and spice—that transported her back to the night in the cabin.

As she looped and knotted the tie, she couldn't help brushing fingers against his chin. His breath hitched.

A smile played at the corner of her mouth.

He'd shaved the skin smooth. She missed the bristles and wanted them rubbing against her skin.

"I can't find my perfume in my purse," Ginika called out. "I'm going to pop back to my room and get it."

Xandra's body trembled, knowing she would be alone with Ebuka for a few minutes. Tension oozed off his body too.

As soon as the door closed behind his sister, she couldn't keep away any longer. She leaned her body against his, boobs crushed to his chest, the bulge of his erection rubbing her thigh.

"I've missed you," she whispered before brushing her lips on his. He gripped her nape, angled her head and devoured her mouth.

She moaned long and deep as she sank into him, loving his strength, loving the contact. Her hands slid around his back. She stepped into him, as physically close as they could be with clothes on.

What happened to her whenever this man touched her? As if being in his arms was where she should be.

A rattling noise at the door broke them apart when Ebuka shoved her away. Then he picked up his leather wallet just as Ginika walked into the room.

"Found it," she announced, holding up a small bottle of perfume.

"Good." Xandra forced a smile. Her body still shook from the impact of the kiss and the abrupt way it ended.

"You look wonderful with the tie. In fact, I'm taking a picture of both of you." She pulled out her smartphone and waved it. "Go on. Get closer together."

If only she knew how much closer Xandra wanted to get to Ebuka. She glanced at Ebuka, but he wasn't looking her way.

"Do we have to?" he grumbled.

"Oh, come on. It's just a phone. It's not going to trap your soul, you know," Gigi teased.

Xandra chuckled as she took a step to Ebuka and put an arm across his shoulders. "You have nothing to worry about. I'll protect you from soul snatchers."

Ginika giggled, and even Ebuka serious face broke in a smile.

"Well, okay then," he said. "Since you both promise to keep me safe, I guess I can survive one photo session."

She set them where she wanted them to stand, took a couple of snaps and then squeezed between them and took a few more of the three together.

They headed out to Nweke's mansion, which was up a private, winding road at the top of a hill in a location Ebuka described as millionaire row. He had opted to not move into the government-appointed housing.

"How he could afford to live here on the SAG's salary is anyone's guess," he said as they pulled up the gravel drive that curved around a stone fountain.

"I suppose he has a few business interests outside of the SAG's office," his sister said. There was about an acre of lush green lawn in front with a section of landscaped plants.

Ebuka pulled up in a parking space where the attendant directed him. From the limousines and sports cars all lined up, it seemed the crème of the city had turned up.

Xandra opened the door and helped Ginika off the truck. Ebuka came around to join them.

"Gigi, head up to the house. I just want to chat with Allie quickly."

"Okay." She walked off.

Ebuka leaned forward, his voice low. "What happened tonight at the hotel between us is never going to happen again."

Jerking, Xandra was stunned by his vehemence. "Why? We kissed. No big deal."

"No big deal?" His hands balled into fists. "My sister nearly walked in on us."

Feeling irritated by his attitude and refusal to acknowledge this thing between them, Xandra crossed arms over her chest and eyeballed him. "What are you afraid of?"

His eyes narrowed. "Look. I can't get involved in a relationship. I'm still trying to get myself out of the last one."

She flinched. "What the hell does that mean?"

He turned away and scrubbed a hand over his short hair. "It means that I was married. Technically I'm still married, awaiting the divorce, although we're separated. So, I'm sorry. But this is over. If you do what you did again, I'll be forced to let you go."

Xandra's stomach congealed, and bile rose in her throat.

How in Hell did she miss such information from his dossier? Not that marital status was necessary for a kill contract. But it helped to understand the close family of the target.

Unfamiliar emotions coursed through her, making her listless. She latched onto the one she could understand and deal with—anger.

Anger at herself for not checking out the information about him. Anger for letting herself care about him and his sister.

He was no different from anyone else, the nuns who had sold her and the man who only took her so he could turn her into a killing machine.

Her back stiffened and she straightened from where she leaned on the truck, glaring at him. "It looks like you don't want me here. So, I'm going to leave tomorrow."

Something flickered in his gaze. It was gone so quickly she couldn't decipher it.

"That'll be a good idea." He turned and walked towards the house.

Xandra stood there for a few seconds as her gut clenched and her chest tightened. Fuck. What was going on with her? Why couldn't she let it go?

She hadn't felt this shitty when Osagie had ended their arrangement. So why did she have this hollow disappointment wrecking her now?

She finally found her feet and went inside. The mansion had a mix of old and new done very well—crystal chandeliers dangling from the high ceilings, classic paintings on the wall and Persian rugs covering marble floors. Everything and everyone seemed to glitter.

Ebuka and Ginika were in a group chatting with people she didn't recognize.

She didn't approach them. Instead, she stood in the shadows, watching. She had never been great in social situations.

Tell her to kill someone, and she could walk right up to the person and put a bullet in their skull. However, approaching someone and talking was not her thing. A leftover from when she was a child and all the other kids would play together, and she would sit on a pile of sand playing by herself.

To be fair, with the status of the people at the party, this was probably not as bad as she'd imagined it would be. She didn't drink often, but she grabbed one of the passing flutes filled with champagne.

Halfway through the event, Nweke in another shiny expensive suit, this time blue, which seemed to be the theme, announced his bid to run for governor. There were cheers and toasts to him.

Ginika was chatting with another woman. Xandra wanted to walk over and ask her about Ebuka's wife. She imagined the woman would be beautiful and charming and full of life. Had Ebuka been in love with her? Why were they separated?

So many questions. The only person who could provide answers was Ebuka. Xandra scanned the space, searching for him, inside and then out in the garden.

Her heart jolted when she saw a couple sitting in a darkened alcove—Ebuka and a woman she didn't immediately recognise. They spoke in low voices, and their body language showed they were intimate.

Xandra's stomach hardened, and a burning sensation spread across her chest. Yes, he'd said they were over. But how could he move on so quickly?

Her breathing became coarser, faster. Her chest burned hotter.

The feeling was strange, unfamiliar. She didn't know how to stop it.

The woman stood and spoke loud enough for Xandra to hear. "I'm going to the ladies, and then you're taking me back to your hotel room."

No! Say, no!

Ebuka didn't say anything as she sashayed away.

Xandra took a secretive shot of her face and used her image identifier app to scan. Her photo showed up on social media.

Xandra's stomach dropped as she stared at the name. Sabina Dede-Njoku.

Ebuka's wife? She was as beautiful as Xandra imagined, flawless skin, round curves and petite.

More information about her showed she was a lawyer who worked in the SAG's office with Ralph Nweke.

This was getting more complicated by the minute. Was she as corrupt as Nweke?

Xandra followed her into the bathroom and waited outside the stall until she came out.

Sabina jerked back and placed a hand on her chest, giggling. "You frightened me, standing there like that."

Xandra flashed a smile full of teeth and little humour and stepped forward so that Sabina backed up against the wall. She locked the bathroom door and leaned on it.

"What's going on?" Sabina asked, a frown marring her otherwise flawless skin.

"I brought you a message. When you leave the bathroom, make your excuses and go home. Not with Ebuka Njoku."

"Or what?" the other woman sneered.

"Or I'll break your neck."

Her breath hitched, and she pulled out her phone. "You can't threaten me."

Xandra snatched it from her, tossed it on the floor and crushed it under her shoes.

She opened her mouth to scream.

Xandra covered her mouth with one hand before she could make a sound while wrapping the other around her neck as she struggled.

"I can break your neck right now," Xandra whispered against her ear from behind, pressing Sabina's front to the wall.

Sabina froze, pulse racing as sweat broke on her skin.

"Are you ready to do what I say?" Xandra asked.

She nodded and made a muffled sound.

"Good. Leave and head to your car. Don't talk to anyone about what just happened. And don't go back to Ebuka. I promise you won't live past tonight if you do."

She nodded again, and Xandra released her.

She bent forward, leaned against the wall and panted for breath.

"Have a good night, Ms Dede-Njoku," Xandra said before walking out of the bathroom. She didn't look back. She didn't need to as she could hear Sabina coughing.

Xandra rounded the corner and waited for her out of sight. Sabina came out and headed to the car park in a hurry.

Xandra turned towards the party where she found Ginika.

"It looks like you're driving me back to the hotel. Ebuka is grabbing a lift with someone else."

"No, he isn't," Xandra muttered.

"What did you say?" she asked.

"Nothing."

Ebuka appeared a few minutes later. "It seems I've been abandoned. Come on. Let's head to the hotel."

Xandra said nothing on the drive back although Ginika chatted for most of it. In her mind, she saw Ebuka and Sabina and her blood boiled hot.

She was resolute in her decision.

If Ebuka wanted her gone tomorrow, she would go. But she would kill him tonight.

As soon as she could, she bid them good night and went to her room. In quiet solitude, she hacked into the hotel system and changed the code to her card so she could get into any space. Then she waited another hour to make sure Ebuka would be asleep.

She opened the safe and took out her weapons. A small bottle of liquid sedative. She pulled the required dose into a syringe and capped it. Then she took the handgun. It was a backup. The plan was to make it look like he drowned in the bath. He put the gun, suppressor and syringe into her jacket pockets.

Following the steps needed to complete a kill, she turned from Allie the farmworker to Xandra the assassin. She became focused on the objective— terminate a life.

Finally, she changed the camera angle in the hallway so it would leave a blind spot at Ebuka's door.

She left her room and strode across to Ebuka's. Hearing nothing, she opened the door and slid in noiselessly, shutting it.

Darkness surrounded her, and she blinked to adjust her sight.

Ebuka lay in bed, covered in a white sheet. She pulled out the syringe and walked up to stand beside the bed.

The needle caught the light and glinted. Ginika's face came into her mind, making her pause. Ginika in tears and broken-hearted after finding her brother dead. She pictured Nweke's face when he found out Ginika was now at his mercy.

Xandra's chest squeezed tight, aching. There would be no one to protect Ginika because she would have to return to Jokogi. The thought of Nweke getting his paws on Gigi made Xandra's skin crawl.

She had never considered the families of the people she killed before. Why was she obsessed about Ginika?

Xandra lowered the syringe, but her fury remained.

Why the hell did she have to do what anyone else wanted? Ebuka wanted her gone, and Nweke wanted him dead.

She wasn't ready to leave Ebuka, and she wasn't prepared to kill him.

Perhaps she was living in a bubble of deceit that she had built. But she wasn't ready to burst it.

She would rather kill Ebuka than have him fuck anyone else.

But she wasn't done fucking him yet. He would just have to get used to her being around for a while.

Capping the syringe, she pocketed it and then removed the jacket, flinging it over the chair as she picked up Ebuka's silk tie.

He stirred in bed. "Allie? What are you doing here?"

He flicked on the side lamp, bathing the room in a dim orange glow.

She turned and faced him.

His expression was a mix of sleep and surprise. The sheet only covered his hips, and his chest was bare, revealing a small trail of hairs disappearing in a v shape under the sheet.

He looked fuckable.

Her mouth watered as she stepped close to the bed. "Thing is, I'm not done with you yet. And I don't think you're done with me. You just don't want to admit it."

She stretched the tie taut between her clenched hands.

"Allie, don't fuck with me." He growled the words.

"Oh, I think that's the general idea." She winked.

He tried to get up. "I swear— "

She shoved his chest and cut him off. "No. You don't. Do you think you can kiss me in this very room and then within a few hours end up with someone else?"

His eyes widened. "You know about that?"

"I saw you two. You were going to bring her back here and fuck her."

"It's not what you think. She's my soon-to-be ex-wife. We were just going to talk."

"No. I don't like it. You don't get to bring her to your hotel room."

"Allie, we ended it."

"No, *you* ended it."

He tried getting up again, and she shoved him down. They wrestled like they had done the night in the rain. This time she had the upper hand as he was beneath and she used the sheets tangled around him to her advantage so he couldn't move his legs in a wide range.

She knotted the tie around his wrists, the other end hooked on the lamp above the bed, panting and sweating, same as him.

He could yank the lamp off the wall if he tugged hard enough. But the upright man in him wouldn't want to damage hotel furniture. The items on the bedside table had crashed to the floor. He wouldn't want to explain how the damages occurred.

They stared at each other as she sat on top of him. His gaze was filled with intense heat, and his dick beneath the sheets had hardened.

"You know when I get out of these bonds, I'm going to belt your ass raw," he said, glaring at her.

"Yes, boss," she replied as she got off him and started taking the rest of her clothes off.

She watched him as he watched her. Her nerve endings tingled, her need heightened.

"Untie me," he ordered when she pulled the sheets back to reveal his nakedness.

He wasn't tamed. Just a wild tiger caged for the moment.

"No," she said. "This obele needs to teach her boss a lesson."

TEN

EBUKA GROWLED as lust flooded his veins.

The threat in Allie's voice floated between them, adding to the violence that vibrated in the air.

He lifted his bound hands, trying to sit up.

"Stay where you are." She pulled his legs, dragging him down the bed, so the tie was stretched tight.

He glared at her, and she only smiled in return.

If he could sit up, he'd be able to loosen the knot on the lamp and eventually free his hands. He could yank hard. But that would damage the wall furniture.

There was a time he wouldn't have cared about damaging property. A time he wouldn't have let anyone tie him up.

But he'd outgrown that boy. Moved on. Gone legit. Become a gentleman.

Still, there was a reason his ancestors had coined the proverb "whether it is dead or alive, do not touch a lion by its tail" because you didn't know if it would jump up and bite you in the ass.

Someone should have warned Allie.

Because she was stirring the beast inside him. The part he'd tried to bury.

In any case, Ebuka had nothing to prove to her. So, he'd allowed her to tie him up. However, it seemed she had something to prove.

He'd never seen her like this. Like a changeling.

She'd been cold and distant at their first meeting. Warm and passionate during their night in the cabin. Determined and diligent while working on the farm. Playful and protective with Ginika over the past few days.

Now her eyes blazed with jealousy and fury. She was willing to defy his order, knowing the outcome would be punishment.

"Allie, let's talk about this." He tried to reclaim some control.

She climbed onto the bed on her hands and knees—naked body, tawny brown skin, scars on her back, and intense amber eyes filled with lust.

His heart stuttered. The urge to touch her made his palms itch and his mouth water. Oh, he would make her ass sore, but he would fuck her.

"Your version of talking is you telling me what to do." She crawled across the bed, smooth like a cat. "Now is the time for you to listen to me."

Mesmerised, his words froze in his throat. He blinked, watching her move until she stopped between his spread legs.

"Don't think that because I choose to yield to you that I have no say in what happens between us?" She wrapped her warm hand around his dick, grip rough.

A ragged moan ripped out of him. Heat spiked through his blood. His limbs weakened, thighs falling apart.

"I have an equal stake in this." She stroked him, up and down.

He opened his mouth to dispute, but the words died as all his brain cells focused on feeling instead of talking. He shook his head instead.

"You might think I have no stake in this," she continued. "But I have as much to lose if things go wrong. You're going to have to trust me on this."

She watched his face as her other palm covered his balls. Unable to stop his response, he groaned, moving arching hips.

He shouldn't be responding like this. He shouldn't let her control the situation.

But there was something about her, the way her amber eyes stayed glued on him, flashing with deadly need, making it futile to resist her.

His arousal spiked, even knowing she dared him.

"So, you don't get to tell me when it ends. And I don't get to tell you when it ends. When the time comes, we'll both know it."

She leaned forward, her burning gaze still fixed on him as she opened her mouth and swallowed the head of his dick.

A sound broke from his throat. Pleasure assaulted him, spiking from his balls to the tips of his fingers. He couldn't breathe. Couldn't do anything but watch her take charge of his body.

Her head bobbed, and his cock hit the back of her throat.

His hands balled into fists. The sound of his heavy panting filled the room.

Her lips stretched around his girth, wetness trailing as she slid up and swirled her tongue around the sensitive tip.

Fuck!

She had him. No doubt about it. Any fight he still had vanished, and he sank into the pleasure like velvet over his skin.

She came down again, taking him deep, her nose grazing the hairs on his groin.

He closed his eyes, jerking his hips, trying to get as deep inside her as he could. If she carried on like this, he was going to come. He also didn't want it to end.

He gritted his teeth, fighting the overwhelming need for release.

She hummed, sending vibrations down his length, to his balls and the base of his spine.

"Allie!" Her name ripped out of his throat in a guttural sound.

She lifted her head, released him with a pop. Her hands stayed on him, left one on his balls, right one gripped his cock.

"Did you want something, boss?" she asked in a tone all too innocent.

Mouth agape, he panted, filling and emptying his lungs in shallow breaths.

"Don't play with me," he managed to say.

"I wouldn't dream of it. I just thought you wanted something."

"Yes. I do. Your mouth. I want to fill it with my cum."

She lowered her head, a devious glint in her eyes before she sucked him again.

On second thoughts, perhaps it wasn't best to let her continue. He had basically handed control back to her.

He cried out as he fought the thrill fizzing through him, bucking hips to get her off.

She didn't let go. Instead, she hollowed out her mouth and hummed, her throat contracting around his length.

His harsh groans filled the room. Instead of fighting, he started thrusting, fucking her mouth as his dick swelled and hardened.

Allie didn't pull away. She took the solid, relentless plunges, her fingers gripping his hips as she held on, her gaze locked on his.

She looked sexy, her mouth stretched around him, saliva dripping down her chin. They stared at each other as she took all of him.

She was right. He wasn't done with her. He wasn't sure if he would ever be done with her. She would leave one day. Until then, they would be together.

The sound of her whimpers got his attention, and he slowed his hip action, letting her take over again.

She swiped her tongue on the underside of his cock slowly from root to tip.

The climax rushed out from nowhere. The base of his spine tingled, and heat spread out to his limbs.

She seemed to know what was happening as she worked him tighter with her mouth, encouraging him to let go.

His balls tightened. With a shout from his hoarse throat, he rammed his hips upward, seeking her warm, wet mouth only to find cold, empty air.

Allie pulled her lips away, only her hand gliding over his dick.

Semen arched through the air and splattered on his stomach and thigh in several bursts.

He lay there, eyes closed, body trembling as the sound of rushing blood in his ears subsided and his panting breath regulated.

The mattress shifted, and she untied his hands. He lifted his lashes.

She stood by the bed, hands to her back, her expression withdrawn. "It's the end of the lesson, boss."

Exhaling a heavy sigh, his gut tightened as he rubbed his wrists, working the circulation around the numb fingers.

He was disappointed because she hadn't taken his cum in her mouth. But he understood she had been protesting against his actions.

He needed to resolve the misunderstanding. She stepped out of the way as he got out of bed.

He walked into the bathroom, ran some water into the sink and cleaned up.

Although he'd come, he wasn't flaccid. A few minutes to rest and he'd be ready to go again. Would she stay or leave?

He got his answer moments later when he returned to the bedroom. She stood by the bed, hands behind her back.

He picked up the linen trousers he'd worn earlier and pulled them on without bothering with any underwear. Then he approached her, stopping at arm's length.

She didn't retreat or shift, showing no fear.

Good. He didn't want to inspire that kind of rapport. They had a connection. No need to fight it anymore.

"So, you'd like us to be in a relationship?" he asked in a calm voice, brows raised in query.

She frowned, touching the base of her neck, her expression childlike. "A relationship? I didn't exactly say that."

His lips tugged at the corners. His chest tingled with warmth. "If we're fucking each other exclusively, and you're working on my ranch while we're living under the same roof and playing house, what else would it be?"

Although he hadn't overtly given her any attention while at the ranch, he'd observed the way she worked. All the reports from the other workers about her had been positive. She'd accomplished every task, no matter how menial. Every evening he'd sat at the dinner table in the kitchen and had watched her interactions with Ginika. They joked and laughed about whatever was trending on social media. Ebuka wasn't big on social media, so most of it went over his head. However, it seemed a good friendship had developed between the two women.

Ginika needed the connection with a female her age, not just the virtual ones. She trusted Xandra.

Now Ebuka found himself discarding his old wariness.

The lines on Xandra's forehead deepened.

He suppressed the urge to smooth them out with his lips. Needing the distance to think clearly, he maintained the little space between them.

He wanted to understand all her needs if this was going to work.

"I hadn't thought about it in that way. But I want all those things with you. So yes, I would like a relationship with you," she said, her gaze steady.

"Good. I'd like that too. But let's get somethings clear. Firstly, Sabina is my ex. Our relationship might be complicated, and the divorce process even more problematic. But I don't want her back in my bed or in my home. I look forward to the day I can get her out of my life for good. Make sense?"

"Yes," she said.

"The second thing is about us. I like you, and I want us to explore this connection between us. But you should know that I can be quite intense. I don't share."

"I like that." Her face widened in a smile, making the band in his chest loosen.

"You are beautiful and strong, and I would never disrespect you. When you yield to me, you offer me a precious gift. Something you don't give others. Something for me to cherish. Do you understand?"

"Yes, I do."

"Good." Relieved, he reached for her, placing the left hand on her hip while the other went to her nape.

Pulling her close, he kissed her aggressively. The second she responded, he pulled away, leaving her panting and wanting more from the expression in her eyes.

It was time to administer her chastisement.

"You remember that I said I would spank your ass raw when I got out of the binding?"

She flinched. "Yes, boss."

A wicked smile curved his lips. "And when I told you to untie me, you disobeyed me."

"Yes, I did." Her breathing became shallow.

"And knowing I wanted to come in your mouth, you still denied me the pleasure."

She lowered her gaze and nodded.

"Obele, I want words."

"Yes, boss." She looked up.

"Yes, what?" he raised a brow.

"Yes, I knew what you wanted, and I didn't carry it out."

"And in all of it, you were insolent."

"Yes, I was, boss."

He didn't include being tied up as a reason to punish her. He could've fought harder if he'd wanted. But wrestling with her had been a turn-on, and he'd wanted to see what she would do once she had restrained him.

Slowly, he pulled out the brown leather belt from the loops of the trousers. "Now it's time to take your punishment."

Her breath hitched as her eyes widened. But she didn't look scared.

"You don't ever have to doubt anything I tell you," he said as he stepped back and folded the belt in his hand so that he held the buckle and the round end in his grip. "Face the bed and lean over it with only your hands touching the mattress."

Without a word, she obeyed, her round ass cheeks presented in a perfect position. Her skin there was so smooth, so unmarred compared to the scars on her back that looked like cane welts that weren't treated and hadn't healed properly.

The thought that someone had left their marks on her made him feel murderous. But he didn't want to disrupt their session by digging into her past right now.

However, he looked forward to making her bum sore with the belt. To reasserting his authority and claiming her. To giving her what she wanted. She liked pain if their night together was an indication.

"For your insolence and disobedience tonight, you will receive ten strikes. Count them out."

"Yes, boss," she replied in a calm, resigned tone.

Standing by the side, he lifted the right hand in a medium arch and brought the leather down on her ass.

Thud.

She gasped, and her grip on the sheets tightened.

"One," her strained voice rang into the quiet room.

ELEVEN

XANDRA'S BODY flushed hot, and sweat beaded her skin by the time the last thud of the leather belt hit the already tender flesh of her bum.

"Ten," she called out, voice a little breathy.

Her arms trembled from the strain of staying in a stiff position, but she didn't move even when he stopped. She sucked in a deep breath and exhaled it, relief flowing through her along with the sense of purification.

"Obele, you're so good when you want to be," Ebuka said as he stepped away, the heat of his presence shifting and chilly air from the AC caressing her backside.

She should be full of indignation at his use of the diminutive 'obele' which translated to 'little'. This implied she was the 'little' to his 'Daddy'. She had no interest in age play or kink.

She would shut him down immediately if he ever mentioned dolls or dummies or fluffy toys. She shuddered at the imagery.

However, every time he used the pet-name, something fluttered low in her belly, her heart warmed, and she wanted to smile like an idiot. Maybe because the name was unique and no one else had given her a nickname, although Zoe shortened her name to Xan.

For a woman who never got emotional in sexual interactions, Xandra was still shocked at how much Ebuka made her feel, many of those reactions conflicting and confusing.

Today, she'd run a full gamut from feeling murderous at the sight of Ebuka with his wife to now wanting his body wrapped around hers as his shaft pulsed inside her.

She suppressed the smile blooming on her face. She shouldn't be smiling when her bottom was sore from his belt. Especially after she'd taken matters into her hands by wrestling, restraining and disobeying him. She had proven her point and had earned his reprimand.

He trailed a palm over her ass. She flinched at the sensitivity.

"Every time you move, you will feel me on your skin." He caressed her backside. "I'm thinking of borrowing a leaf from Ginika and taking photos of you like this to celebrate as the marks will be gone in a few hours."

Muscles tensing, she locked her elbows, so she didn't push off the bed and get away from him.

Photos were dangerous things. She didn't want any evidence of her in a vulnerable position ending up in the wrong hands.

She turned her head and looked at Ebuka. Her breath caught.

Damn! The man was too damned irresistible standing there, belt in hand, bare-chested with the top of his navy slacks undone to reveal his groin hairs and the base of his partial erection.

She remembered the salty taste of his shaft and the ache in her mouth as he'd repeatedly rammed into her throat. It had been a shame to waste all the creamy cum. But she had to finish what she'd started.

"Did you want to say something?"

His words pulled her from the memories to the present.

Many women had fallen victim of men posting their images on porn sites. Although any person who tried that with her would die an excruciating death by her hands.

"Will the photos be for your eyes only, boss?" Using the honorific always subdued her need to control and put her in the mind space to hand over control to someone else. It worked well with Osagie and was working wonderfully with Ebuka who seemed to understand her need to hand him the power.

"Yes. I won't use them for anything else. Do you trust me?"

"Yes, I trust you."

A smile spread across his face. "That's the best thing you've said to me. Don't move. Let me get the device."

Xandra didn't suppress the smile as he stepped out of view. She stared ahead, determined to allow him to do whatever he wanted.

"Right," he said. The camera on his device clicked several times. "Turn around. Lie on your back."

She did as he ordered.

He clicked away, giving a few more directions.

"Spread your thighs. Caress your pretty pussy. Show me how much you want to come."

Click. Click.

"Lift your legs. Part your labia lips. Show me how much you want me inside you."

Click. Click.

She panted heavily. Blood rushed rapidly in her ears, matching the throbbing in her clit. The combination of his words, her aching bum and showing off her body to him was going to make her come soon.

She focused on slowing her breathing. He wouldn't be pleased if she came without his permission. She probably wouldn't get fucked. And she wanted that more than she wanted to come.

"Shove your fingers in your hole. That's it. Prepare yourself for me." Breath locked in her lungs.

His left hand held onto the camera while his right hand stroked his dick through the fabric of his trousers.

With her legs pulled up, she shoved a finger into her slit. Closing her eyes, she exhaled a sigh of pleasure. It felt good, but she needed more. She added a second finger, slid it in and out, and added a third.

Cold gel drizzled down her pussy. She opened her eyes.

Ebuka watched her directly, lust burning in his gaze. It seemed he'd forgotten his camera already. He tossed the device onto the table, and it clattered as he popped the cap of the tube and squeezed lube onto his hand before reaching into his trousers and pulling his swollen dick out. He tugged his length twice before he grasped her thighs, her bum hanging at the edge of the bed. Her fingers slid out of her slit, but it didn't stay empty for long before the mushroom head of his dick breached her.

Hooking her legs over his arms, he rocked his hips forward, knocking the breath out of her as he slammed all the way to the hilt. He was firm. Unyielding.

She couldn't do much but lie here and take whatever he gave. And she didn't feel threatened by another person leaning over her, driving into her. First time ever.

She didn't have to prove that she was powerful. She had nothing to prove and was happy to be under him, enjoying the pain as it morphed into pleasure.

"Fuck, Allie. I can't get enough of you," his voice was husky, on edge.

He pulled out and slammed back in, working a slow rhythm that was excruciating and driving her crazy. He carried on for a few minutes.

The pleasure was insane. She wanted to crawl out of her skin and stay there all at once.

Sweat dripped down her body. She clenched her inner walls around him.

"Please, Ebuka. You're killing me."

He leaned over, pressed his weight onto her body, and kissed her mouth.

He felt good. So good. His weight on her. His mouth on her. His dick in her. She was covered in Ebuka and filled with Ebuka.

He lifted his head, still leaning over, his left hand hooked over her right thigh, his right hand holding the back of her neck, his groin grinding on her pussy with his motions.

They were in sync. When he exhaled, she inhaled. When she exhaled, he inhaled. She had never felt better.

Suddenly, the frustration of his slow thrusts morphed into euphoria as he continuously hit her sweet spot.

Her core tingled with an upcoming orgasm. "Boss. Can I... come... please?"

He pressed his lips to hers briefly. "Yes, obele m. Show me how much you enjoyed this."

He stroked her again. Once. Twice.

"Ebuka!" She came with his name on her lips in a long shout of pure bliss. Her pussy clenched, again and again, her body writhing.

"Ezigbo obele m. Gwa ụwa niine na o mụ nwe gị."

She understood the context of his guttural words if not their literal translation. He was claiming her and happy for the world to know it.

He grinned at her and leaned back before turning his thrusts fast and hard. Soon he came with a slam and a heavy grunt. Then he flopped beside her on the bed to catch his breath.

Her legs fell to the bed. She winced as her sore bum contacted the mattress. "Come on then, let's clean you up."

He stood and carried her into the bathroom, the shower was quick.

"Is it okay if I stay the rest of the night?" she asked while drying her body with a towel.

"Of course, you're staying the night," he said as he tossed his towel on a railing and kissed her lips.

"Thank you." She strode across to the bed and climbed in, lying on her side.

He climbed in behind and spooned her, wrapping his arm around her.

"Obele, who put their marks on your back?" he asked in a gentle voice.

Her heart skipped a beat, and she stiffened.

She hadn't been prepared for the question. Hadn't thought he would ask since he hadn't the first night.

"It's nothing. Not important." She muttered.

"It is, to me. You're mine now. I want to know if it was consensual. And if so, why didn't they take care not to break the skin or put healing salve on afterwards."

"And if it wasn't consensual?" she asked out of curiosity. Why did he care so much?

"If it wasn't consensual, then I want to know the person so that I can give them several doses of their own medicine."

Huh? This was Ebuka Njoku, quiet farmer, reserved gentleman except when he was a freak in bed. Could he hurt anyone? It was probably just talking. Ordinary people did that all the time. Was Ebuka like that? Would he say things he didn't mean?

She turned her head and looked at him with confusion. "You would torture the person for me?"

"Yes. I wouldn't just torture someone for no reason. But if they hurt you. I would hurt them."

Intuitively, she believed him. He wouldn't say it unless he meant it. "Okay."

"So, tell me how you got the scars."

She sighed, knowing she would have to tell him some if not all of it.

"The scars are cane marks, and they were consensual. I refused aftercare, so the welts didn't heal properly."

He sat with his back to the pillow. "You refused aftercare. Why?"

"Because I equated it to affection and affection is dangerous and deceptive. People are nice to you one minute and then stab you in the back. I don't trust nice people."

He frowned. "But you trust me?"

She shrugged. "You're different. Not like the people I know. I see the way you treat Ginika and your workers. You seem to genuinely care about your people, and I like it. I want some of that too."

He slid down the bed, leaned over and kissed her on the cheek. "I don't know who you've been hanging with. But I'm glad you're here now, and I promise to take care of you."

"I'm glad I'm here too."

He turned off the lamp. "Obele, ka chi foo."

That she understood. "Goodnight, boss."

Her eyes drifted shut, and eventually, she slept.

Sunlight streaking into the room woke Xandra. Ebuka lay on his back, head on the pillow, asleep.

She watched him for a few seconds, her heart squeezing tight.

What was she going to do about him? There were a few more days before she had to complete the job. She had accepted a contract to kill him. And she had never broken a deal before.

Yesterday had changed something inside her.

Going to Njoku farm had changed something inside her. Living as Allie for the past few days had been liberating. Had shown her a life she never knew she wanted. An experience where someone else could genuinely care about her. A life where people around her didn't look at her and see a freak.

Still, there was no getting away from the kill contract. If she didn't kill Ebuka, someone else would turn up to do the job.

And then she'd also end up on someone's hit list.

All the thoughts unsettled her, and she got out of bed. She got dressed, gave him one last look over her shoulder and left the room silently.

In her room, she showered and pulled on a pair of jeans. She was pulling the t-shirt on when her device beeped, indicating she had a message. At the same time, a loud knock came through the door.

She ignored the gadget and walked to the door, peeking in the hole to see who it was.

Ebuka stood on the other side.

She undid the lock and pulled it open.

"Thank God you're okay," he said as he walked into the room before she could welcome him. Then he pushed her against the wall and kissed her hard, making her breathless.

She kissed him in return before they broke apart.

"What's going on?" she asked.

He paced away and scrubbed a hand over his head. He looked dishevelled as if he'd rushed to dress in yesterday's clothes.

"I had... a nightmare. It was about you." He turned to face her. "In the dream, I was in bed with you, and then I woke up from sleep, but you weren't in bed. So, I went looking for you only to find you dead in the hall. You'd been shot."

He puffed out a long breath.

"So, when I woke up just now and didn't find you in my room, I got worried, and I had to come and check on you."

His hands clenched and trembled. He must have been scared she was dead.

Her legs weakened, and she had difficulty breathing. She had never seen anyone genuinely concerned about her before.

Himba and the family didn't care if she lived or died. If something happened to her, they would replace her with someone else.

They were people she had known most of her life.

But she'd only known Ebuka a few days. And still, he cared.

She didn't know whether to be happy or sad. This was the man she was sent to kill, after all. Everyone on her hit list was as good as dead. He was a dead man walking.

Her footsteps were heavy as she walked over to him and wrapped arms around him, leaning head on his shoulder. "I'm fine. Nothing is going to happen to me."

He wrapped himself around her. "I know. The dream unsettled me, that's all. I should get back to my room and clean up."

She pulled back. "Okay. I'll be there soon, and we can have breakfast. Is that okay?"

"Of course."

He kissed her again before heading for the door. Once it shut behind him, she went to check the message. She logged into the encryption server and decoded it.

New non-exclusive contract issued. Target: Ebuka Njoku.

Price: $500,000.

Details attached.

Fuck! She dropped the device on the bed and rubbed a hand over her mouth.

Ebuka's kill contract had gone non-exclusive, which meant it had gone into the open market. Xandra wasn't the only assassin after him.

What the fuck was going on? She had never had a contract pulled from under her before. She picked up the phone and dialled Zoe Himba's number. If anyone knew what was going on, she did.

The phone rang for a while.

"Xan, how are you?" She sounded out of breath when she picked it up. She'd either been having sex or working out in her private gym, which was quite likely.

"Not good, Zoe. I noticed the contract is on the open market." Although she didn't specify, the other woman would know exactly what she was talking about. It was never good to speak openly on an unsecured line.

"Yes, I know. The client changed his mind. Said he wanted more options. More bidders."

"Fuck! How did this happen? I get at least two weeks, and the time isn't up."

She sighed. "You know how it is in this business. Things change all the time. Anyway, I know you can still handle this, right? You can still win the bid."

"Of course, I can."

"Good. See you soon." She hung up.

"Fuck! Fuck! Fuck!" Xandra tossed the phone on the bed. Her life just got fucking complicated.

TWELVE

XANDRA NEVER got involved with non-exclusive kill contracts.

It meant dealing with amateurs who got in the way of the actual professionals. Any goon who knew how to use a handgun or sniper rifle or explosive would want in on the action. Which meant they would be sloppy and end up spooking the target into running or going into hiding, making the job even trickier for those who knew what they were doing.

This would be the time to back away.

She ran a hand over her head and gripped it tight. No fucking way.

Ebuka was hers. He belonged to her.

She didn't care what Nweke or Himba wanted.

All her life, she had followed orders, first in the orphanage, then the training camps and finally working for Himba. She never stopped long enough to claim anything for herself. Everything she'd done had been for others.

Always the freak. Never welcomed. Only tolerated. Owning nothing.

Now there was a chance to be part of something more. Something substantial. Something better than her.

This was probably a suicide mission. She would probably spend the rest of her life looking over her shoulder. But if she planned it properly, it could work.

She picked up the tablet and sat in the armchair, rereading the message. It was Ebuka in the picture. It must have been taken last night at the party as he was wearing the same navy suit and white shirt.

Nweke was such a bastard. He'd invited Ebuka to a party only to send more assassins after him.

The message seemed to have gone live late last night while Xandra was in Ebuka's room. Which meant it could take anything between a few hours and a few days for assassins to start arriving.

She had a limited amount of time to act.

First, she needed to convince Ebuka to send Ginika away. She wasn't the target, but she could quickly become collateral damage. No assassin would hesitate to kill her if she got in the way of their work or to use her as a bait to lure Ebuka out.

Then, she needed to get to Nweke and get him to withdraw the contract, or she'd terminate him. She would've liked to do that straight away, but she couldn't be sure there wasn't an assassin already in this hotel or on the way to the ranch. She couldn't leave Ebuka or his sister alone.

She picked up the phone and called Ebuka's room.

"Ebuka, it's Allie," she said when he picked up. "Did you order room service?"

"Not yet. I just got out of the shower."

"Good. Don't order anything. We'll go out and eat on the way back to the ranch."

"Okay. That sounds good."

"Great. I'll let Ginika know. One more thing. If someone turns up at your door claiming to be room service, don't open the door."

"What? Why not?"

"It's your dream. It made me remember something I overheard last night at the party," she lied.

This wasn't the time to reveal who she was to him. He would bolt and not trust her, only ending up in the pathway of someone who would kill him. She had to protect him.

"You heard something? Why didn't you tell me?"

"Well, I was a little preoccupied and angry when I saw you with Sabina that I forgot. It's only after you left my room that I remembered it. I'll explain when I get to your room. It's not safe to discuss it on this line."

"Okay. Get over here and tell me what's going on."

"I will."

She hung up and called Ginika, who was in the process of dressing, informing her to pack up. Xandra would meet her in the room shortly.

Afterwards, she rigged the hotel camera system so she could see the full length of the corridor between the rooms and who was coming and going on her tablet.

Then she packed up the rest of her things, placing the handgun in the jacket with spare ammo as well as the syringe sedative she would have used last night.

Packed, she dragged the case out only to find Ginika leaving her room with her luggage, dressed in jeans, t-shirt and pink boots.

"I told you to wait for me." Xandra was a little miffed that Ebuka's sister hadn't done what she'd said. This kind of thing could get her killed. More reasons for her to leave.

"I couldn't wait. You promised me breakfast." Smiling, she batted her lashes.

Xandra shook her head and returned the smile.

"You said your mother was staying with her sister in Iguocha. Why don't you go and visit them?" Xandra said as she knocked on Ebuka's door.

"I'd love to go. But I can't leave Ebuka by himself on the ranch."

"He's not by himself. He's got the team and me. We can survive without you for a few days."

Ebuka pulled open the door. He was fully dressed and packed, judging from the luggage standing by the door.

"Please tell Ginika she can go to Iguocha for a few days and that we'll be fine without her," Xandra said as soon as she stepped in and the other woman followed.

He looked from her to his sister. "What's going on?"

"Allie suggested I should go and visit Mum and Aunty," she said, as she flopped onto a chair.

"She thinks we can't cope without her for a few days. But I said we'd be fine and she needs the break." Xandra met Ebuka's enquiring gaze, holding her breath, hoping he would back her up. Their lives depended on him trusting her.

He nodded and looked over at his sister. "Gigi, I think it's a good idea for you to go and see Mama."

Xandra exhaled in relief, glad he trusted her for now at least.

"Really? I can go?" Ginika's eyes sparkled with excitement.

"Of course."

"Thank you. I'll make the arrangements when we get home."

"There's no need for that," Xandra said. "You don't need to get back to the ranch. We're already in the city, and the airport is twenty minutes from here. You can be on a flight by the time it takes us to get to the ranch."

"Today? But I have to get home and pack." Her gaze bounced between them.

"You already have a suitcase full of stuff, and you can buy whatever you need over in Iguocha.

You have your ID card with you, don't you?" Ebuka said as he pulled out his device.

"Yes..."

"So, you can get on the flight," her brother spoke again as he tapped the screen. "There's a flight in three hours. We can go grab breakfast and then we're taking you to the airport. Come on, let's get out of here."

"Oh wow, I'm really going to Iguocha," Ginika said in a daze as they headed out.

Xandra kept ahead, scanning the corridor and pressed the button for the lift. No one else got into the ride as they descended to the lobby.

The reception area was empty apart from the guy at the desk. While there didn't seem to be any immediate threat, the quietness made her uneasy.

"Give me the keys to the truck," she said to Ebuka. "I'm going to load our things in."

"Okay," he said and pulled out the fob and bunch. "Give me your room card, and I'll check out for you."

She slipped it out of her pocket and handed it to him before taking Ginika's suitcase. The sliding doors opened, and she stepped out into the sunshine.

The parking area was filled with cars. Theirs was in the second row to the right. She looked up at the buildings across the road, looking for any tell-tale signs of a sniper on a roof like glinting metal or glass reflecting the sun. Finding none, she listened for sounds that could be out of place. But with the flowing traffic and pedestrians, nothing stood out.

Luggage left outside the building, she walked down the steps to the truck and listened for any ticking devices. Nothing. Although some explosive devices only ticked when armed.

Tyres screeched, and a blacked-out SUV sped from the road into the car park, nearly hitting a pedestrian on the pavement.

Xandra's nape prickled. Shit. Something was wrong. She swivelled towards the hotel entrance.

Ebuka and Ginika sauntered out of the building, smiling, chatting, unaware of the danger.

"No!" She shouted, waving hands as she ran in their direction, pulse racing. "Get back!"

Ebuka stopped, held onto Gigi. "What is it?"

Xandra didn't have time to respond. She was at the edge of the ramp about five metres away.

The car slowed as it neared. A round metal object flew out of the car window. A grenade.

Shit.

On instinct, she jumped, placing her body in its path. She used her palm like a racket and swiped the weapon, changing the direction. It smashed into a nearby parked vehicle.

An ear-deafening blast went off. The force lifted her about ten feet into the air and onto the bonnet of another car.

She must have blacked out for a few seconds. When she opened her eyes and tried to move, everything ached. Disorientated, her ears rang. Blood dripped from a cut on her head. Pushing past the pain, she slid down and planted feet on the tarmac, gaze sweeping the environment frantically.

Mangled cars lay amongst the fire and smoke. The speeding blacked-out SUV was gone. Ebuka cradled a shocked Ginika as they ran in her direction.

"Thank God. You're okay." Ginika hugged her tight.

Ebuka's eyebrows were drawn together, his expression pained as he placed a hand on her shoulder and looked her over. "Are you hurt anywhere? We need to get you to the hospital."

"No. I'm okay. We need to get inside," she said, conscious of being out in the open. The assailants could return with more weapons.

She leaned weight on her left leg and winced.

"Let me help you." Ebuka bent and swept her up in his arms.

She didn't argue with him as she might have done with another person nor spend time analysing why when she was trying to protect him. It was more important to get indoors quickly.

The car park was now filling up with onlookers and staff from the hotel. Inside, Ebuka lowered Xandra into a chair. Ginika and the team brought their luggage back in.

"What happened?" Ginika asked.

"I don't know. I was going to put the luggage in the truck, and then a car came speeding past. I just felt something was wrong and ran back towards the hotel. Next thing I knew, kaboom."

She met Ebuka's gaze. He looked as if he thought there was more to the story, but he didn't say anything.

The emergency services turned up. The police asked questions, and Xandra kept to her story. Onlookers backed her up about the blacked-out speeding car before the explosion. When they asked about her address, Ebuka gave his residence and contact details in case they needed to get in touch.

The medical team wanted to take Xandra to hospital, but she refused, so they bandaged her sprained ankle and sealed the cut on her head. The fire service extinguished the flames and confirmed the cause had been an explosive device of some sort.

With the amount of police around, Xandra relaxed a little. The attacker wouldn't try anything with so many law-enforcement officers everywhere. He or she would wait for another opportunity without the fuss.

She reminded Ebuka that they had to get Ginika to the airport. He agreed. Although Ginika protested about leaving now, he insisted she couldn't stay until they found out what was going on.

Xandra excused herself and headed to the ladies to clean up. Checking the cubicles to make sure they were empty, she pulled out her phone and sent an encrypted message to Osagie.

I need your help to make someone disappear. Alive, but invisible. Urgent.

Putting the phone back in her pocket, she changed out of the bloody t-shirt into a clean one. She was washing her hands in the sink when Ebuka walked in.

He stood beside her, looking into the mirror at her reflection. "Is someone trying to kill you?"

Her mouth dropped open, and she turned to stare at him. What an irony. He thought she was the one in danger. She couldn't lie to him about this.

She lowered her voice. "It's not me they're trying to kill. It's you."

His eyes widened, and he stumbled backwards. "What? Who wants to kill me?"

She stepped close to him and whispered, "Nweke."

"You're out of your mind. He might be a lot of things, but he's not stupid enough to try that. He was my best friend, for goodness sake, even if we don't see eye-to-eye these days."

She lifted her shoulders and eyeballed him. "He wants you dead now."

He stared at her for a minute and then said, "We're going to take Ginika to the airport and then we're going to see Nweke."

THIRTEEN

EBUKA'S GRIP on the steering wheel of the truck tightened.

Every time he remembered stepping out of the hotel and finding Allie flying due to the impact of the blown-up car, a chill ran down his spine even as his blood boiled.

Dread and anger warred within him.

When Allie had landed with an almighty thud on the car bonnet, his gut rolled as he imagined the worst—her not getting up again. Last night's dream of finding her dead had flashed through his mind.

He'd wanted to rush to her side. Only the sight of Ginika crumpled to the ground in shock had stopped him. She'd been upset too at the thought of Allie being killed. She cared about her, perhaps as much as he did.

Gigi was close to her age, and they got on very well. Being on the ranch was tough on her. She didn't get to interact frequently with people her age. So, Allie's arrival had been a godsend.

He glanced over to where they both sat. Ginika had her head on Allie's shoulder, and Allie had her arm around her.

A vice clamped his chest. He struggled to breathe.

Allie was quickly becoming a part of their family. And the idea that someone was trying to hurt a member of his family infuriated him as much as it filled him with dread.

Crazy thing. Allie thought Ebuka was the one in danger.

What would be the reason for his life being threatened? He'd disengaged and distanced himself from the lawlessness of his youth.

The only question mark was Ralph Nweke. Had their disagreement degenerated to the point of Ralph wanting to kill him? Would his former best friend stoop to that level?

He would find out soon enough when he confronted the man.

He glanced at Allie. He'd only known her a short while. But she made him feel alive for the first time in years. The thought that something could happen to her made his heart skip a beat. Perhaps he should also send her somewhere safe while he dealt with Nweke.

However, she behaved like someone who could handle any situation. Even though she'd had minor injuries, another person would have been more distraught about nearly being killed.

Instead, she'd been composed and coherent as the police officers had questioned her. Since they left the hotel, occasionally, she would twist to look out of the back window. Ebuka recognised the action. He'd been that cautious once upon a time.

She was checking to see if they were being followed.

He started checking the rear-view mirror too. Traffic wasn't heavy, so if someone was following, it wasn't obvious.

Ebuka met Allie's gaze over his sister's head. Her chin was set with purpose, but the lines wrinkling her brows also showed she was worried. Concern for him lay in the depth of her amber eyes.

Lifting one hand from the steering wheel, he covered her arm with it and squeezed to reassure her.

If Nweke was involved with the explosion, then Ebuka would make sure he paid. No one threatened his family and got away with it.

He found a spot in the busy airport car park. Allie helped Ginika out of the truck while he brought down her luggage. Luckily, she still had time to get on the flight. She was teary-eyed as she hugged Allie and him goodbye, making them both promise to be safe.

Allie promised she would take care of Ebuka.

A lump lodged in his throat. They waited and watched as she disappeared through the security checkpoint.

They walked side by side back to the truck in silence. Remembering the explosion, he checked for any cars or people behaving suspiciously.

"Just wait here a minute. Let me check the truck?" she said, glancing around.

He glanced at the truck, looked around the area and back at her. "Check the truck. Why?"

She lowered her voice and leaned into him. "Just in case there's a bomb."

"A bomb?"

"Shh."

He lowered his voice. "You think someone planted a bomb on the truck? That's crazy."

"If they are crazy enough to throw grenades out of a moving vehicle, they are crazy enough to install explosives onto a car. We have only been gone a few minutes. A bomber wouldn't have had the time to plant one properly. But I want to be sure."

She had a valid point. Whoever tried to kill them at the hotel could have followed them. She stepped forward.

Ebuka gripped her arm. The image of her flying through the air this morning replayed in his mind. His blood ran cold. "I'll check it."

She raised her brow. "Do you know what you're looking for?"

He grimaced. He wasn't a bomb expert. "Not exactly."

"Then let me do it."

"No. We'll both do it."

She nodded and pulled a small device from her back pocket that looked like a phone. She pressed a button, and a blue light flashed at regular intervals. She held it out toward the truck and got on the ground as if searching for something under the car.

Ebuka's body flushed from hot to cold as he knelt on the concrete, looking under the truck for anything out of place.

"What does that thing do?" he asked, rolling his tight shoulders, expecting to hear a ticking sound or worse.

"If it starts flashing red, that means there's an explosive device on the truck," she replied as she moved around the vehicle.

He followed her, keeping pace. He wasn't big on technology except where it helped to run the ranch. There were now apps for practically anything. "You have an app that detects bombs?"

She glanced over her shoulder with a wry smile and shrugged. "Comes in handy occasionally."

He frowned at the implication of his words. Why would she need a bomb detection app? How did she know what to check for? Who was she? So many questions he would ask. But not right now.

They completed the circumference of the car, and she stopped. "There's no bomb here."

Exhaling in relief that they weren't going to be blown to bits, he gripped her shoulders and squeezed.

They stared at each other for a few seconds both aware of the reprieve.

The world around them seemed to stand still.

He wanted to kiss her. Instead, he pressed the fob to open the door.

She nodded, accepting the unspoken wariness. There were things they needed to resolve before they could relax. She walked around to the passenger side as he climbed into the cab.

"What's your plan with regards to Nweke?" she asked as she got in and shut the door.

He started the ignition. "I'm going to confront him about the incident at the hotel."

"You think he's going to tell you the truth?"

"Maybe not. But I'll know if he lies."

Glancing in the mirrors, he reversed out of the spot and drove out of the airport towards Nweke's house. He took the highway that bypassed the city as the location was at the other end and it was quicker than being stuck in Saturday traffic.

He glanced at Allie, who was typing something on the smartphone with her thumbs. What was that about?

He shook off the need to question her and focused on the road, checking the mirrors occasionally.

"We have a tail," she said eventually as they neared the turn off they needed.

"We have?" He checked the mirrors. The cars behind kept the required distance for the speed. None drove erratically like you'd seen in the movies. "Where?"

"Two cars back on this lane. Black saloon. It's been there for about twenty kilometres."

He looked again and saw the car. He flicked the indicator and changed lanes. Sure enough, a few seconds later the vehicle changed lanes too but didn't come any closer.

"They seem intent on following us, but they're not doing much else," he said as his body tensed and his pulse sped up.

"Yes. I suggest we carry on as if we haven't noticed the car. We'll wait and see what happens."

Made sense. There wasn't much they could do until whoever it was did something.

Still tense and with all senses heightened, he carried on as usual. He lost sight of the car when he drove up Nweke's tree-lined avenue. At the gates to the mansion, the security men let them in.

He drove onto the drive and parked in front of the house. At least the truck was safe from tampering, here. If it was Nweke sending killers, he wouldn't want to blow up his own home in the process.

"I have the number plate details of the car, and I sent it to your phone," Allie said as she got out and waited for him to come around.

"You got it? Great. We can give it to the police, and they'll pull the driver."

They walked up the multi-tiered steps of the white mansion. The massive door had an arch carved into the wall around it and a solid black iron knocker which he used. A few minutes later, the slab swung back, and they were let in by a woman in the uniform of a housemaid.

"Oga is by the poolside. Please follow me," she said. She led them through a well-lit corridor with arches cut out of the wall instead of square windows.

The pool was a rectangular shape with terracotta tiles decked around it. Plants in decorated pots stood the low walls at the edges, along with two palm trees. Lounge chairs occupied by Nweke, who was dressed in white lined shirt and trousers and a woman in a red bikini Ebuka didn't recognize.

Ralph had done well for himself. No doubt about it. And he'd offered Ebuka the opportunity to get in on the money. Ebuka didn't want any of it.

"Ralph, we need to talk," he said when he approached his former friend.

"Ebuka, how now?" he said, sounding more cheerful than he'd been in recent times, and waved to the chairs. "Come and sit."

"In private." Legs planted apart, Ebuka didn't move from the spot as his jaw set with suspicion.

"Of course," Ralph said, smiling and standing. "Bridget, entertain the guest."

Ebuka nodded for Allie to stay and followed Nweke into the house.

In the living room, Ralph walked over to the bar and pulled out a bottle of whiskey before pouring some into two glasses. Then he came back and handed one over before sitting down.

Holding the drink, Ebuka sat opposite him on a cream brocade settee.

"Have you changed your mind about what we discussed?" he asked after taking a sip of his whiskey.

"No. I'm here because someone tried to kill me this morning in an explosion," Ebuka said in a slow, deliberate tone, watching the other man.

His welcoming actions came across as forced. Something wasn't right with him.

Ralph frowned and then his eyes narrowed. "What? That was you? I saw something about an explosion at a hotel in the city. Are you okay?"

"You mean apart from nearly being blown to bits? Yeah, I'm okay. But it seems someone is trying to kill me. We were followed on the way here."

"You think someone is trying to kill you? I'm sure the police will do their best."

Ebuka's spine stiffened at his dismissive attitude.

"I need you to make sure they investigate and keep my family safe," he replied in a stern voice.

"Well, I can make sure nothing happens to you and your family. In return, you can do me a favour and allow your ranch as one of the stopover routes for the business we discussed." He relaxed into his chair.

Ebuka leaned forward. "Hang on a minute. Are you blackmailing me?"

Two years ago, he'd offered a proposal to use the Njoku ranch for one of his business partners. Ebuka soon found out the business involved trafficking people. Because they were close to the borders of two territories, they were in a strategic location.

Ebuka had rejected the deal, and their friendship had disintegrated afterwards, especially when other revelations came to light.

Ralph shrugged. "I'm asking you to do something for me while I do something for you. It's a simple exchange."

"It's your job to keep the citizens safe. That's why you are the State Attorney General."

"If you're murdered, I'll be sure to prosecute the culprit. Until then, my hands are tied. The explosion at the hotel could be attributed to other things. It's happened before."

Slamming the glass on the table, Ebuka jerked upright and strode across to where he sat, leaning over him. "Listen up, Ralph. If anything happens to any member of my family, I'll kill you. You know what I'm capable of doing."

"Let's hope you live long enough." He sneered.

Ebuka jabbed his right fist, connecting with the other man's nose.

"Ouch!" His head snapped back, and blood dripped. He withdrew a handkerchief to press against the nostril. "You broke my fucking nose."

"Anụ ọfịa! I'll do worse than that if you don't call off your dogs." Ebuka spat before walking out.

FOURTEEN

STANDING BY the pool, Xandra stayed alert to her surroundings—the bikini-clad woman fiddled with her phone. The housekeeper decanted refreshments from a tray onto a table. The security men remained at the front entrance.

Satisfied there wasn't any immediate danger, she asked for the toilet. The woman said it was down the corridor on the right.

Xandra went back inside. She didn't go to the toilet. Instead, she stood in the hallway listening to the conversation between Nweke and Ebuka in the living room. Not that she was monitoring her lover. She wanted to make sure that Nweke didn't try anything stupid.

A smile curled her lips when she heard the impact of crunching bone, and Nweke yelled.

Ebuka could hold his own.

Her lungs expanded to their fullest as she took a deep, satisfied breath.

Ebuka came out. His body vibrated with his rage, his feet stomping on the stone tiles leading to the front door.

Outside, he leaned against the truck and puffed a breath. "That asshole tried to blackmail me."

He rubbed his knuckles.

"You hit him." She smiled.

He looked up, and a slow grin spread on his face. "Yes, I did. I haven't thrown a punch in years."

"From his whining, it sounded like you still have it."

"I could kill that man for what he's doing."

He sounded furious enough to want to. But was Ebuka really a killer? Most decent people didn't have it in them. And Ebuka was decent.

It didn't matter though. Xandra would do whatever it took to protect him.

"What do you want to do?" She pulled open the truck door and climbed in.

He joined her inside. "We're going back to the ranch, and I'm going to try and find someone in the state assembly or the police department who isn't corrupt. Someone's got to have something on him we can use to get him off my back."

"That's going to be difficult, isn't it?" She glanced at him as the car rolled down the drive and out of the gates.

"Yes, it is. But I'm going to find it."

His determination resonated with her. She was going to do whatever she needed to do to help him.

"I can hack into his computer to see if there's anything you can use," she said, keeping an eye on the road for a tail.

"You can do that?" He glanced at her.

"Yes. If he uses an unencrypted network, then it'll be easier. I doubt it'll be that easy, though."

"Okay. What do you need?"

"Just network access. I can do what I need on my device." He nodded.

She met his gaze. "You don't mind that I'll be doing something illegal by hacking into the SAG's files?"

"That man has no right to be State Attorney General after what he said today, and if that's what's needed to bring him down, then you do it. Understood?"

"Yes. Does that mean you wouldn't consider hiding out for a while just until the storm blows over?"

"Hide? Hell no!" He glared at her. "I'm not going to run from this. Njoku farm is my home. My father started it as a small-scale farm, and I built it up to what it is today. I'm not walking away from it. If Nweke wants a fight, he's going to get it."

His dark eyes burned with the fires of resolve and determination. He was an impressive man on any day. But now Xandra understood why she found him attractive. He possessed explosive power that had the potential to be ruthless if needed. If he was going to survive what was to come, he needed to be relentless.

"Got it," she said.

He had just declared war on Nweke and possibly Himba, and it wasn't going to be easy combat to win.

The tail didn't show on the way to the ranch.

While Ebuka went to make some calls, she took the time to check out the security of the house. She secured open windows and made sure there weren't any corners hiding an intruder. Mama Ebele claimed there hadn't been anyone on the ranch since they left aside from Hector and Adiele.

In Xandra's room, she took out a long-range binocular and climbed up to the top of the house tower. She did a three-sixty-degree check of the area around the ranch as far as she could see, even past the tree she had climbed on the first day here. With no sign of anyone lurking about, she went downstairs.

Ebuka asked Mama Ebele to serve dinner early. They hadn't eaten properly all day aside from a quick snack and drink before driving Ginika to the airport.

After they cleared up the kitchen and the men left for the night, Ebuka took Xandra into his office so she could set up what she needed. She was about to pull up the leather chair when she got a message notification. Pulling out her device, she decoded and read the message.

Deliver the package to Lori Osa. Code 7030. All will be taken care of.

She had sent a message to Osagie to help as one of her options was to put Ebuka in hiding until she resolved this thing with Nweke and Himba.

But Ebuka didn't want to hide, and she couldn't blame him. They would play it his way until they ran out of options. Hopefully, she would find something tangible on Nweke's system tonight for them to use as leverage against him.

In the meantime, she hoped they would get through the night without assassins breaking down the door. But that was wishful thinking.

"Wow. You're good," Ebuka said when she got through the firewalls and past the security hurdles into Nweke's file network.

"Thank you," she said and concentrated on locating the files they needed.

Most of them looked like case files, court rulings, house of assembly decisions, etc. Nothing stood out until she found an encrypted folder. It took a while to decode it. And when she did, it looked like they'd hit the jackpot.

It was a spreadsheet containing what looked like names, bank account numbers and sums of money transfers with dates too.

"Bingo," Ebuka said, as he read the file over her shoulder. "If this is what I think it is, we've got enough to nail Ralph to one of his palm trees."

"It looks like it." She plugged in a storage device and started downloading the file. Halfway through the download, a ten-second countdown began on the screen.

"Shit," she yelled and started typing furiously on the keyboard to stop it, heart pounding hard in her chest.

"What's happening?" Ebuka asked, staring at the screen.

"The file is set to self-destruct if its hacked." She pulled the storage drive out as soon as the download completed and the names and numbers were wiped off the screen.

"Fuck! It's all gone." Ebuka's face crumpled.

She lifted the device in her hand and grinned at him. "No, it isn't. I got them all."

"You did?"

She nodded.

"You're brilliant." He grabbed her face and kissed her, dipping his tongue into her with such passion.

She gripped his nape and held him tight, enjoying the feel of his soft lips and forgetting their troubles for a few seconds.

He lifted his head and whispered against her mouth. "One day you're going to tell me where you learnt all these skills. But for now, I'm going to lock that storage device in the safe and then we're going upstairs to bed."

Smiling, she remembered the last storage device she had taken from a safe. "I have a better idea about the memory stick. Do you have an empty opaque pill bottle?"

Pulling back, he eyed her. "Yes. There's one in the bathroom upstairs. Why?"

"Trust me. Most safes won't stop someone determined to get into them. But simple ingenuity might stop them from finding this. Just give me a minute."

She ran upstairs, found the empty pill bottle and came back to the office. She slipped the device inside, making sure it was well padded so it wouldn't rattle. Then she sealed it and took Ebuka's hand, leading him to the pantry where she had noticed a loose brick in the back wall.

She pulled out the brick, placed the bottle in the gap and replaced the brick.

"So only the two of us know where this is hidden." She grinned at him.

"Clever. I'm going to lock up, and then I'll meet you upstairs, in my room."

"Okay." While packing up, she still listened out for any sound that wasn't Ebuka.

She locked her kit away in her room. She heard him coming upstairs and met him in the hallway.

He opened the door and reached for her. She took his hand, and he led her inside, turning on the overhead lamp. The space seemed like an extension of the man—solid furniture made from wood and metal, the furnishings in varying tones of brown and the walls the same sun-kissed cream tone as the rest of the house.

Without hesitation, she switched off the ceiling lamp. Silver light from the moon beamed in. She strode to the expansive windows and pulled the shutters. Then she walked to the table lamp and angled it so that it didn't cast shadows of them and turned it on.

"Why did you do that?" he asked as he watched her move across the room.

"The light and open windows make us sitting ducks for anyone good with a sniper rifle."

"Makes sense. But the things you think of astound me. Makes me think you were in the military."

"Special forces."

"No shit."

He stared at her with open admiration. "It explains why you take orders so well."

"And why you wouldn't want to turn into a tyrant." She grinned.

He chuckled. "Obele, I wouldn't dare."

It was great to find humour in their situation even when she knew someone was probably on the way to the house intending to kill them.

"So, I don't need to ask if you know your way around a gun." He strode to his closet and opened a storage unit. Inside were two shotguns, one pistol and ammunition. He closed the cabinet but didn't lock it. "You know where they are if we need them."

"Good to know. But I'd say 'when' not 'if.' And I hope you don't mind, but I'd rather use my weapons. Just give me a minute." She hurried to her room and grabbed the pistol.

"That looks impressive," Ebuka said when she returned. "Can I take a look?"

"Sure." She held it out in an upturned palm.

He picked it up, weighed and sighted it before handing it over. Then he walked over to the right side of the bed and sat on the mattress.

She went to the opposite side and did the same, placing the gun on the bedside unit before pulling her boots off. But she didn't remove the socks in case she needed to put the shoes back on in a hurry.

They both shifted into the bed fully clothed. As she placed her head on the pillow, he switched off the light, rolled over and put his arm over her.

Sighing, she relaxed a little as she felt his body close. The need for him still shimmered in her veins. But the need for survival superseded the need for sex.

Neither of them spoke nor slept for an hour.

"You can sleep," she said. "I'll take the first watch and wake you in two hours."

"I'm not sure I can sleep," he said.

"Try. You need the rest." She turned to face him. "I'll keep you safe."

His face was shadowed, but she could feel the tension in his body. "You're the one I saw, dead in my dream."

"I promise you I won't die." She hoped. At least, not tonight. She leaned forward and pressed her lips to his. "Sleep."

After another fifteen minutes, she heard his breathing even out, and he was asleep.

An hour later, she heard something that sounded like feet crunching on gravel. It was very faint, and she couldn't be sure, but she couldn't dismiss it either. Sitting up, she focused and strained to listen. She heard it again. It was faint, but it was there.

Her pulse rate picked up. Moving to the edge of the bed, she pulled her boots on and picked up the weapon. Then she patted Ebuka on the shoulder. He stirred and opened his eyes.

"There's someone outside the house," she whispered.

He scrambled out of bed and raced to the cabinet for the guns. He held the rifle and a pistol.

"Put your boots on and stay in here," she said.

"I'm not hiding in here while there's an intruder in my house."

She gripped his shoulders. "This is what I do. Trust me."

He nodded after a heartbeat.

"And if anyone comes through this door, shoot them. I'll call out if it's me coming back." She turned to leave, but he gripped her nape, his fingers rough and gentle at the same time.

"Obele, stay alive," he ordered.

Something lodged in her throat, and she coughed to dislodge it. "You too, boss."

They both nodded, and she left him.

Her heart rate soared as she crossed the threshold into the hallway. Adrenaline flooded her system, making sure her muscles had the vital oxygen it needed to survive. Her body prepared to react to threats.

Unfortunately, an increased heart rate wasn't right for using fine motor skills, the same abilities she needed to line up a shot accurately. She couldn't afford to miss a target.

She took several deep breaths, pulling the air into the bottom of her lungs, into each alveolus. She held the inhales for a count of four before exhaling. This slowed her escalating heartbeat enough for her to function at optimal levels.

A scuffing sound came from downstairs. She moved swiftly, silently, the stone floors muting her footsteps. She reached the bottom of the stairs just as a shadow moved out of the kitchen.

Aiming, she squeezed the trigger, releasing two successive shots as she rolled across the floor into the living room. Bullets whizzed past her from a semi-automatic, hitting the sofa behind her, making cracking sounds.

She paused and listened out for where the sound came from. There were scratching sounds in the hallway, moving slowly towards the stairs. If she moved quickly, she could intercept him from behind.

Hang on. There was a second set of sounds, thuds, coming from the direction of Ebuka's office.

Two intruders?

Professional assassins didn't usually work in pairs. They were lone wolves by nature.

Except... a pair of assassin brothers. The deadly Soraya Psycho Twins.

Fuck.

Moving quickly, she raced across the room as another round of bullets peppered the air, punching holes through the furniture and only missing her by a hair's breadth. She fired into the corridor, counting them out—three, four, five—so she didn't lose count. She peeked into the hall just as she heard a heavy thud on the floor.

Rounding the corner, she fired another bullet into the heart of the man on the ground just to make sure he was dead.

The sound of several gun blasts from upstairs meant the second assassin was up there already. She jumped over the dead body and raced up the stairs. On the landing, she crawled as she listened. Heaving gasping. Both men were injured.

Adrenaline spiked in her body, and she lunged across the floor towards the open door in time to see the second intruder reaching up to shoot. She released two successive rounds into him, and he slumped back on the floor.

Dragging herself up, she jumped over him to where Ebuka lay on the floor. He'd dropped his gun and was clutching his side. Hands trembling, she checked him over.

Seeing him wounded made fear seize her heart for the first time in her life. If assassins kept coming, one would eventually hit its mark. Ebuka would be dead. She couldn't let that happen. It was time to implement the backup plan.

"What happened?" he asked with a groan.

She tore his shirt apart to see where blood was seeping out. "You've been shot twice."

Another wound bled on his thigh and a nasty gash on the back of his head where he'd hit the cabinet. He drifted in and out of consciousness.

Sitting him up, she hooked her shoulder under his arm and dragged him up to the bed.

She turned on the side lamp before racing into the bathroom to get the first aid kit.

Luckily, the injury by his side was no more than a flesh wound. She cleaned it out and wrapped a bandage around him.

The bullet in his leg was trickier, lodged in his thigh, near arteries and shit.

She couldn't afford to take him to any hospital. He wouldn't be secure.

She sedated him with one of the syringes and proceeded to dig the bullet out with her knife. Afterwards, she cleaned it out and cauterized the wound before sealing it with bandages.

She dressed Ebuka again and left him sleeping before focusing attention on the bodies of the dead men. Carrying their bodies outside, she loaded them into the front seats of Ebuka's truck and poured fuel on their bodies.

Back inside, she cleaned the blood from the floor. Forensics would find traces, but she wasn't going to make it easy for them. The best thing would've been to use professional hit cleaners, but there wasn't the time right now.

She returned upstairs, changed her clothes and loaded her car with her luggage. Then she carried Ebuka downstairs and lay him down across the backseat of the vehicle.

She returned to Ebuka's truck and stuck a long rag into the fuel tank and did the same with the SUV of the assassins. Then she lit the tips before getting into her car and driving away.

In the mirror, the fire blazed, and a massive blast turned the two vehicles into fireballs. They were a safe distance from the house, and hopefully, the other men would be there before any of the animals could be hurt, and Ginika would still have her home.

She drove for hours, stopping only at a rest stop to buy tea, food and use the ladies. Lori Osa was at least twelve hours away and the one place she had to get Ebuka to keep him safe until she dealt with Nweke and Himba.

FIFTEEN

THE RENDEZVOUS in Lori Osa went as planned, and Xandra handed a still unconscious Ebuka over to the contact Osagie had given her. She paid for him to be kept in a secure location for a few weeks until she came back to get him. Although his movements would be restricted, he would have food and shelter. Most importantly, he would be out of reach to any assassins.

She followed the news of the explosion at Njoku farms. The initial reports said Ebuka Njoku and one of his workers had been killed.

DNA would show otherwise, so she hacked into the State Medical Examiner's laboratory system and doctored the results. She hoped the lab technicians were sloppy and wouldn't notice. It worked. The final report identified the burnt bodies as Ebuka Njoku and Allie Momodu.

This bought her some time to deal with Nweke. At a rest stop on the drive to Jokogi, she logged the kill and half an hour later got confirmation of payment of the balance into the account of a dummy business corporation she used.

Her phone beeped a few minutes later.

"Come see Papa when you get into town," Zoe said when she picked the call.

Something niggled at the back of Xandra's mind. Zoe usually congratulated her on a job well done after an assignment, but she hadn't mentioned it.

"Okay," Xan said. "Are you alright?"

"Sure," she replied in what seemed an overly bright voice. "When are you back?"

Something was off with her. To be on the safe side, Xandra lied, "Tomorrow. I'll visit your father in the evening."

She would be in the city later tonight, but she needed some time to plan before seeing the Himbas.

Four hours later, she drove into the garage of her house. Each time she went away, getting back and going through the security routine helped to relax and compartmentalize her last kill.

This time as she went through the checks, she didn't feel the same sense of peace when she completed them.

For one, Ebuka was on her mind. He was safe. But she needed to work to get him back on the ranch doing his thing. This meant getting rid of Nweke.

Secondly, as a skilled, efficient killer, she had always completed jobs before. She was dedicated to what she did. Loyal to the crime family that gave her a sense of belonging. It defined her.

Now all of that was up in the air. She was walking in a different direction.

She wasn't foolish enough to think she could take on the entire Himba family singlehandedly and survive. But she could get rid of Nweke permanently and give Ebuka and Ginika the chance to live their lives without having to look over their shoulders.

Even if it meant Xandra wouldn't be part of their lives.

The next day as she went out to do her usual chores. The hair on her nape stood erect like she was being watched.

At the supermarket, she watched the mirrored surfaces but didn't notice anyone. If she was being followed, then whoever it was superb. At the dry-cleaning shop, she watched the reflections of the people walking the street in the shop windows across the road.

It was then she saw the man sitting at a table outside a tea shop. She had seen him in the supermarket car park.

She went into the dry-cleaning shop and dropped off the clothes. When she came out, she strode casually to her car parked outside, took out her gun and a newspaper she'd bought from the supermarket to cover it. She walked across the street to the tea shop and made a show of going in before sitting at the table opposite the man.

His eyes widened, and he made to stand.

"Don't move." She lifted the newspaper so he could see the muzzle of the gun pointed at his chest. "Keep your hands on the table where I can see them."

He did as she said and licked his lips, looking up from the weapon to her face. He appeared calm for a man with a gun pointed at him. "Ms Gowon, I don't mean you any harm."

"Who the fuck are you and why the fuck are you following me?" she asked in a low voice.

"My name is David and Mr Peters sent me."

Osagie?

"Why?"

"Don't know. My instructions are to keep an eye on you and report to him."

Why would Osagie send someone to follow her?

Gun still trained on him, she withdrew her phone and pressed the button for Osagie.

A few seconds later, it connected.

"Yes," he said in his usual deep, accented voice. They rarely ever spoke to each other on the phone because it wasn't secure.

"Why do you have someone following me?" She didn't bother with pleasantries.

"Oh, you found David. I knew you were good." He sounded like he was smiling.

She tried not to roll her eyes. "You know I'm better than good. You haven't answered my question."

"He's just keeping an eye on you. When you contacted me, asking for help, you raised my curiosity."

This was why she rarely got other people involved in her life. "You know better than to interfere in my business. Curiosity killed the cat."

"I'm a Bini tiger, and you know better than to threaten me."

Osagie wasn't someone she wanted to piss off no matter how irritated she was that he was having her followed. She had to remember Ebuka was in one of his safe houses.

Exhaling a sigh, she conceded. "That's not what I meant. I just don't want a babysitter."

"Then think of David as your guardian angel. We all need them, occasionally. You can thank me later." He hung up.

Ignoring David, Xandra stood and walked across the road to her car.

One thought kept swirling in her mind as she headed out to Zoe's. Did Osagie know something she didn't know?

The time she'd spent with Ebuka had made her understand Osagie better. She could see similarities between them—the power they exuded, the loyalty they inspired, and the fierce need to protect their own.

Osagie believed she was his responsibility. Had always thought so from the first time she allowed him to take the cane to her back. To mark her with his stripes.

Of course, Ebuka didn't know her as Xandra. Didn't see or understand the woman who needed the punishment to clear her conscience and find inner peace.

At the restaurant, the two men sitting outside playing a board game nodded their greetings as she strode in. Instead of Zoe meeting her as usual, Norbert 'Little Devil' Gemade, another of the capos, sat at the bar. His nickname said it all. What he lacked in height, he made up for in deadliness.

He wasn't usually here when she came to see Don Himba. He didn't get involved with the kill contracts, which were Zoe's area. But he was also the person likely to be promoted to be next underboss and possibly Don, one day. And he was the Himba enforcer.

The prickling she'd felt in her scalp earlier returned.

"Xandra, how're you doing?" Norbert waved at her.

Hiding her surprise at seeing him, she strode over. "I'm doing great. It's been a while."

"Yes, it has." He tilted his head and pursed his lips. "Have a drink with me."

He leaned over the bar just as Zoe entered the restaurant.

"Xan, you're back." She came over and gave the customary hug and kiss before walking around the counter.

"I think I should see the don first. If you're still here when I come down, we can have the drink." Xandra nodded towards the stairs as she settled on a stool.

"Papa isn't here yet. So, you can relax." Zoe smiled as she picked two more glasses from under the counter and poured another two shots of whiskey.

She took a glass. Norbert lifted the one he'd been drinking from, and Xandra picked the third.

"Here's to another success." She tossed back the drink in one gulp.

Xandra emptied the glass in her mouth and swallowed, feeling the burn down her throat. Five seconds later, a sweet aftertaste hit her palate just as the floor shifted. She stared from Norbert to Zoe, whose images seemed to double as the space expanded and contracted.

Xandra tried to step down from the stool and stumbled, gripping the counter. Her senses were scrambled, the world full of white noise and yet muted.

"What did you give me?" Her words came out slurred.

They had drugged her. She glanced at Zoe, who just stared at her blankly. Zoe had drugged her.

Xandra had trusted the woman. Foolishly. She was a Himba, after all.

Feeling a presence behind her, Xandra reached for the gun inside her jacket. Too slow.

Too late. Something hit the back of her head. She fell forward into the darkness.

The world was still swaying when she woke, tied to a metal post bolted to the floor and ceiling of an empty warehouse. Her numb hands and feet were bound tightly behind her.

This wasn't good. Had they discovered Ebuka? If so, how? She needed to get out of here. She tried to wiggle her fingers to see if she could work them. Perhaps her brain wasn't sending the signal, or her fingers weren't receiving them because she couldn't move them.

The drug was still in her system.

Footsteps echoed off the concrete walls.

"Good, you're awake," Norbert said, standing in front of her. He smacked a metal pipe against his right hand continuously.

"Where is Zoe? Why the fuck am I tied up?"

"You were seen at Club Arufin," he said in a strained, cold voice.

"This is about Arufin? About what I do in my personal time?"

"This is about you going to a sex club and being a perverted freak," Norbert spat out.

Relief washed over her that they hadn't found Ebuka and she started laughing uncontrollably.

"You think this is funny, freak?" He sneered at her.

"You said that one already."

"We don't want your kind in the Himba family."

"What? Because I didn't kneel for you? Because I didn't let you fuck me? Sorry, I'm not interested in little pricks like you."

She probably shouldn't taunt him. But what right did he or anyone else have to tell her how to live? Laughable that even gangsters could be puritanical and judgemental.

"You don't deserve to live." He swung the pipe like a baseball bat, and it smashed into her ribs.

Blistering pain flashed through her as he swung it again and again, hitting her thighs, arms, stomach until she couldn't feel her body. She was white-hot pain all over.

She stopped fighting the agony, welcomed it, let it consume her, lifting her into a heady space where she floated above it all.

Then there was a flash, and she could smell fabric burning. A different hurt consumed her, taking her to Hell for all her sins. She burned. And then she was in darkness.

She woke to the sounds of beeping machines. Her body throbbed, ached. Only one eye worked, the other had a covering. She tried to lift her arms, but they were heavy and bound in bandages.

"Don't move," a soft female voice said.

She turned her head to find Zoe sitting on a chair. She opened her mouth to talk, but her throat hurt.

"Don't try to speak. There's a tube in your throat to help you breathe. You have second and third-degree burns on your legs and hip. One of the bones in your arm is broken."

Her eyes became watery, and she lowered her head. "I'm so sorry, Xan. It was never meant to get this far. Papa told Norbert to teach you a lesson. Just a little beating to make you think again about going to Arufin. But he took it too far."

Her head was bowed as she held Xandra's hand.

Did she honestly think a 'little beating' was going to cure Xandra's deeply rooted deviancy?

She wanted to rage at Zoe for not warning her about what was coming. For drugging her. For proving why no one was a friend in the cartel world.

Then again, she couldn't blame her. Would she have done any better if she had been in her shoes? What was the point of rage? She was alive and grateful.

Xandra squeezed Zoe's hand, bestowing forgiveness.

"There's a man outside. Says he's your guardian angel," Zoe said after a while. "They attacked the warehouse and rescued you. Norbert is injured. He wants revenge, but I convinced Papa to let it be, considering what's happened."

Xandra smiled internally. Osagie was still watching out for her. After Zoe left, she drifted in and out of consciousness.

Healing was agonizingly slow—surgery, medication and physical therapy. Days turned into weeks. Weeks into months.

With each painful breath, each tormenting step, each excruciating moment, she lived through it all with one person in mind—Ebuka Njoku—and the day she would see him again.

PART TWO

SIXTEEN

Six months later

HE WAS close by. Xandra knew it. Sensed it deep in her tightening gut. The man she wanted. The reason she had broken her months-long seclusion.

Stepping out of the underground car park, she stood and gazed at the bright lights around her.

Once upon a time, she had been a significant part of vibrant city life. Carefree, only concerned about fixing her boss's problems. Now, she was nothing more than a ghost, non- existent to many.

Cars honked jumbled with people's conversations. The world carried on without her input.

A few months of isolation had skewed her view on life.

She had never been a big fan of Lori Osa. A city full of pretentious people all vying to outdo each other with their unrefined attitudes. It is said, 'money can't buy good taste,' and the statement stood steadfast for many of its residents.

Still, this was the one place where she could acquire what she needed. Anything could be bought, even if it wasn't for sale.

At the foyer of her destination—Madaki auction house—the retinal scanner beeped before the glass screen allowed her through the security archway.

The doorman tipped his head in respect. "Welcome, Ms Gowon. Weapons and electronics, please."

Smile curling her lips, she pulled out the FN Five-SeveN from the shoulder strap under her jacket and the phone from her pocket, placing both on the counter.

The rules of the auction house stated no weapons allowed as part of their terms and conditions. There were other ways of killing, not always as efficient, yet effective.

He placed both items in a metal box in a vault behind the counter and locked it before handing her an electronic key card. Pocketing it, she ascended the stairs to a short corridor.

Madaki was an exclusive and discreet auction house, and clients came from far and wide.

In the foyer of shiny dark surfaces and diffused lighting, an usher led her to the seat. A VIP box with a one-way glass screen, designed to ensure that she could see the stage and the merchandise being auctioned. Still, no one outside the room could see in.

The raised platform stage was lit with low lights while the rest of the auction room lay in almost eerie darkness. No other bidders were visible, probably sitting behind screens too.

The usher offered refreshments as she relaxed into the seat. No alcohol on offer.

She settled for the sparkling mineral water. Taking a sip, she reached for the tablet device on the table and read the message.

Welcome. Place your card on the screen to begin.

Following the instructions, soon she browsed the electronic brochure. Not a regular at these events, this was her first time. But she had something specific, albeit unusual, in mind. It had taken weeks to track this item, and she had it on good authority that it would be on the blocks today.

She scrolled through until the merchandise appeared on the screen. Her breath caught in her throat at the fierce beauty on display.

The lights on the stage pulsed as if in warning that the auctions were about to begin. The background music faded and silence reigned as the first item was brought to the platform.

How many potential rivals did she have bidding for this? She didn't know, but she would acquire it today, even if it cost her life... and it probably would.

SEVENTEEN

A BRIGHT beam of light nearly blinded Ebuka as he shuffled onto the stage, the clinking sound of metal a dismal musical ensemble, the platform cold beneath his bare feet.

"Raise your hands," one of the guards said, a short-haired burly, Hausa man who probably spent his leisure time lifting weights.

Gyms were not places Ebuka visited. He had worked the land, one way or the other. After months of captivity with restricted rations, the sinews of tight muscles showed in his reflection off the mirrored walls as he obeyed the instructions without resistance.

They bound his outstretched hands and widened legs to a pulley system of ropes and chains that made him look as if he was nailed to a cross.

Assume a submissive posture. The words drilled into him. He bowed his head, while his mind rebelled, his gaze fixed at the grey metal beneath his feet.

For months, he'd fought against his captors' attempt to break him. Why had he been taken from his home, away from the people he loved? No answers came.

It didn't help that there were gaps in his memory. He woke up one day in a strange house with no recollection of how he got there. He had sustained head and body injuries. But the strangers in the house couldn't tell him how it had happened. Only that they were instructed to keep him locked in the place. They had fed him, cleaned and changed his bandages and given him new clothes.

After he tried to escape and failed, they started locking him in a barricaded room and only bringing food when he promised to behave.

Then one day, several weeks later, everything changed. They moved him to a different location which looked like a prison with cells. When he resisted, he received beatings, starvation, and degradation. The excruciating pain eclipsed all else. Madaki, the owner of this perverted establishment, had given him a choice— submit to the upcoming auction or suffer a slow, torturous death.

Ebuka had nearly laughed in the man's face.

He wasn't afraid of death. It came to the best people.

But, he wanted something else more. Vengeance. The chance to find those responsible for destroying his life and wrecking theirs.

So, he had agreed. They had cleaned him, fed him, and given him a room with a futon mattress instead of the cold cell floor he had slept on for weeks. Still a shadow of his pre- captivity self, but he could hold his own weight, and his mind was returning to full function.

"Lot number three-fifty-two is a fine specimen of a man." Madaki's voice echoed although Ebuka couldn't see him.

The pulley swivelled slowly so that his naked form rotated three-sixty degrees for however many people were out there bidding for him. "He is rough, hard, and good looking. Bidding starts at fifty thousand dollars."

Damn. Someone out there was going to pay at least that amount for him?

His nostrils flared, and his grip curled into fists around the chains holding him. The world had gone mad.

"Lift your head," Madaki said.

Ebuka's jaw tightened at being put on display like cattle, and his body curled tight with the urge to smash a fist into the man's face. Counting to five, he inhaled a deep breath as he remembered the endgame.

With head raised, he stared straight ahead into the darkened auditorium, swallowing the simmering rage in his stomach.

In his peripheral view, the auction house owner stood before a large monitor, with a microphone headset and fingers padding across the screen. A lanky Hausa man, clean-shaven.

The first time Ebuka met him, he had thought the man appeared gentle. Delicate. Boy, had he been wrong. The man was a sadistic son of a bitch. He got a sickening enjoyment from watching others suffer.

Ebuka shuddered as he remembered the torturous use of a cattle prod.

Since no one else could be seen or heard, he assumed the bidding was being done anonymously via electronic devices.

Eventually, Madaki turned to him.

"Congratulations, Ebuka," he said in a soft voice like he was talking to a child who had pleased him. "You have a new owner."

Taking a deep breath, Ebuka suppressed anger. For the first time in weeks, a kindling of hope ignited within him. The future remained uncertain, yet he wouldn't lose the one thing that had kept him together.

He would escape this degrading life. He would reunite with his family and mete out revenge on those who had wronged him.

Hope. He clung on to it as the guards returned and untied him from the pulleys, leading him down the bright corridor accompanied by the sound of shuffling footsteps and rattling chains. The holding cell had nothing in it but stripped back brick wall.

"On your knees," Guard Number One ordered.

Usually, his tone would've irritated Ebuka. Now he was indifferent as he complied, the only thoughts in his head of getting out of here.

He removed the metal cuffs and chains attached to Ebuka's wrists and ankles. He rubbed the unbound arms, getting the circulation going again.

The other man tossed some clothes at him. "Put these on."

Baring his teeth, Ebuka glared from the items on the floor back to the guards. Even two against one, he could take them down and make a run for it.

Easier said than done though, considering he still had the damned electronic collar around his neck. The contraption was nasty. It delivered crippling electric shocks to the wearer. He knew from first-hand experience how much it hurt.

The guards smirked as if they knew what he was thinking. He could do nothing to harm them now. One day perhaps. Not today.

Suddenly, the men stiffened and stepped outside the room. Eyes narrowed, Ebuka wondered if Madaki was back. But it wasn't the purveyor of flesh blocking the doorway.

Breath caught in his throat.

A woman in a fitted black jacket and trousers, a dark-blue shirt and flashy sneakers. Expensive shiny fabrics and immaculate tailoring. Her hair was short, curly and suited her heart-shaped face and petite body.

Ebuka was a plaid shirt and faded denim kind of guy. So, he could smell rich city slickers a mile away. But she didn't project the usual arrogance associated with spoilt rich people.

She had short brown hair, and a slender, feminine body. Her cold and piercing eyes got his attention—the most intense irises he had ever seen.

She showed no emotion, neither smiling nor frowning.

Still, his body temperature rose under her gaze, and he resisted the urge to adjust his position.

Damn, she didn't even blink.

She stepped into the room and shut the door, leaning against the bare wall.

Once they were alone, it seemed her demeanour changed. Her expression softened—steady eyes contact, large pupils, fingers skimming jawline.

Was that admiration?

What was there to admire about a man who had been sold to the highest bidder?

Still, his pulse raced, and his skin tingled under her gaze. Warmth spread through his body, converging at his groin. The last thing he wanted was to sport a hard-on while he was naked in front of this stranger. As a distraction from his unease, he asked, "Who are you?"

Asking a direct question when he hadn't been spoken to was asking for trouble. Madaki would've punished him. He braced himself for her retribution.

Instead, she frowned, jerking back. "What do you mean? You don't know who I am?"

His body tensed. "No. I've never seen you before."

"Wow. They told me you had suffered some memory loss. I thought it was a ruse." She narrowed her eyes and rubbed her chin. "I admire your resilience after everything you've been through."

Her voice was soft and almost intimate. She reached for the clothes on the floor and handed them to him.

His mouth dropped open. Warmth bloomed in his chest.

This was the first nice thing anyone had said to Ebuka in weeks, probably months. Since his captivity.

The corner of his lips tugged in a would-be smile, but he suppressed it.

In praising him, she offered deference to him, a power swap. It was subtle. But it was there.

Her words called to Ebuka's protective instinct. The confident, generous man who had almost disappeared with the onslaught of the past few months.

"It's surprising what the human spirit will do to survive when tested. I'm sure you would have done well under the same circumstances," he said in a gentle voice.

Her eyes sparkled, and she nodded toward the clothes in his hand. "Put those on for now. I'll provide you with better clothing when we get home."

Reminded of his current state of undress, he pushed off the hard floor and pulled on the loose-fitting sweatpants and shirt. They were more than he'd had to wear for a long time.

"Home?" he asked in a tense voice, giving her a side glance.

A word filled with distant promise. Would he get to see his soon? A ranch house that had been in the family for a few years; acres of land for livestock; his sister and mother gathered around the dinner table.

He pictured their smiling faces. His throat tightened, chest aching.

"Yes, you're coming home with me." The stranger's words augmented his despondency.

Ebuka shook off the crushing disappointment weighing down his shoulders and straightened to his full height.

"You just paid for me. What am I, your slave?" Tired of bowing and scraping, he spat the words out, not caring about the penalty of the rash words.

She flinched, jaw tightening. "You won't be beaten or debased in any way."

Lips flat and jaw set, he narrowed his eyes. What did she take him for? A fool?

"Lucky me. I suppose I'm going to be your sex toy. Is that it?" His words dripped with sarcasm.

Something flickered in her gaze, and she shifted from one leg to the other. "No. I won't treat you that way."

If she was trying to play the benevolent owner, he could play too. "So, can I go home to my family whenever I want?"

"No." She shot the word at him with vehemence she hadn't shown before. "You can have anything else you want, but you can't leave."

***

You can't leave.

The finality of the words rattled in Ebuka's head as they left the auction house, enraging him. The muscles on his neck corded and his nostrils flared as he rushed his breaths. The idea of being confined permanently sent his brain into overdrive, and he assessed all the possible chances of escape. It became imperative now more than ever.

They were escorted by guards down to the car park, where his new owner allowed him to sit in the front passenger seat of a grey BMW. The guards left, and it was just the two of them.

It was the first time he had been this close to another human in months without being restrained.

In the enclosed, intimate space, he smelled her clean, feminine scent—flowers, citrus and musk.

The urge to lean into her made his skin itch. Made him picture their bodies aligned, writhing together.

Fuck!

He nearly laughed out loud as the word bounced around in his mind. He needed to fuck. It had been too long. Too fucking long. Sucking in a deep breath, something in her scent was familiar and comforting.

Had he known her before today?

Shaking his head, he shoved the thought away. It was a dangerous idea to develop at this moment. Needing a distraction, he stared at the switches and dials on the control panel.

"How am I to address you?" he asked.

Others demanded they be called 'master' or 'mistress.' He couldn't picture using any of those honorifics.

"My name is Xandra."

Xan. He rolled the word around in his head.

Even the sound of her voice was familiar, like a lover's, making his heart lurch.

But he couldn't have taken a lover because he was only recently separated from Sabina, his wife and he had sworn off women.

A pounding started in his ears as it always did every time he thought about his old life.

His fingers curled into fists, digging into the flesh of his palms.

There were so many questions that needed answers. The last place he wanted to be was in this car, especially since it was taking him further away from the people he needed to see again.

"Do you promise to behave for the duration of the journey? That way I don't have to anaesthetize you."

Her words drew him out of his thoughts. He frowned.

Had she read his thoughts of escape somehow? Weeks of torture had obviously demolished his ability to hide his expressions.

Damn her. Damn Madaki. Damn the whole lot of them. Jaw clenched, Ebuka gave a taut nod.

"I need your verbal agreement," she said.

Turning, he glared at her. "Yes."

He had a twinge of guilt at telling a lie, but she was a fool if she expected him to go home with her without a fight. Never.

"Good," she said.

She drove out of the car park and onto the street. Soon they left the bustling metropolis of skyscrapers and lights onto the highway leading out of the city and then there was nothing but headlights against the inky night.

Xandra pressed a button, flicking radio stations.

Seizing the opportunity, Ebuka lashed out, hitting her across the chest. Her neck snapped back, and her head hit the backrest.

With the other hand, he unclipped the seat belt and reached for the controls.

Any other person would've passed out cold from the impact. Not Xandra.

She lunged at him, and they struggled, their bodies hitting the panel. The car jerked to the side and swerved all over the road.

Pressed against her lean body, he felt primal and exhilarated, a heady rush of arousal and adrenaline. Her strength and agility surprised him. Turned him on.

Something pricked his nape. A sharp pain shot down his spine, and his limbs became heavy.

Frustration bubbled in his chest, making him growl. He slumped onto the seat and fell into darkness.

EIGHTEEN

EBUKA OPENED his eyes to the streak of sunshine through open windows. A gentle breeze cooled his face as he blinked and studied the environment.

He lay on a bed, soft mattress and cool white sheets that smelled like the outdoors. White walls and large pane glass windows. From this angle, the clear blue sky stretched forever. The sound of crashing waves made him stir.

Standing from the bed, he walked naked toward the window. His head swam. Waves crashed against rocks more than one hundred feet beneath him.

Sweat broke on his forehead. His stomach lurched at the weird sensation of almost walking on air. What crazy person built a house hanging off the sheer face of a cliff?

Images flitted through his mind. Was it last night that he had been sold to Xandra and they had fought in the car? He had blanked out.

Did Xandra bring him here? Was this her home?

Moving away from the windows, he opened one of the tall drawers, searching for something to wear. He pulled out a white T-shirt and pair of shorts that were perfect fits.

He wandered the rest of the house filled with white furniture and glass surfaces, a minimalist haven. Xandra must have an army of servants. How else could she keep everything shiny?

Peering into each room, he checked for any sign of life, he called out, "Xandra?"

No one responded. He walked past an open-plan living room overlooking the sea into a kitchen. The sight of the teapot made his mouth water. He hadn't had tea in months.

He ignored it and pushed open the door leading out into a garden filled with shrubs and flowering plants. Somebody had gone to great lengths to create a tropical paradise here.

He stood still and lost himself in the sounds of chirping birds and the beauty of the architecture of the house which blended with the breath-taking landscape.

After months of being locked up and staring at brick walls all day, he felt as if he was in Heaven with the salty breeze on his tongue, the hot sun on his face and the grainy sands under his toes. His limbs loosened, and his breathing slowed down. Lifting his face, eyes closed, he pictured living here.

You can't leave. The image of Xandra from the auction house loomed over him.

His eyes flew open, the brief peace ruined.

The anger that had been festering inside him for months returned, eating away at his gut like acid.

He would be damned if he would become a rich girl's toy.

He stomped across the sand, down a slightly rocky path. The sun wasn't high yet, and the trees provided cool shade. A little walk away, he came to a timber hut beside a small waterfall and sparkling pool. But still no Xandra or any other sign of another human.

Was she hiding somewhere, watching through cameras?

Madaki liked playing games, testing him. Looking for opportunities to punish and mould him into a better captive. Was this what Xandra was doing?

Balling hands, his knuckles cracked as he swivelled and headed in the direction of the much cooler house.

Xandra had to learn that he wouldn't be easily cowed. At least Madaki had the sense to restrain him. But there were no cuffs on his wrists, chains around ankles, or collar weighing down his neck.

Why hadn't Xandra done the same? After he had fought her in the car.

Lips flattened and brows wrinkled, he entered the kitchen, suspicion spiked.

His new owner was playing games for sure. He would bide time until he figured it out.

Rolling shoulders to shake off the tension, he opened the white cabinets until he found a white porcelain mug. He poured some tea and strode over to the beechwood table, pulled out a matching chair and settled on it.

He took a sip and savoured the dark liquid. Sighing with pleasure, he lowered eyelids, letting the smooth taste and rich aroma permeate him.

"I see you're awake."

Eyes flying open, he sat up and put the cup down on the table. Muscles tensed, adrenaline rushed through him, ready for a fight.

How did she get in here without any noise?

Xandra stood in the doorway to the kitchen in sports leggings, long-sleeve top, and trainers. Sweat dampened her hair and clothes. A casual version of the woman he'd met last night. Had it been last night?

His heartbeats seemed loud and fast. The strange pang he felt in his chest when they met at the auction returned. His grip around the mug tightened as he shoved the feeling aside.

"About yesterday," he started. His attitude had always been to deal with issues head-on. No better time than now. And by bringing it up, he gained the upper hand. Regained some control over the situation.

"I'd rather forget about what happened. It's done. No need to rehash it," she said as she pulled the fridge door and took out a bottle of water.

Head tilted to the side, he watched her with narrowed eyes. Did she not mind that he'd been rebellious? She had bought him at an auction, paid at least fifty thousand dollars. She owned him.

The fuck she did.

Chin lifted; his teeth ground together.

She believed it.

Still, she didn't look perturbed about her slave who sat at the kitchen table drinking tea. Instead, she held a plastic bottle of water to her lips and drank her throat rippling.

Like that, Ebuka was ensnared in lust. Warm blood rushed to his groin. His shorts constricted his rapidly swelling cock. He fought the urge to reach down and adjust himself.

Watching her drink water had to be one of the most erotic things he'd ever seen. He pictured her mouth wrapped around his dick. His tongue darted out, licking the bottom lip as the urge to taste the salt on her skin made his mouth water.

He lifted his gaze.

Xandra stared at him, need burning in the depths of her grey eyes.

His annoyance returned. She was the damned enemy, and his dick couldn't seem to get the message.

He stood from the chair, wood scraping stone tiles. "I couldn't resist the tea. What is my punishment?"

The sooner she got to behaving like Madaki, like the owner of a slave, the better for them.

Jerking her head back, she lowered the bottle in her hand. She looked dazed as if surprised by his question. "Punishment? Why?"

Did she expect him to buy the innocent act? "Yes. I drank tea without your permission.

I'm sure there are probably other rules I've broken this morning."

She stared down at her hands for a couple of heartbeats. Then she lifted her head, giving him an empty stare as she spoke in a monotone voice.

"There are no rules here. You won't get punished for drinking tea. You are welcome to use anything you find for your pleasure."

There it was. The trap.

Ebuka could've sworn she meant more than just the food and drink. It sounded like she was offering herself for his pleasure. He wasn't falling for that one.

"Okay," he said in a nonchalant tone.

Nodding, she dumped the empty bottle in the sink. "I'm going to have a shower. Would you like to join me?"

Was she flirting?

She stood close enough to touch. Too close. Those eyes seemed to lack any reflection.

The heat from her body surrounded him. She smelled of musk and sweat and woman.

Very tempting.

Heart thundering, his breath caught. She had to be baiting him.

He still ached to touch her. To be touched by her.

After months of being starved for TLC, he craved pleasurable human contact. Stepping back, he raised the mug to his lips. "I'd rather finish my tea."

She shrugged and walked off. "I'll make breakfast when I come out."

Puffing out the breath he hadn't realized he'd been holding, he sat on the chair. Was she going to leave him alone while she showered?

He could run away. From the looks of it, they were close to the sea. There would be a boat, surely. And although he hadn't seen any other houses earlier, she would have neighbours and a means of escape.

But his rumbling stomach indicated he needed to refuel and regain some energy before planning any getaway. After last night, she'd be a fool not to put in measures to keep him restricted.

Ebuka doubted he would get far, especially in such an unfamiliar location.

Ten minutes later, Xandra was out, dressed in a blue long-sleeved linen shirt, navy jeans slacks, and bare feet.

NINETEEN

"I'M GOING to sit outside," Xandra said as she put the last dried plate away. They just had dinner—grilled peppered fish with steamed plantain—which she had cooked. "Would you like to join me?"

Ebuka looked up from the magazine he was flipping through. He'd been reading it as a show, so he could watch her discreetly while she washed up.

Her skin had prickled with awareness throughout.

"Sure," he said, closing the magazine on the table. "I'll take the bottle of wine and glasses out to the veranda."

Flipping the kitchen towel over her shoulder, she watched him grab the items and head out through the door.

He had changed from the man she met months ago. The effect of his confinement was visible not just physically in his weight loss, but mentally in his attitude. He'd become an angry, mistrustful man.

And she was to blame for it.

All her plans had gone wrong. First, she hadn't seen the ambush by Norbert coming. Thankfully, Osagie's team had rescued her. Then, the months she'd spent in hospital and healing meant she hadn't gone to pick Ebuka from the safe house, and the agreement had expired because she hadn't kept up the payment. This meant he ended up in Madaki's auction house.

A week had passed since she brought Ebuka to Laroca. They had settled into a kind of routine. She went for a run every morning before breakfast. On the second day, he joined her, and they followed the same route every day, running in a circular path around the island.

Laroca was part of an isolated cluster of small islands in the Atlantic Ocean. The nearest inhabited land was hundreds of miles away—Nigeria to the north, Cameroon to the east and Equatorial Guinea to the south.

She had noticed Ebuka checking out the area, trying to figure out how to escape. With no boat in sight, if he managed to climb down the sheer rock face of the high cliffs, he'd have to swim through violent waves and razor-edged rocks.

After their exercises, he would make the tea while she showered. Then she would make breakfast while he washed. Every morning, she invited him into the bathroom. Each time, he refused.

And every morning, she died a little inside when he rejected her.

She hadn't realized it would be this tough being close to him again. To have him look at her with anger and hatred. She never thought she would care this much. But after everything they had shared, her gut hardened with nausea when he looked at her like a total stranger.

As Xandra, she was a stranger to him.

But his memory loss meant he didn't even remember Allie, his obele.

The back of her throat hurt, and she gripped the sink tight. Why did it hurt so fucking much?

It was partly why she refused to bring up Allie or the short time they had spent on the ranch.

It was easier to be Xandra, cold and aloof.

Anyway, she didn't want to pretend any longer. She needed him to know Xandra and accept her the way she was.

Sighing, she hung the towel on the rail and headed outside to join him. He sat on the lounger, legs stretched out, a glass of red wine in hand.

She took the drink he'd already poured and settled in the seat on the other side of the table.

A flock of migrating birds flew across the setting sun and orange sky. A gentle breeze fluttered the leaves in the trees.

"Do you ever get any visitors?" he asked in a softened voice.

The first time she heard him speak gently, all week, reminding her of the man she had known. She glanced at him, hiding the surprise with the raised glass.

Leaning forward, his head was tilted to the side, his focus on her.

Awareness of him increased. He looked at her as if he was trying to figure her out.

He raised his eyebrows when she took long to respond, giving a glimpse of the old Ebuka, a man who was ready to step up and take charge.

She wanted to push this Ebuka into being that man again. She needed the old Ebuka.

"No." She shrugged as if it didn't matter, masking her thoughts with a faraway expression.

"Surely you must have friends that want to visit once in a while," he probed.

"I have no real friends. Not in the way that normal people have them," she replied.

There was Osagie, and although he'd appointed himself her guardian angel, she wasn't clueless enough to call him a friend.

"Family?"

"None."

The Himbas were the closest thing she had to a family, and they'd proven that family couldn't be trusted.

In contrast, Ebuka had his sister, mother and a host of extended family members. She expected to see his mouth twisted with scorn at her revelations.

Instead, his facial features turned down as he placed his glass on the table. And his hands dropped limply to his sides.

He reflected the sense of loss, of loneliness, that twisted inside her sometimes. He must miss his family. They had been such a crucial part of who he was.

Exhaling a deep breath, he picked his drink again. "What exactly do you do for a living?"

This was an important question. For him. For her.

She met his gaze, his dark eyes unwavering. "I'm an assassin."

His breath hitched. Beads of sweat broke across his forehead.

She knew the effect those words had on people, and it was no different on Ebuka. She saw the fear ripple through him almost as if she had told him she was an evil spirit.

As a hit-woman, she was an adult's worse nightmare. Questions flashed across his eyes.

Did he wonder how she had become a hired killer?

"How old are you?" he asked with the boldness that was pure Ebuka. There was no hint of the person she had bought last week.

"Twenty-four."

His eyes widened, and he shook his head as if he struggled to believe her. "How did you become a contract killer at such a young age?"

"It was what I was trained to do." She never discussed this with anyone else. But she wanted him to know. To know Xandra. So, she told him.

"I grew up in an orphanage run by nuns. I didn't fit in and didn't get along with the other kids.

One day the reverend mother told me I was going to new parents. A car showed up and took me to Tiye Himba's house. But Don Himba didn't want a child. He already had a daughter. It wasn't until I was older that I found out the nuns sold me to the Don. Instead of living there, I was put on a private jet and sent to a place in Europe. It was a mix of academic school and military camp where I was trained to fight, learned to code and hack computers as well as other survival skills. When I turned eighteen, I returned to work for my sponsor."

He swung his feet down and faced her. "What kind of school was that?"

Her gut tightened as she remembered the time there. "It's a cross between an academic school and a military camp. We learned all the usual subjects, but we were also taught martial arts skills. They were training an advanced army of children. I can write a computer program to take down a financial system as well as I can fire a weapon at a human target."

"Why would the nuns sell you?"

"I don't know, and I don't care. It doesn't change anything. They did what they did, and I'm who I am." She gulped down the rest of the wine and poured some more into the glass.

He shook his head when she tried to fill his glass and kept watching silently.

She felt awkward, so continued talking. "A few months ago, my life changed. I had to go off-the-grid. I'd bought and built this place a while back as a safe house. It made sense for me to come out here."

Feeling his gaze warming her skin, she turned attention to the turquoise ocean, the sound of the waves crashing against the shore filling the silence.

"Why would you lock yourself away from the world? It must be lonely living out here on your own."

Turning to him, a sad smile curling the corner of her lips. She couldn't tell him the whole reason she was living here alone. Not yet. "I'm not alone anymore. I have you."

Something flickered in his gaze too close to pity, and she hated it. She didn't want pity.

"Buying a slave just so you can have company isn't right," he said in a disdainful voice.

The muscles on her neck tensed, and she stood abruptly. "I may have paid for you. But I've never treated you like a slave."

She was self-sufficient on the island, growing fruits, vegetables and herbs. Occasionally, she had to go to the mainland to buy items, but she made the most of what was in her environment.

She did all the cooking and cleaning. She provided everything he needed. Treated him like a king. Like he was the master.

And he was still complaining?

She paced a few steps away and turned, glaring at him with fury, hands clenched by her sides. "Who exactly is the slave here? I do everything for you. I've even offered my body to you, and you rejected me. I—"

"Hang on a minute." He cut her off and stood, chin high, tightness around his eyes. "When exactly did you offer yourself to me?"

"Every morning, after our run, I invite you to the shower."

"But... you were inviting me to fuck you?"

"Yes."

His mouth opened and closed a few times before he finally spoke. "What?"

His clenched hands loosened, and he widened his legs.

She saw it then, the tenting of his fly.

"Hang on. Why?"

"Remember the first morning when I met you drinking tea, I told you that you were free to use anything in this place for your pleasure."

Jerking his head back, he stared at her as if he didn't believe what she was offering him. "That offer included you?"

"Yes, and it still stands."

TWENTY

THE NEXT morning as Ebuka pulled on his running shoes and joined Xandra for the jog around the island, regret wound tight and knotted like vines in his gut.

He'd thought his life was messed up. But Xandra's was on a different level.

Her story about her lost childhood had affected him in ways he hadn't thought he would feel again. She was an enigma and yet all too human.

The adoration on her face had weakened him.

He'd nearly allowed her to fulfil the promise in her eyes.

But there were too many unanswered questions, and he couldn't indulge in pleasures when he hadn't resolved them.

Sometimes he had flashes of images, memories. But like a scrambled jigsaw puzzle, he hadn't been able to put them all together. He needed to get off this island soon.

"You better keep up, boss," Xandra called out as she ran ahead.

A chill travelled down his spine, and he stumbled.

"Are you okay?" Xandra marked time beside him and eyeing him curiously. He leaned a hand against a tree trunk and caught his breath.

"Fine," he said in a gruff voice. "Did you call me, 'boss'?"

The word was intimate, familiar, and he heard a soft voice whispering it to him, but the image wouldn't come. But the reference also had other connotations he didn't need reminding.

"Yes. You like it when I call you 'boss'."

"No, I don't. My name is Ebuka," he snapped, turned and sprinted to the house. He did quick stretches, took his shoes off and headed inside just as she arrived.

The fresh shower helped to wash away some of his tension and jumbled thoughts. The smell of fresh tea had him dressing quickly and going back to the kitchen.

Breakfast was laid out on the table, and Xandra was wiping down the counter as he strode across to the teapot and poured a cup.

Pulling out a chair, he sat and bit into the warm croissant before taking a sip of tea.

He could get used to this luxurious isolation—morning runs, breakfast served, a beautiful woman at his beck and call, the lack of expectation.

He wasn't the same man who'd run a ranch a few months ago. His life had been consumed with providing and taking care of his family. Now he was overtaken by anger and the need for revenge. Even when he got off this island, he wouldn't go back to farming. Not until he had covered his hands with the blood of his enemies.

"Aren't you going to join me?" he asked, watching her standing stiffly by the counter. He should've picked up the clue that something was wrong, but he was too engrossed in his thoughts.

"I'm sorry," she said, avoiding his gaze and shaking her head.

"What's... wrong?" His words came out slurred, and his body became heavy. He slumped against the chair before the world went dark.

The whizzing of an engine made him peel groggy eyes open. The sun was high in the sky. He tried to sit up but couldn't. His legs and arms felt weighted with lead. He tried to remember what had happened. Breakfast and then nothing.

"Xan," he called out before drifting off to sleep again.

Next time he woke, the sun was low in the sky. He dragged himself off the sofa and went in search of Xandra. The woozy feeling was the after-effect of being drugged. Xandra had tranquillized him. Again.

Pounding rose in his ears, and he felt like punching a hole in the wall. He heard a sound and rushed into the kitchen to find her dumping a box of groceries on the counter.

Before she could do anything, he ran full pelt at her and slammed his body into hers. "Bloody bitch!"

Her back rammed against the counter as she tried to fight him off. "Ebuka, wait."

Despite her plea, he didn't let up, smashing his elbow into her side.

She doubled over, emitting an oomph sound.

He opened open a kitchen drawer and pulled out a knife and the roll of duct tape.

"This shit ends today. On your knees," he demanded, pointing the sharp edge of the blade at her throat.

Without protest she obeyed, eyes fixed in an even, soulless stare that would've unnerved someone else.

Not Ebuka. Not with the adrenaline coursing in his veins. "Stretch out your hands."

She did, and he bound her wrists with the tape. He pushed the placemats off the table.

"Spread yourself on it, face down," he said, using the knife to point at the empty table.

With her hands tied, she was still dangerous. She was an assassin. A deadly, cold-blooded killer.

He couldn't kill her anyway. He needed Xandra alive to get off this island.

As if to emphasize his dilemma, she stared at the knife in his hand. It would not stop her if she wanted him dead. The determination in her eyes matched the steel of the blade.

Yet, she submitted, reached for the table edge and stretched across, lying flat on it, her movement deliberate and sinuous and silent.

He kicked her legs apart and taped each to the table posts.

He recognized what she had done, capitulating to him. It said, "I'm as strong as you and deadlier. But I want you to have the power."

His anger abated, replaced by arousal.

In this posture, she was a sight to behold. Beautiful. Sexy. Tempting. What would it feel like to slide his dick inside her pussy from this angle?

He moved, circling the table.

"You're going to tell me what the hell is going on." He pulled the collar of her t-shirt, pressed the flat knife surface against her neck for emphasis, so she would know he meant business.

There was tension in her shoulders for a moment as she froze. Her grip on the table became tight.

The need to uncover the truth about her rippled through him. She was always fully dressed and tight-lipped. She would be after he was done.

He dug the sharp tip of the knife into her top and tugged.

She relaxed as the shirt ripped from top to bottom.

He continued slicing and cutting until the tattered shirt hung like confetti on her body. Then he turned attention to the silk trousers, giving it the same treatment. He swept the fabric aside and revealed her bare body to his gaze for the first time.

Ebuka gasped.

Mottled scar tissue marked her legs and hips while welts covered her back.

"Stand," he said.

As if reluctant to show and yet reluctant to disobey him, she pushed off her elbows slowly.

The dark scars continued to her belly like a rising wave.

His mouth dried out, his heart aching with concern for her.

"What happened to you?" his voice was low.

She turned her head away, jaw clenched. "I was in a fire."

He couldn't explain the overwhelming need to protect her. He wanted to wrap her in his arms and tell her nothing would hurt her again.

Reaching across, he tried to touch her.

She flinched, jerking the table.

"It's okay. I won't hurt you," he said, voice gentle.

True, he'd been angry with her for drugging him.

But seeing the scars flipped his anger at the circumstance that caused her to hurt. He wanted to hurt whoever hurt her because now he understood her loneliness. It echoed the desperation he'd felt the past few months.

Sometimes when he watched her, and she didn't know, she seemed like someone weighed by troubles, like a soul tormented. In those unguarded moments, he saw a haunted woman, and his constant anger and suspicion subsided. The protectiveness he felt for the people he cared for came to the surface.

He put the knife down on the counter. "Can I touch you?"

She stared at him for seconds that dragged. Then she nodded.

Lifting his right hand, he traced the smooth, raised, hard skin on her side gently, moving up to her back. The demarcation between the different damaged areas was visible.

Now he understood why she chose clothes that hid them even in the warm weather. She hadn't worn shorts or skirts.

He traced fingers on her belly. She twisted away.

"Let me touch you," he said gently, trying to coax her.

"I'm grotesque," she said in a tight voice. "You didn't want me before. I know you won't want me now."

Frowning, he leaned back. "Why do you think I don't want you?"

Her shoulders lifted and fell. "You didn't want me last night."

"Look at me," he ordered.

He had slipped into his natural, instinctually assertive role. Binding her to the table, contributed to the switch in his brain.

Then again she hadn't put up a fight just now when he tackled her. Not like she'd done in the car.

So, when she obeyed and turned her head to meet his gaze, a mix of concern and pleasure skittered across his flesh. He was falling into her snare and yet delight skittered along his nerve endings when she gave herself without reserve.

"Do I look like someone who doesn't know what he wants?"

He surveyed her body. She was lean, muscular, breast and bum equally proportioned, dark, taut nipples, flat tummy and strip of bush over her pussy. The scars and welts only added to her beauty.

He still wanted to explore her body, stroke her flesh, pinch her nipples and taste her pussy.

"No," she murmured.

"Last night, I wanted you." He walked around to her back and pressed his groin against her bum.

Her breath hitched as he leaned in and whispered close to her right ear. "I still want your hot mouth on my dick. I want to savour sliding across your wet lips and watch you swallow my cum."

Her breath came out in shallow pants.

Blood rushed in his ears as his dick filled out. He rocked his hips. "Can you feel how much I want you?"

"Yes." Her voice came out raspy.

He slid hands around her, fingers tweaking one nipple while a palm covered her labia.

She shivered and let out a sigh.

Her skin was soft and slippery as he pushed an index finger against her slit.

Her body tensed briefly and relaxed as he pushed inside her warm wet flesh. Her breathing became heavy, and she clenched, sucking his digit all the way to the root.

He slid it out and added another one, controlling her. The other hand moulding her breasts, one after the other.

"So, you know how much I want to fuck you, fill you up and stretch you until all you can feel is me?"

"Yes," she moaned as her insides contracted around his fingers. He withdrew his hands.

She moaned in frustration.

Smiling, he walked over to the sink and washed his hands before facing her.

"I've wanted you from the first time I saw you. But I'm not going to fuck you until I get some answers from you."

Her gaze searched his before she nodded. "Ask me what you want to know."

"I will." He traced her stomach with fingertips. His heart clutched in his chest.

The fire had been merciless and melted the skin, and it had been grafted with healthy skin. But there was a trace of welts at the edges around her hip where it still seemed to be healing. He touched the scars tentatively.

"Does it hurt?"

"No. But it's a little sensitive."

He tangled fingers in the short hair on her nape. The scars on her body fascinated him, but he saw beyond the physical marks to the damaged and lonely woman.

"You're beautiful."

"Don't say that."

She sounded fractured, lost. A broken assassin.

And he yearned for her. He hadn't realised how much until now.

Were his feelings for Xandra clouded because she was the first person to show him affection in months after the ordeal he'd been through? Was his mind playing tricks?

Whatever the case, he had to show her that she could trust him.

"It's true, and I'm saying it." Standing beside Xan, he held her head still so she could meet his gaze.

There was much to deal with beyond these walls and this island. A family who needed him. But right here and now, Xandra needed him too, and he couldn't let her down. "You're a beautiful woman."

He kissed her lush lips. The familiar sensation sizzled down his spine, images of the two of them in a room flitted quickly through his mind and was gone.

She let out a moan and opened to him, body relaxing in his hold.

He lifted his head and said, "Don't ever doubt anything I tell you."

"It's tough to do that." The tone of her voice and the expression on her face said that it was more challenging for her to admit the flaw. "I struggle to let people close. You're the only one who's seen me like this, apart from the medics who treated me."

Eyes widening, he studied her. "Surely you had friends visit you while you were healing."

Someone must have helped her.

"I had a caregiver visit the house in the city to change the dressing and top up my prescriptions, but I didn't want anyone else to see me like this. As soon as I was strong enough to drive, I came out here."

His breath constricted, and his chest felt tight.

She had been out here on her own, recovering. He couldn't imagine not having any support. The loneliness. The isolation.

Xandra had chosen to insulate herself.

Leaning his forehead against hers, he gently massaged her nape. "You're not on your own anymore. I promise you. But I must go home. I have a ranch, and family members who I'm sure are anxious about me. Let me go and take care of them. I promise you I'll come back to you afterwards."

She stiffened and pulled back.

"Nobody ever leaves this island," she said in a sombre tone.

A finger of dread travelled down his spine. "What do you mean?"

"I mean that anyone who comes here doesn't get to leave. Nobody apart from me knows about this island. It's my haven. My safe place."

He stared into her eyes that looked like cold grey metal. She was deadly serious.

"That can't be right. What about the people who built this place? They know about it."

"They knew about it. Now they're all dead."

His stomach rolled. "You killed them?"

"I had to. I couldn't take the chance that one of them would talk."

He scrubbed a hand over his face. This was who she was. It didn't sit well with him, but he had to accept it.

"I promise you, I'll come back. I just can't stay here not knowing what's happened to my family."

"The last time you made a promise, you broke it," she said in a matter of fact voice.

His cheeks heated. He had promised to behave in the car and hadn't. "We didn't know each other well enough then. I didn't trust you. I trust you now."

"Then you should know that if I let you leave and you don't come back to me, I'll hunt you down and kill you."

TWENTY-ONE

EBUKA STIFFENED and backed away.

Never had a threat to his life sounded deadlier, even though the person who had spoken the words was currently tied to the table immobile.

Xandra had uttered the words with clear intent and in a relaxed manner. It seemed as if danger oozed from her pores.

He had no doubt she would carry out the threat.

Ebuka paced the kitchen. Late sunlight beamed in, casting long shadows of the furniture.

Under normal circumstances, he would like to come back to this island.

She has worked with the environment to create a sustainable lifestyle, the same as he had done at the ranch.

But did he want to get involved with a person like Xandra? A cold-blooded killer. Once upon a time, he would not have minded. But he had turned his back on that life.

However, the likes of Ralph Nweke had been harassing him since, thinking he had turned soft. And he still needed to get to the bottom of how he got abducted and imprisoned.

What other choice did he have? He needed to get off this island.

And Xandra was the key to getting the answers he needed. He would have to deal with the implication of coming back here when it happened.

He returned to Xandra.

Surprising that she still hadn't moved from the spot. She was naked and tied up in her own house, and she didn't look perturbed.

She was a complicated person. A master who took pleasure in service. A killer who had no qualms about being tied up. If she wanted to cause him harm, she would have broken out of the bond and hurt him already.

He swallowed the lump in his throat. "I can tell you now, I won't tell anyone about this island. Once I sort out what I need to do back at the ranch, I'll come back here if you still want me."

Would she accept his words? His heart thudded as he waited for her to speak. She stared at him for several seconds.

"Okay. We'll go to the mainland so you can do what you need to do," she said finally.

He puffed out the breath he'd been holding as relief washed over him. He stepped up to her and gripped her nape, staring into her grey eyes before kissing her briefly.

"Thank you for trusting me," he said.

Her mouth curled up at the corner in a slow smile. "Well, if you're not going to fuck me, maybe you should untie me so I can get dressed and we can talk."

He chuckled. "Yeah. Good idea."

He loved seeing her bare, but if they were going to talk practicalities, then it was best to get some clothes on her before he lost control and did what he'd regret. He took the knife from the counter and sliced the tapes off.

While she headed out to find some new clothes, he cleared out the mess from the torn ones. Then he loaded the pantry and fridge with the items from the grocery box. He opened the grill, stuck two beef steaks on it and set about preparing a salad to go with it.

"What are you doing?"

He turned to find Xandra standing by the door in a pair of shorts and a tank top. This was the first time he saw her in shorts. There was some scarring visible on her calves and thighs. Now that he'd seen the rest of her there was no point wearing clothes that hid all the scars.

"I'm making dinner," he said and waved at the table. "You can get the table ready."

Her eyebrow arched, but she didn't say anything as she went about wiping the surface and putting out the placemats and eating utensils.

How did he end up in an almost domestic situation with an assassin? He finished the preparation and served up the food.

"Did you sedate me because you had to go out for groceries?" he asked, stabbing a string of green beans with the fork.

She glanced up, shook her head and carried on chewing. He waited as she took a sip of water.

"Not exactly. I must go away for a few days on a job. I went out to buy the items for you so you'll have enough until I get back."

"You were going to leave me here alone?"

"As I said before, I had no intentions of letting you leave this island. I knew you'd be safe here until I got back." She shrugged. "It doesn't matter now. You'll come with me to Opal City when I head out in a couple of days."

Exhaling in relief that she would keep to her promise of letting him off this island, his pulse rate picked up at the thought that she was going on a job to kill someone.

Somebody out there had a hit on their head.

His chest constricted, and he struggled to breathe.

Standing, he took the empty plate to the sink. "I thought you said you were staying off the grid."

She came to stand beside him with her dishes and placed them in the sink. "I am. It's a special request from Tiye Himba. He wants me to do a job for one of his associates. I got more interested when I saw the name of the target. A high-ranking member of one of the most prominent families in the Yadili network."

Interest piqued, he turned and leaned on the counter, flipping the towel over his shoulder.

The name Himba sounded familiar. He'd heard Ralph Nweke mention him. "Himba is your boss, right?"

"I wasn't on his payroll if that's what you mean. But he introduced me to the game and took me into his fold. As a sponsor, he takes a percentage of my fees for each kill."

"And he wants to kill a cartel boss?"

"Not him. An associate of his. The Baron." Xandra poured more wine into his glass. "Who's that?" he asked, surprised she was talking about all this.

If she was going to trust him enough to let him off the island, then she should trust him enough to tell him this. In for a penny, in for a pound.

"John Bull Owo. He's the kingpin up in Lori Osa. Controls the drug routes and the brothels. Also connected with the political elite."

"I know of him." He turned and put away the dried plates that Xandra had washed. These people were heavy hitters. Dangerous. Deadly.

Why was she going to Opal City when Lori Osa was a different region? "So, the person you're going to kill. Is he a rival of Owo's?"

"Not that I'm aware of. The Odilis own casinos. Gambling is their thing. I can't see how that clashes with Owo's drug cartel."

Gambling he could live with. Drugs not so much. His scalp prickled though.

"How does this work? They call you up and say, 'we want you to kill x, y and z', and you decide I'll kill x and y but not z?"

How did she justify killing these people? How did she live with herself afterwards? He wanted to understand her.

"It's not my place to determine who lives or dies. I'm the executioner. I look at the name, gather info and do the job."

"Really? You don't feel any kind of guilt or remorse when you go out to do these things. Those are human beings you kill. Someone's son, father, brother, uncle or friend. Don't you care?"

Her body stiffened, and the shutters came down. He had gone too far.

"Why should I care if some guy out there lives or dies? If they're on my list, then they are not innocent." She paced away and came back. "And why are you bothered about Duke Odili? He is an underboss, heir apparent to the Odili clan. He's part of this life, and he knows what it entails. Death comes to the best of us."

His brain got stuck on the name, and he barely processed the rest of her words. He knew that name. "Did you say Duke Odili?"

She frowned. "Yes. Do you know him?"

"No." It wasn't a lie as he didn't know the man personally, just his family. Xandra studied his face as if she didn't believe him.

So, he added, "The name sounds familiar like old family friends. I used to know an Odili family when I was a child."

It was the truth. His father, Oganiru, had worked for Daniel Odili, his wife Bisola and their son Duke. The last time Ebuka saw Duke, they'd been boys.

She nodded as if in acceptance of his words.

"I didn't mean to shout at you. It's just that I couldn't help thinking about the situation and what it would feel like to be the target."

The lines around her eyes softened, and her shoulders relaxed.

"I understand," she said in a soft tone. "But trust me when I say, any man who makes it onto the hit-list is a dead man. Because even if I don't kill him, someone else will take up the job and finish it. Duke Odili is a dead man. At least this way, I get the fee that comes with the contract."

Something niggled in Ebuka's mind.

"At the auction house, you said that the two of us knew each other before. How did we meet?"

She leaned her body against the counter and looked at him. "Are you sure you want to know the answer to that question?"

"Of course, I do. Tell me."

"Then I'm going to sit down because it's a long story and I want to be comfortable." She grabbed the bottle of wine and headed outside.

Ebuka followed her and settled on one of the deck chairs on the veranda.

She poured wine and gulped down the full glass without taking a breath. "I'm going to need something stronger than wine to talk about this."

She shifted, pushing off the chair and entered the house.

Ebuka followed and placed a hand on her shoulder when she opened and slammed the door of a drawer. "Stop."

She bent over the counter. Her body trembled.

"Hey, what's wrong?" He coaxed her gently until she turned. But she kept her gaze fixed away.

He'd never seen her like this, looking distraught. "Tell me what's wrong."

She shoved his chest, but he didn't budge.

"Do you know how hard it is to talk about what happened? When you look at me like I'm a stranger? Like you've never held me close, or kissed me in the rain or held me in your arms until I fell asleep?" She squeezed her eyes shut, and a tear dropped onto her cheek. "I don't even know what's wrong with me. I've never been this jittery about anything before. Why the fuck can't I talk about what happened without feeling as if the world is going to implode. I need to get over this shit. I need another drink."

Damn. It sounded as though asking her to talk about how they met had been a kind of trigger that unlocked her trauma.

He pressed his body into hers, caging her against the counter. "Slow down. Let me hold you for a minute."

He wrapped his arms around her.

"No. I just need a drink." She stood stiffly, hands trembling.

He didn't let go. Eventually, she sighed and relaxed against him, head on his shoulder, arms around him. Her panting breaths evened out.

He kept holding her, though. "I like having you in my arms."

She grunted, and her grip around him tightened.

A smile curled his lips, and he leaned back, looking at her face. "I kissed you in the rain?"

"You did more than kiss me in the rain," she mumbled against his shoulder.

"Uh-oh. That sounds interesting. Did I fuck you in the rain?"

She lifted her head, and her eyes sparkled with warmth. A smile lit up her pretty face, making his chest squeeze tight. "Yes."

"Where? Outside the house?" Where were Ginika and Mama at the time?

"No. Outside the remote cabin at the range. You held me down by the stone steps in front of the veranda and took me from behind while the rain pelted our naked bodies. You were a fucking god that night."

Her description was accurate.

She'd been to the farm. She *knew* him.

More to the point, the imagery made him as hard as a rock. "Jeez. You're killing me, woman."

Giggling, she tipped her head, looking at the tent in his shorts. "I can help you with that."

TWENTY-TWO

XANDRA DIDN'T know what happened to her.

One minute she was discussing her next contract kill. Then Ebuka had asked about how they'd met, and a big ball of emotions she couldn't decipher had knotted her throat, chest and belly.

She had been overwhelmed, unable to breathe, unable to think.

Until Ebuka had hugged her and after a few minutes the world had righted itself.

Perhaps it was his musk in her nostrils or the strength of his arms around her and his soothing voice. Maybe it was just having his warmth cocooning her.

Whatever it was, it had returned some of her sanity. She still couldn't figure out what had gone wrong.

She was never the clingy sort, never got emotional. Always dealt with issues with detachment.

Not since she brought Ebuka to the island, though.

It was almost as if her mind had decided that Ebuka was her safety net and she could break down safely.

She couldn't afford to fall apart.

People were relying on her to do her job.

After the incident with Norbert, she hadn't been offered any jobs.

So, fulfilling the new contract would be her way of telling the world that she was still Xandra. Unbeatable. Indomitable.

She needed to start by proving to Ebuka that she was strong. That she wasn't a weakling.

That he didn't have to console or comfort her.

She covered the bulge in his shorts with her hand and traced his erection. "Use me." He groaned, closing his eyes. "That is tempting."

Sighing, he gripped her arm. "I have something better in mind."

He grabbed her hips, lifted and swivelled her, then sat her on the kitchen table. Growling, he crushed her lips with his.

Her breath hitched as if someone had punched her lungs. For the second time this evening, her world spun.

Ebuka kissed like a champion. His lips were perfect, rough and soft all at once. He held her as if she belonged in his arms.

Her pulse skipped, and her bare toes curled against the wooden posts. Her core heated, clenched.

She forgot the fight to prove her strength. When he held her like this, she melted. Became all woman. His woman.

Her body was on fire after the week of seeing him and physically craving him.

It was as if all those months they were separated had vanished, as if he knew her, remembered her, wanted her on the same deep level they had shared.

She clutched his shirt, tugged him close, returning the kiss.

He cupped her face, his touch tender, possessive, the other hand on the small of her back. He made another growling sound and pulled back a few inches. His eyes burned hotter than they'd been since his arrival.

"I'm going to take you to the bedroom," his voice rumbled.

She swallowed the lump in her throat. "Yes."

"In there, I'm going to take your clothes off. Then I'm going to spread you on the bed, settle myself between your wide legs, and eat your pretty pussy until you start screaming."

Jeez.

With his dirty talking, she would start screaming right here on the kitchen table. Her knickers were soaked, and her pulse raced. Her nipples hardened, and her body ached for him.

What was it about Ebuka?

Where was the Xandra who would baulk at this level of intimacy? Who wouldn't allow this to happen? Should she step away? End this?

She didn't move. Right here was where she wanted to be. Miles away from anyone else, with Ebuka all to herself.

"I want everything on offer," she whispered in a husky voice.

His lips curled into a hungry grin, and he scooped her into his arms and strode down the hall into the bedroom he slept. Then he lowered her onto the mattress and covered her body with his before his mouth descended on hers.

She moaned, tasting him—wine and Ebuka—swirling her tongue in his mouth.

His hands touching her body made her tingle and throb, and he groaned into her. He tangled fingers in her short hair, pulled her tight, while the hand on her thigh was rough.

Lord, she wanted him.

She tugged at his clothes, forgetting the sensual promise he'd made in the kitchen, wanting to feel him skin to skin.

He lifted his head, looking down at her. His expression was full of heat and raw intensity.

He looked like he finally saw her, saw Xandra and Allie, and still wanted her. Like she was all he wanted.

"You are amazing," he said, his voice filled with awe.

He sat on his haunches and tugged the hem of her top. She lifted her arms so he could pull it over her head.

Although she never had a problem undressing in front of a man before. This time felt different. Her heart raced.

Perhaps because he was the one undressing her. Probably because her burn scars would be visible to him. She still wasn't used to showing those off.

She was happy to wear a cane welt as a badge of honour. But the burn marks made her feel ugly and undesirable.

Ebuka didn't seem to care as he lowered the zip of her skirt and pulled it down along with her knickers.

"Roll over," he demanded. She flipped onto her stomach.

He grabbed her hips and tugged her to her knees, body and ass bare to his gaze. He would see how wet she was for him.

"Xan, fuck." A sharp intake of breath, and then he groaned.

It was the first time he'd used the shortened form of her name, and it sounded good to hear him say it.

He slid his palm down the dip of her back to her hips, squeezed her bum cheeks, cupped her. He rolled his hip against her. Something massive and hard throbbed against her bum. His erection.

His hand returned to her thigh, travelled up and then stopped between her labia. One thick finger dragged over her slippery wetness.

She moaned, clenching inside.

His other hand gripped her tight, spreading her open for the other fingers to push into her hungry contracting slit.

Her breath caught. Her body shivered in bliss.

His finger curled inside her, stroking the sweet spot, making her clench and tremble. He settled closer, his breath on her bum, his fingers playing her inside and out. Then his tongue joined in, sliding over her pussy.

She caught fire, gasping, clutching the sheets, arching her back as his mouth settled around her clit. The pleasure was a drug in her veins, sweeping her slowly to the edge as he

fucked her with fingers and mouth. She rolled her hips shamelessly around his face, using him for her pleasure, thrusting against him, clenching tighter and tighter.

For the first time in months, she felt desired. Truly desired.

And he didn't stop. Didn't relent. He licked her labia, her clit, pushing with his tongue, rolling, sucking, while his fingers rammed and curled and gave her pleasure again and again.

Then he upped the ante, sliding his tongue up her crack, his mouth teasing her tight forbidden hole.

"Boss?" she cried, the title slipping out easily, forgetting he'd rejected it the last time she used it.

"Yes," he replied against her skin. He didn't seem to mind. His tongue swiped her hole. "Did I fuck you here?"

She gasped, moaning loudly, head to the sheet. "No."

He licked her again. One hand spread her open. The other between her thighs, wreaking havoc, thumb on her clit, fingers in her slit.

"No part of you is out of bounds to me, Xan. Did I tell you that already?"

"Yes," she said breathlessly as pleasure frazzled her brain. "On our first night together." "Good. Then you know that I'm going to claim every available hole in your body. I look forward to the day when I plug your pussy with a vibrating dildo and ride your ass for as long as I want." He bit her bum cheek hard.

The pain was just what she needed, and she hurtled towards an orgasm. "Boss, please."

"I know you want to come. I want to taste your sweet cum." His tongue returned to her pussy, his mouth sucking her clit while his fingers rubbed her g-spot.

She trembled and clenched, fire building in the pit of her belly and spreading until it erupted at her extremities.

He sucked her hard, and she let go, screaming in pleasure at the climax that slammed into her. Wave and wave of pleasure crashed over her until he released her.

She collapsed onto the bed, a quivering mess, his body around her a cocoon of blissful warmth and comfort.

TWENTY-THREE

"STAY THERE," Ebuka said, getting off the bed.

"Yes, Boss." Xandra stretched languorously as he covered her with a light sheet. In the relaxed state, she looked young and vulnerable.

His heart clutched. He felt connected to her even when he couldn't remember everything about their first meeting. Like they truly belonged together. But there were so many unanswered questions that left him uneasy about trusting her.

Shoving the heavy thoughts out of his mind, he pressed a quick kiss to her forehead before going to lock up.

The location was remote, and there was little chance of anyone walking in the front door. However, there were wild animals and birds, so the door had to be locked properly. Mesh sheets across the windows excluded flies and mosquitoes.

The house was powered by solar energy via panels affixed to the roof, making it possible to live here without interference from the outside world.

He returned to the room with a glass of water. "Have a drink."

She leaned on her elbow and took the tumbler. When she finished, he put it on the nightstand and joined her in bed, naked.

They were curled up with arms around each other when she started talking. "I was sent to kill you. That's how we met."

She said the words without emotion. Simply. Like she was reading the weather forecast. A chill slithered down his spine. He froze in place.

Suspicious, he had wondered how his path could have crossed with an assassin's considering the quiet life he'd led. Hearing the truth was like smashing through a brick wall that had kept him imprisoned. Rage simmered in the pit of his gut.

He shifted, leaving her warm and sitting on the edge of the bed, feet on the cold floor, back to her. "When?"

"About six months ago."

He waited for her to continue. She didn't.

Her silence fuelled his anger. This wasn't the time for her to become mute. He wanted to know everything. Who? Why? What?

He grabbed the shorts he had discarded, shoved his feet in and stood. Reaching for the wall, he flicked the switch and bathed the room in an orange glow. Finally, he turned to face her.

She lay on her side, head on a pillow, arm tucked beneath. Her eyes were closed.

Was she sleeping? She couldn't have delivered such troubling news and fallen asleep.

She was that cold-hearted, was she?

Her breathing pattern hadn't evened out. She was awake.

Still, how could she look calm when he wanted to rage? Smash. Kill. Make someone pay.

His months-long captivity had become a poison in his vein, tainting everything. Tainting his mind. Although a part of him warned against blaming her, against lashing out, he couldn't absolve her. Couldn't release her from the urge to avenge his circumstances.

"Is that why you brought me here? You decided to keep me as your pet instead of killing me? Am I supposed to be grateful?"

Her dark lashes fluttered, and she met his gaze with deadly scrutiny, her eyes cold as ice and sharp as knives.

Tension rippled the air. She shuffled out of bed, tugged the discarded shirt over her head. The hem dropped to cover her bum, just about. It showed off her long slender legs. The legs that led to the treasure hidden beneath the top. For a second, he forgot his anger and recalled her flavour. Her sweetness. How he'd nearly come in his shorts as he'd eaten her pussy. How she'd trembled and begged, crying out and gushing as she'd climaxed. How he wanted to bury himself in her lush wet heat. His dick jerked, hardened.

"Taming a wild lion would have been more fun if I'd wanted a pet."

Her words yanked him from his thoughts to the present. The comparison to a lion would have made him smirk if he wasn't already wound tight. However, his expression turned to a grimace as she stalked to him and stabbed his chest with fingers.

"You know what? You should be grateful that I didn't kill you. Okay? I had many opportunities to end your life. But stupid me, I worried about how your death would affect your family. I worried about leaving Ginika in Nweke's clutches."

His stomach rolled, and he narrowed his eyes. "What has Nweke got to do with this?"

She glared at him, dropping her hand. "He's the one who took a contract out on you."

He staggered back, stunned by the revelation. "Ralph Nweke sent you to kill me?"

Although he asked a question, he believed her. His former best friend had been trying him for years. Pushing to see how much Ebuka would tolerate. However, when did their disagreement degenerate to Ralph wanting him dead? He'd once trusted that man with his life. He was now paying for the folly.

"Yes. At first, it was an exclusive contract, and I was the primary. But when I didn't kill you within a week, he extended the contract to others and made it non-exclusive. Other assassins showed up. One nearly blew you up outside a hotel in Bakili. We had to send Ginika to your mother and aunt in Iguocha for her protection. But when we got back to the ranch, more assassins came."

She stopped talking and stormed out of the room.

Assassins in his home? His heart slammed into his chest. Thankfully, they had protected his family. What about his employees, the livestock? Did they survive the attack?

He followed Xandra. He needed to know what happened. To fill in the blanks.

Maybe something would trigger his memories to return.

He caught up with her on the veranda which ran the length of the back wall. The lights automatically came on when the sensors detected body heat and motion. The sounds from the waves mixed with the chirping of the night creatures.

"Tell me what happened when the assassins came."

She stood by the low wall looking out into the darkness beyond the lit garden of edible and flowering plants.

"You were shot, okay. And you had a head injury. You were slipping in and out of consciousness." She swirled and jabbed her hand against his thigh, where he had a recently healed scar. "I couldn't take you to the hospital. I had to dig the bullet out of your leg. And suture your injuries. I was out of options and had to take you to a safehouse in Lori Osa to hide you while you healed so I could deal with Nweke. But then this happened." She pointed at the burn welts on her legs. "I couldn't go back to get you until it was too late. Fine. Get angry with me because you ended up in Madaki's slave house. But I have no regrets about keeping you alive."

"Oh." The realisation hit him. She cared about him. He heard it in the huskiness of her voice and the passion blazing in her eyes.

His heart squeezed tight. Some of his anger dissipated. Sighing, he placed hands on her shoulders and said in a gentle tone. "You saved my life."

She turned her head away and didn't respond.

He sighed again, wrapped arms around her, pulling her softness into his hardness, her tank top rubbing his bare chest. Pressing his forehead to hers, he whispered against her mouth. "I'm sorry. I'm grateful you didn't kill me. I can't imagine the heat you must have taken on my behalf. Thank you."

She jerked back, looking into his eyes. "But don't you get it. If you go back to the mainland. Nweke and Himba will know you are still alive."

He saw what she didn't say in the depths of her eyes. Fear. She was scared he would be killed. That was why she'd brought him here for his protection.

She had valid reasons to be concerned. Ralph Nweke was connected to influential people.

Men like Tiye Himba. Taking him down could ruin Ebuka if he wasn't careful.

But Ralph would now evade him. He would have his vengeance.

He needed a plan. A name Xandra had mentioned earlier sprang to mind.

Duke Odili. He was a powerful man. If Ebuka could get to him, he would be the key to unleashing his revenge.

Ebuka held Xandra's chin, pressed his lips to hers, brushing gently. She exhaled and relaxed against him.

"Don't worry about me. I can handle Nweke. He won't see me coming, this time around."

A frown creased her face. "What are you going to do?"

He met her gaze full-on so she would know he was serious. "I'm going to kill him."

***

Two days later, Xandra showed Ebuka the speedboat which had been hidden in a secret alcove covered by the waterfall he had seen on the first day. The source of escape had been in plain sight all along. The whirring engine he'd heard the day she'd drugged him had been from its motor. She was intelligent, his Xandra.

He'd come to appreciate her quirks over the past few days as they'd gotten to know each other better and she'd told him of their time together on the ranch.

They loaded the craft with what they would need for at least a week and headed to the mainland. Once they left the choppy waters around the island, the sea was mostly calm, and they made good time according to Xandra. Warm clothes and water-proof jackets protected them from the lashing wind. They were silent for most of it. The noise of the motor didn't allow for conversation unless they shouted.

Neither of them seemed interested in talking.

Ebuka's mind went to Ginika and Mama. His pulse raced. He felt breathless and lightness in his chest. He would see them in a few days.

First, they had business in Opal City. Then, they would travel to Bakili and eventually the ranch.

Two hours after leaving Laroca, the mainland came into view. Xandra avoided the busy shipping port and headed up the river. As she steered the boat into one of the deltas, she said, "Take the wheel for a minute. I want to send a message."

They changed position, him at the helm while she sat on the bench, phone-in-hand. He wasn't a mariner and liked to keep his feet on Terra firma. But keeping the boat clear of obstacles seemed straightforward.

"Each time you travel on the boat, you're alone?" he asked, suddenly aware of all the things that could go wrong out here. Bad weather, rough seas, pirates, equipment breakdown. The list went on.

She came to stand next to him. "Yes."

A chill permeated his bones, and he shivered. "What if something bad happened?"

She shrugged. "That's always a possibility. But I mitigate it by sending a message to my maintenance man before each trip. He'll be there to meet us, and he checks the boat while I'm on the mainland and makes sure it's ready for use when I return."

"But that still doesn't help you if you're stranded out in the ocean."

She shrugged again. "The shipping lanes get busy, and there are naval patrols to combat pirates, so someone would find me eventually. Anyway, I'm not worried. Since fire didn't kill me, I'm not worried about a little water."

His mouth dropped open. "It's the fucking Atlantic Ocean, not a little water!"

She giggled, eyes sparkling.

"What's so funny, woman?" he snapped.

How could she find this amusing when his gut was wrenching with dread at her being stranded? Without help. Without him.

"Calm down, sailor." She leaned into him sideways and curled her arm around his waist. "I'm happy because for the first time you reminded me of the old Ebuka. A man who cared about me like no other man ever did."

"Oh," was all he could say.

She pressed a kiss to his cheek. "It was that fierce expression on your face, of love, of tenderness that kept me going while I was in the hospital. It made me determined to get better, even after I saw the extent of the damage on my body. I swore I was going to get back to you. Then when I found you and you couldn't remember me. That was crushing. The pits."

"I'm sorry." He tugged her so she stood in front of him and his arm caged her to the wheel. "Not remembering is painful for me too."

"I know. It must be frustrating. That's why I cheer whenever you go all caveman because I feel like I'm getting my Ebuka back and soon your memories will return."

"I hope so." He leaned down and kissed her nape.

She sighed with pleasure but stiffened as a small secluded harbour came into view about thirty minutes of travelling inland.

A man stood on the wooden planks that formed the jetty. He was dark-skinned, wiry and probably in his forties. Empty fishing boats bobbed in the water.

"That's the maintenance guy," Xandra said.

"Okay," Ebuka replied.

"Aunty, you don come?" the man called out.

"Benji, na so. How now? How everybody?" Xandra threw the rope.

The man caught it and tied it to a post. "We dey. I see say oga don better."

She climbed onto the pier. "Yes. He don better."

"Oga, welcome," Benji said.

"Thank you. Please, help me carry the bags out," Ebuka replied.

"No problem." He took the luggage as Ebuka passed them.

"Wait here. I'm going to get the car." Xandra walked onto the sandy shore along what looked like a dirt road to a large shack made from wood and corrugated zinc. She unlocked a door, went inside.

Ebuka dragged the travel cases to the edge of the pier and waited.

A few minutes later, a BMW pulled along the shore. Xandra's BMW. Not long after the car was loaded and they waved goodbye to Benji.

"What was that about oga getting better?" Ebuka asked.

He sat in the front passenger seat as Xandra drove, reminding him of the night she'd bought him at the auction. His body tensed, and he shoved the horrors of that place out of his mind.

"The day we arrived, he helped me get you into the boat because you were still under the effect of the anaesthetic. I told him you'd been in hospital and I was taking you home to recover."

Nodding, he glanced at her. "Does he think I'm your husband?"

She shrugged and said nothing. Didn't look at him. Just continued driving. At the end of the dirt road, she turned into another widened dusty road through a small town.

Sparse low brick houses. Children with jerrycans on their heads. Women with babies strapped to their backs and bundles on their heads. Wooden stalls, multicoloured wares, hawkers chasing cars on foot. Construction workers taking shade under trees, drinking and laughing.

The thought of being her husband didn't annoy Ebuka considering the troubles with Sabina. Instead, warmth bloomed through him. But he couldn't hide his status from her. He cared about her too much.

"Do you know about my wife?" he asked.

"Yes. I met her," she said stiffly and glanced at him; expression closed. "What's the deal between both of you? Why are you still married to her?"

Talk about direct. He liked Xandra's directness. Liked her. A lot. Not like Sabina at all.

"It's a long story," he said.

"It's a long drive," she replied.

He scrubbed his hands over his face and head. She had a point.

He didn't like talking about Sabina. But Xandra had bared her soul to him. It was only fair to do the same, even if he hurt in the process.

"I can't really talk about Sabina without talking about Ralph. Ralph and I were best friends. We met in high school and went to the same university. We even joined the Yadi fraternity on campus, which is loosely linked to the Yadili syndicate, on the same night."

"Wow. You were that close." She glanced at him; eyebrows raised in a shocked expression.

"Yes. We were brothers, inseparable."

"What happened to change it."

"It was a series of things. In my final year, I started dating Sabina, who was in her first year. At the time, I was in love with her. She was smart and beautiful and the daughter of the state governor. She was out of my league. I wondered why someone like her would even give me a second look. But it became clear later that she'd dated me for a reason.

I was the leader of the Yadi fraternity and on-campus that made me king. So, dating me automatically made her the queen of the campus."

"Really?"

"Yes. She told me she wouldn't have stooped to date anyone lower than the Yadi 'general' which was my title at the time. Her father was our godfather and was campaigning for the governorship. He wanted to hire the Yadi fraternity to intimidate his opponents. I was against the idea and discussed it with Ralph. Yes, the boys had gotten into scrapes before. But it was usually just intercampus rivalries and skirmishes. Nothing that heavy. We were kids transitioning into adulthood. Also, that kind of stuff went against the Yadili values which we were supposed to be upholding. Ralph saw it differently. He was about getting what he wanted anyway possible. Sabina's father was godfather, and we shouldn't refuse our godfathers anything."

Ebuka stopped talking as he conjured up the stress from years ago. It had been a painful period for him for so many reasons.

Xandra pulled into a service station and parked the car in one of the available spaces. She unclipped her seatbelt and turned to him. "So that's why you fell out?"

Ebuka released himself from the harness, scrubbed a hand over his face and puffed out air. "Not exactly. About the same time, my father fell ill, so I had to go home for a while. As my captain, I left Ralph in charge of the frat boys. While I was away, he started using the boys to run interference for Sabina's father. Harassing and intimidating supporters of the opposition. When I found out Ralph, and I had a big fight because he had no rights to overrule my decision since I was still the frat leader, and he was my second-in-command. So, in the end, I stepped down and handed the frat leadership to him.

"At that point, my focus was changing anyway. I was more interested in graduating with a good degree, not the paper one I could have bought by paying off lecturers. Not that I had that kind of money to waste anyway. But Chief Dede, our godfather had guaranteed we would all graduate somehow. My father always said, 'you shouldn't always take everything you're given. Some 'gifts' carry a hefty price'. He never liked Chief Dede. He said the man was too egotistical. That he was more interested in filling his pockets than taking care of the people. I didn't quite see that at the time. Afterall, Sabina's father was a member of the Yadili which was set up for the progress of the people. Much later, I saw the man beneath the gloss.

"And then my father died, and my focus shifted to taking care of my mother and sister. Meanwhile, I did my youth service and then came home to work on the farm. I had plans. At first, Sabina didn't like it. She wanted me to go and work for her father. He was the state governor and could offer me a position in one of the ministries. I wasn't interested in politics or civil service. Plus, I wanted to build on what my father had started on the farm.

"Ralph went to work in his father's law firm. His father had been the state chief justice, so it was inevitable that Ralph would follow in his footsteps since he maintained the political connections over the years. After Sabina graduated, we made plans to get married. She had big expensive plans for the wedding. Honestly, I couldn't afford a lot of it. Her father footed most of the bill. That should have been a warning to me. But I loved her and wanted to give her what she deserved. After we got married, she started going on at me about joining her father in politics. She said if I got close to her father, I would get all kinds of contracts. She wanted to live like a politician's wife, not a farmer's wife. She had a good job, working at first with Nweke Law firm. I told her she could keep her money and do whatever she wanted with it."

"And that wasn't enough for her?" Xandra asked quietly.

"It never was." He fell silent after that and Xandra didn't push him for more.

TWENTY-FOUR

AS THEY drew close to Opal City, Ebuka became restless. His mind was on Duke Odili. How was he going to prevent the man's death?

Ebuka's father, Oganiru, must be watching over him, expecting him to stop the assassination. It wasn't just coincidence that his path crossed with Xandra's or that Xandra kept him alive.

He believed in a higher power. A greater purpose. This was his chance to contribute to do his portion.

Ebuka had to do something. He had to save the man's life. Even if it meant interfering with Xandra's kill.

Opal City was one of the largest cities in the region and was the old regional capital city known for its opal mines.

By the time they arrived and checked into the hotel, it was late. The next day, Xandra headed out. She said she had to see some people and plan.

Ebuka used the opportunity to visit the hotel's computer suite and search for any information on Duke Odili. From everything he found out, it seemed even more likely the man in question was the same person he'd been thinking about.

He needed to get hold of him. But reaching a man like Duke would be difficult since he was listed as CEO of the casino chain.

He found a contact for the casino and got through to Duke's personal assistant. However, the man was away and wouldn't be back in the office for a few days.

Frustrated, Ebuka returned to the room. The only other option was to get into Xandra's system to get the file on the target. Hopefully, she would have some personal contact details listed on there.

The opportunity came later that evening when Xandra was on her device.

"How do you know the person you kill is the correct person on the list?" Ebuka asked, hoping to find the information he needed somehow. "I mean, I know there should be a dossier. At least that's what happens in the movies. Is that the same in real life?"

She glanced up and smiled. "More or less. There is a file of information about the target that covers everything that could be used to identify him. I won't aim to kill until I've identified the target correctly."

"Can I see what's on there for this one?"

She stared at him for several seconds.

His heart raced, and his hands became clammy.

Eventually, she nodded and passed the device.

He stared at the image on the screen. It matched the man he'd seen earlier on the hotel computers. Duke Odili. There were all kind of details included, from date of birth and address, hair colour, eye colour, height, weight, etc., to things like unique markings like birthmarks and tattoos, and his private contact details.

Ebuka memorized the number before handing the device back to Xandra.

"That's a lot of detail in there," he said. The same level of detail must have been provided about him when Nweke took out a hit. He balled his hands into fists.

She shrugged. "This is a professional business. The client won't be happy if you kill the wrong person. And you don't get paid."

"Is this all about the money for you? Is that why you do the job?" He had to know what she was about.

Money was good. Nothing wrong with making a living. However, there were more important things.

A shadow passed across her eyes briefly. "The money helps me stay alive in a dangerous world. Without it, I wouldn't have been able to buy the island or secure so many safe houses. This is what I'm good at. It's what I trained for. It's in my blood as much as running a ranch was in your blood."

She tossed the device on the bed and walked into the bathroom, signalling the end of the conversation.

He wanted to go after her. But he was jittery enough about memorizing Duke's number and what he would have to do at the earliest chance. He let it drop for now. He had his hands full and didn't want to risk Xandra finding out what he had in mind.

He slept a little better that night. The next day, he left the room early under the guise of going to buy some things he needed for the trip to the ranch. Xandra had given him a money card with his name on it.

He took a cab to the shopping district. He bought a new phone and dialled Duke's number. As expected, he didn't know who Ebuka was when he answered the call. But to his credit, Duke agreed to meet when Ebuka mentioned his father's name. They arranged where to meet and hung up.

While waiting, Ebuka bought a backpack and gifts for Ginika and Mama, so he would have something to show Xandra when he returned to the room.

His stomach knotted for deceiving Xan like this, but there was no other choice. From the shopping mall, he took a cab to the location of the meet. It was in the heart of the old town where the streets were narrow and cobbled, and the houses had white walls and red roofs.

When he walked into the tea shop, there were a group of teenagers sitting at one corner, chatting and laughing. He walked over to the other end and took a seat near the window so he could see the street and know when Duke arrived.

A black SUV pulled up in front of the building, and three men got out. Two of them were in suits. The third in jeans and a t-shirt. He recognized Duke from the online photos of him. He was a striking man and had an aura of power around him. Yet he was congenial as he spoke to a bunch of kids whose soccer ball had landed near the car.

Then he opened the door to the tea shop.

Ebuka stood and walked to the back to sit in a more private booth. He watched the man approach who dressed like a businessman. He wasn't fooled by the man's appearance.

Duke was a dangerous man.

"Mr Njoku," he said, standing by the table.

"Ebuka. My name is Ebuka," he replied. Tension rolled off him as he didn't know what to expect from the man.

Duke settled in the seat opposite. The pose exuded relaxation, but his eyes were vigilant.

The waitress dressed in a white t-shirt with the café logo and black skirt came around. She was probably in her late thirties. She had brown hair with highlights and little makeup on her face, and she took our order.

After their order arrived, Duke stuffed a wad of cash into the woman's pocket and told her to send everyone else away and take the rest of the day off.

Ebuka was impressed by Duke. The man worried about the welfare of the ordinary person, the same as his father had done. He was taken aback by his generosity to the woman. Many men in his position wouldn't have cared and would've ordered the woman to do whatever they wanted without compensation. The money would buy her silence when law enforcement started asking questions.

After they were left alone, the two of them chatted mainly about the assassination of Duke's parents and how Ebuka's father had smuggled Duke out of the house that night.

At one point, Ebuka closed his eyes and raised hands to his face. He was bone-tired, and he wondered if this was even worth it. Was this man significant enough to incur Xandra's wrath? Unfortunately, he was. Family obligations made him necessary. Regret settled over him like a blanket.

His life seemed so far removed from the one his parents led. His father had been a prominent politician and lawmaker. According to Ebuka's father, he'd been a beacon of light and fairness in a world with rising corruption.

Had the governor's son become one of the men his father had fought against?

Ebuka believed Duke could accomplish his father's vision for their people, and he said as much.

Duke laughed as if Ebuka was crazy. "In case you haven't noticed, I'm not a statesman. Just a businessman."

"We both know you are more than a businessman. And you have a lot of influence. Some men do what you say. They will follow you and die for you."

"All this is inconsequential if I'm dead anyway."

Ebuka sighed. "I think I know how to keep you alive. I just needed to know if you're capable of keeping your father's legacy alive."

"And are you satisfied?"

"I think you'll do the right thing when the time comes. I know the person contracted to kill you."

He froze and tilted his head as if listening out for something. Then he stood in a rush, pulling a gun out and pointing it at his head.

"Stand. Keep your hands on your head. No sudden movement," he said, keeping his voice low and urgent.

"What's going on?" Ebuka asked as he stood slowly and did as he said.

He walked behind   and pulled a zip wire from his pocket. "I should be asking you.

Slowly lower your hands to the back and keep them together."

Ebuka let him tie his wrists together, wondering what had gone wrong. They'd been having a reasonable conversation. Now his hands were bound, and a gun was pointed at his head. "Why are you doing this?"

"Your friend is here," he said as he pulled a phone out of his pocket.

Ebuka felt another presence and gasped as Xandra walked into the main room of the cafe.

Shit. How did she know where he was? Did she follow him?

"Yes, I am," Xandra said. Eyes as cold and hard as steel, a black gun with a silencer nozzle in her gloved hand. She looked like the angel of death.

His heart nearly exploded out of his chest and sweat beaded on his upper lip. Duke stood behind him.

Xandra was in front, blocking the exit. Both had guns pointed at each other. This didn't look good.

"Xan..." Ebuka cleared throat. "What are you doing here?"

"I came to kill two birds with one stone." Xandra met his gaze. Her eyes were unforgiving.

He swallowed again. "What do you mean?"

"I find out that my lover has betrayed me, and there's only one way this can end. And Mr Odili—" She tilted her head in Duke's direction, "—was already on my list. You only accelerated my plans on his account."

"No." he took a step in her direction. "Stay where you are," Duke ordered.

Ebuka turned to him. He needed to salvage the situation somehow. He didn't want anyone dead on his account. "Let me talk to her. I can sort this out."

"You mean you want to convince her not to kill you. It's not going to stop her from trying to kill me, even if you resolve your lovers' quarrel."

He hit a raw nerve, and Ebuka eyes narrowed. "Look—"

"Yeah, exactly how do you plan on changing my mind?" Her fury seeped into her voice as well as her eyes. "You fucking betrayed me."

Images flashed of the two of them in a room. Memories. His hands tied. She had the same expression of fury.

Her emotions were raw, exposed. He had to convince her of his good intentions.

He spoke to her quietly, softly and seemed to be getting through to her when he saw the laser dot in the middle of Xan's chest.

Fuck. Ebuka's blood went cold as he froze. He couldn't let them hurt Xandra. "No. Duke, tell your men to stand down."

"Tell your woman to stand down first," he replied. "Weapons on the floor."

"Xan, do as he says." Ebuka's heart pounded. He hoped she would comply without a fight.

Xandra eyed him and then looked down to find the spot on her chest. "Well played, Mr Odili. I was told you were a hard man to kill. But I didn't think you would use my lover as a weapon to keep me distracted. It seems someone dies today, after all."

"If I'd wanted you dead, I would've given the order already," Duke said.

"So, what do you want from me?" Xan asked as she dropped the weapon and it made a dull clatter on the linoleum floor.

Another man pushed in the door with the ding of the bell and stepped in, gun pointing at Xandra. But he didn't say anything, just picked up the discarded gun from the floor and tucked it into the back of his trousers.

"I think that Mr Njoku makes some valid points," Duke said, lowering his gun, so it pointed downward.

Ebuka exhaled a little in relief, but he couldn't fully relax. The red dot was still on Xan's body.

"I'm in the market for good people, and you two seem like good people."

Xandra laughed, and it echoed humourlessly. "You want me to work for you. I already have a sponsor who wouldn't be too pleased with that proposition."

"Yes. Tiye Himba is a tough bastard. What do you think will happen when he finds out about you two? You'll both be food for worms, that's what."

Ebuka exchanged glances with Xandra. Was Himba really that bad? Something in Xan's eyes made him think it was true. He didn't like the fact Xan worked for Himba anyway. And Duke had to be better. Hopefully, he would use his influence for good and make some positive changes.

"So, are you saying that you'll be a different kind of boss?" Ebuka asked.

"I give you my word that the two of you won't be harassed about your relationship if you come to work for me."

"You're offering me a job, as well?" Ebuka asked. "I don't know much about your business."

"As long as you're willing to do whatever is required, there's not much to it." Duke shrugged. "You'll both have my protection."

Ebuka nodded before turning to Xandra. "Let's do this."

"You do realize that would mean that I'll become a target. Tiye Himba won't be happy about this."

"Yeah, you're right." His shoulders slumped. He didn't want Xandra in trouble.

"But on the other hand, this hit wasn't contracted by him. The contract is with John Bull Owo." Xandra walked over and leaned against the counter. He wanted to reach out and touch her. It felt good having her beside him, even if his hands were still tied.

The new man and Duke exchange glances, but they didn't say anything.

"And I don't owe The Baron any allegiances. So, I couldn't care less if he's pissed off," she continued, grinning for the first time. "And I wouldn't mind a boss who was more inclusive and tolerant."

Ebuka chuckled.

"Do we have a deal?" Duke asked. "Yes," Ebuka said.

Xandra nodded and walked over to Duke, offering her hand. "You sure do."

The two of them shook hands. The other man came forward and introduced himself as Mason as he cut the tie binding Ebuka's hands.

Ebuka breathed a lot easier as he rubbed his wrists. He'd managed to avert a bloodbath.

Afterwards, Duke pulled Ebuka aside. "Your father was Yadili. Why didn't you become a member?"

"I was an associate member at University, but I renounced my oath of allegiance to the godfather." He couldn't be a full member without a godfather.

"Oh." Duke's eyes narrowed. "Why did you renounce your oath?"

Ebuka understood the man's suspicions. Renouncing an oath was a bad thing, usually.

But he had good reasons. "It's complicated."

"I still need an explanation. I can't bring you into my clan if I can't trust you."

Ebuka puffed out heavy air. "I understand. Chief Dede and I don't see eye-to-eye on many matters. I cannot in honest conscience accept his methods or support them."

"Chief Dede. You mean Senator Dede?"

"Yes. The same one."

Sabina's father turned his ambitions to the national assembly once he completed two full terms as a governor.

Duke nodded. "Now, I understand. I don't think much of the man either."

"You can say that again. But things are complicated because his daughter is my soon-to-be ex-wife and her father is threatening to ruin me."

Duke whistled.

"And then there is the matter of an old friend who attempted to kill me," Ebuka continued. "Do you know Ralph Nweke? He's the attorney general in Bakili."

"I don't know him personally, but the name has come up in conversations," Duke replied.

"Well, you might know that he is Yadili," Ebuka said. "Since you've welcomed me into your clan, I am obligated to inform you that I intend to kill him and I'm going to need some resources."

Duke tilted his head and stared at him for a few seconds. Ebuka had to get the man's consent so that it didn't come to bite him in the ass later for killing a member of the Yadili. He hoped that since he had saved Duke's life, Duke would be happy to grant him this request.

After a few long seconds, Duke said. "We should formally induct you into the Odili clan then."

TWENTY-FIVE

THE DRIVE to the hotel with Ebuka was silent. Xandra felt a sense of déjà vu.

The first time she met Ebuka she'd been sent to kill him. Spending time with him and developing feelings for him had stopped her. She'd managed to save his life by faking his death. But things had gone wrong afterwards.

Now she'd returned to letting another target go, because of Ebuka.

However, she understood some of Ebuka's reasoning, especially now that Ebuka had been inducted into the Odili clan with an informal oath-taking. He would have to meet the head of the family, Don Sylvester Odili, who could veto it all. However, as Duke was underboss and heir-apparent, that would be unlikely.

Surprisingly, she was relieved she hadn't killed him. Her stomach had been a ball of knots, and her hands had shaken when she'd followed Ebuka. She had suspected something was up when he had asked her for details of the target.

So, when he went out this morning, she had followed him discreetly and tracked him to the restaurant. When Duke and his crew arrived, she knew exactly what was up.

Anger mixed with anxiety. Because she would have killed Ebuka and Duke. Yet both were alive.

Although she had let Duke Odili walk away alive, he wasn't out of danger for as long as The Baron wanted him dead.

But that wasn't her problem. She had bigger fish to fry. Himba.

There was no doubt about it. Himba would send men after her. Most likely Norbert to finish the job he'd started. She had left him alone because she had wanted to focus on finding Ebuka and getting him back. But if their paths crossed again, Norbert wouldn't be walking away.

She pulled the car into the parking space of the hotel lot and turned to Ebuka. "I'm going to Ralph Nweke's house with you."

"No." He looked shocked. "I will handle Ralph myself."

Her anger rose again. He had no right to refuse her after what he did today. How dare he? She got out of the car and slammed the door shut. Then she leaned hands on the roof of the vehicle. "You don't have a choice in the matter. As it is, I can't fucking leave you alone for two minutes without you trying to betray me."

Admittedly, she couldn't stand to see him with other people. It had been bad enough when she had seen him with Sabina. Although he wasn't doing the same thing with Mr Odili, the fact that he'd gone out of his way to warn the man rankled. He'd chosen to risk her wrath to protect another man.

Jealousy boiled in her gut.

"I told you I didn't betray you." He strode around the car and shoved her in the chest, and her back hit the car.

"You chose to save his life and risk my anger. I would've killed you both today."

"But you didn't." He stepped close enough for her to feel his body heat.

Her heart raced, and she yearned to feel him skin to skin. It felt like a long time since that happened.

"I couldn't let you kill him. Ralph is a member of the Yadili syndicate which Duke belongs. Now that we're part of Duke's crew I can tackle Ralph without having the wrath of the entire Yadili network on my neck for killing one of them. I did it to keep us all alive."

"But you're not going to be able to save him from the next assassin that goes for him."

"Maybe not. At least it won't be you pointing the gun at him."

He breached the gap between them and kissed her in public. Someone could see them.

Her breath caught, her lips parting, pulse racing.

He pulled back, his dark eyes intense, his voice husky. "You trusted me today by letting me take the lead in front of Duke and his men. I know it wasn't easy for you to let go of the control and let me take charge, so I appreciate it."

Their bodies were still connected at the hips. The bulge in his jeans prodded her belly as her pussy clenched.

He leaned forward so that his breath feathered her neck, and he spoke in a whisper. "So, if you're good, when we're done with Ralph, I'll reward you by fucking you."

The breath locked in her throat, and she couldn't breathe at the image his words conjured up. Her body felt as if he'd lit it on fire.

"I know you want my dick inside you. You've wanted it, from the first time at the auction. Well, you're a step closer to having it stretching your pussy."

Jeez. He was killing her. It took all her strength not to beg him to fuck her right here. She loved it when he asserted his power over her. He was the first man who didn't make her feel weakened because she bowed to his command.

Her job required discipline and control for her to be efficient. Yet, there were times she yearned for situations where she didn't have to be in control. Where she could hand over the power to someone she trusted.

That person was Ebuka.

She just needed to convince him that inside this killer was a woman whose heart thrummed for him.

He brushed his hand over her short hair before stroking the sensitive skin on her neck with his warm lips. Then he pulled away and turned, heading to the hotel entrance.

She leaned against the car, panting to catch her breath before following him.

***

The next day, they drove east to Bakili, about seventy kilometres from Opal City. With roadworks and diversions on the route, it took about two hours to arrive at their hotel.

Ebuka intended to deal with Ralph before going to the ranch to see his family.

Between meals, they spent the day going over their plans—drawing the layout of Ralph's compound, how to gain access, taking down night-time security, surveillance equipment, confronting Ralph. Xandra was brilliant, making sure they had all bases covered. Since there was only two of them, they needed to make sure there would be no surprises.

Duke's enforcer, Maddox, had ensured they had the ammunition they required.

After midnight, they left the hotel. No other cars on the road, the BMW headlights cut into the pitch blackness as Xandra drove. She parked the car a street away from Ralph's house.

"You ready?" Ebuka asked. He didn't want her here in case something went wrong.

However, she was the best person to back him up in this situation.

"Yep." She replied, stepping out of the car. The street was tree-lined and shadowed. They were parked next to a high wall so had adequate cover.

He followed, opened the boot and took the Berretta out of the rucksack, tucking it into the chest strap. He shouldered the backpack containing the spare magazines and explosives.

Xandra already had her FN Five-seveN in a holster too and a knife sheathed in her boots.

They wore matt black clothing. He'd bought black jeans, t-shirt and jacket earlier today.

He pulled down the black mask and hood, which helped him blend into the shadows of this starless night. "Let's do this."

They jogged up the hill towards Nweke's mansion at the top, keeping to the shadows, avoiding streetlamps and moving quickly.

The area around the gates was well lit. A patrolling guard smoking a cigarette leaned against the wall by the entrance. They could disable him, but someone watching the video feed from the camera would spot them.

Ebuka indicated for Xandra to follow and they skirted the perimeter wall and walked through the dense hillside, checking for a spot to exploit. There was elevated ground overlooking the side of the house. With their position on higher ground, they could clear the fence. But there was a camera positioned there.

"I've got this," Xandra whispered, pulled out the silencer and attached it to the nozzle of the FN. Then she shot at the camera.

Ebuka jumped over, checked the corners and then, whispered into the mouthpiece. "Clear."

Xandra did an acrobatic flip and landed with ease like a cat on the mown lawn, rolling to a crouch.

Ebuka checked the corner, signalled and they proceeded towards the house. There were no lights inside, but spotlights lit up part of the outside.

Footsteps made him stiffen, and he held Xandra, flattened to the wall. He listened, counting down as the guard came close. Then Ebuka grabbed his arm and twisted him into a headlock, arm around his throat. Xandra hit him in the head, and he went limp. Ebuka dragged him to a corner where he wouldn't be spotted so easily. Xandra grabbed his gun.

They jogged through the back garden past the swimming pool.

A second guard appeared. He froze, his expression dazed.

Xandra fired two rounds into him before he could move. The man went down, and an alarm blared.

"Shit. We've been made."

There was no point for stealth. Ebuka aimed the gun at the sliding door glass until it shattered. The rat-tat-tat of gunshots had them diving for cover behind the pool house.

"I'm going inside," Ebuka said, firing at a shooter who was on a balcony.

"I'll cover you," Xandra replied.

Ebuka turned, pressed lips to hers quickly. "Stay alive."

Xandra sighed. "You too, Boss."

Ebuka ran full pelt toward the door, while Xandra blasted shots at the balcony giving the shooter no time to respond. He crashed through the door just as the person at the top hit the ground.

Xandra joined him. "Got him."

That meant all the guards were dead. Only Ralph was left in the house.

They scoped out the downstairs living area before going up the stairs, Ebuka leading the way.

The house was quiet.

As they approached one of the rooms, gunshots exploded through the wooded slab sending splinters flying. They shielded and then fired together before Ebuka kicked the door in.

They stormed the room.

"Don't shoot!" Nweke crouched behind the bed, clutching his arm, his gun tossed on the floor.

A woman lay huddled in the corner, sniffling, head bowed.

"You. Get up," Ebuka said.

He didn't want to hurt an innocent. His beef was with Ralph.

Wide-eyed, she lifted her head. In the dim light, he recognized her. His insides went cold, and his muscles tensed.

"Sabina," he said in an icy tone.

Somehow he wasn't surprised she was here. A few years ago, he had discovered that the two had betrayed him right from when they were at uni.

Ralph had been envious of Ebuka's relationship with Sabina. And Sabina had dollar signs in her eyes, wanting things Ebuka couldn't give her and Ralph could.

Her eyes bulged, mouth dropping open.

"Ebuka?" Her voice shook, and she wrapped arms across her middle.

"Ebuka, is that you?" Ralph asked, scrutinizing him.

Of course, they couldn't see his face. But his voice wasn't so easily covered. He pulled the hood down and took the mask off.

"Oh, God!" Sabina cried, shrinking back.

"It's not true." Ralph shook his head.

"Oh, it's absolutely true. I came back from the dead. You thought you could kill me."

"Look, it was just a misunderstanding. We're friends, right." Ralph raised his arms.

"Friends? You fuck my wife and then send assassins to kill me. I don't need friends like you."

"It wasn't like that."

"Tell me what it was like."

"Sabina and I was just that one time back at uni. And the other thing was business. Himba wanted the land, and you refused to play ball. We could have both made a lot of money from that deal. But you have to be so fucking principled and idealistic. Wake up, man! The two of us could rule this state just like we used to rule in school days. We can still square the deal."

"You know your problem? You have always coveted what other people have. More specifically, me. You wanted my position as frat leader, and I gave it to you. You wanted my wife, and you got her. But my land? I will not give an inch of it to you or anyone else."

"You see what I mean? This is your fucking problem. You've already lost that land just like you lost everything else."

"Half of that land belongs to me, and you know I was going to get it with the divorce," Sabina shouted.

"That's where you're both wrong." Ebuka lifted his gun and fired two shots into Ralph's chest. "I told you I would kill you if you hurt any member of my family.

"Are you mad?" Sabina screeched, scrambling for the gun on the floor. "You're not going to get away with this!"

"Shut the fuck up!" Xandra aimed her weapon.

Suppressed shots hit Sabina between the eyes. She slumped to the carpet.

Ebuka glanced at Xandra.

She shrugged. "She was giving me a headache."

"Come on. Let's get out of here," Ebuka said, puffing out a breath.

Somehow, he didn't exactly feel better, even though he'd had his revenge.

Ralph and Sabina had been a part of his life for so long. It was hard to break the connection in this manner.

But he was relieved his family would be safe. That was more important to him than anything else. He'd promised his father he would keep them secure. A promise he would never break.

Now he had to go home and see them.

When they got back into the car and headed down the hill, the eastern horizon had a hint of dawn's grey.

TWENTY-SIX

THE DRIVE to the ranch was quiet. Njoku farms was a little over an hour from the city. Yet it seemed like ten hours.

Xandra's gut churned, and her grip on the steering wheel tightened. It was unlike her to feel any anxiety or fear. She glanced at Ebuka whose gaze was fixed out of the window.

He hadn't said anything since they left Nweke's house. His expression was pensive, brows pulled in. Occasionally he would tap his left index finger on his bottom lip.

Was he reflecting on what they had done earlier? Did he regret killing his former best friend and wife?

As far as Xandra was concerned, those two deserved what they got after what they had done to Ebuka. And once he had shot Nweke, she had to shoot Sabina.

For one thing, they couldn't leave her as a witness. And Xandra didn't want Ebuka to live with the guilt of shooting his scheming bitch of a wife.

Ebuka wasn't used to killing people, nor was he cold-hearted. He cared about others too much.

So Xandra had done it for him. Her gift to him. Now she had to get him home to his family.

Then, she would go to Jokogi and face the double trouble that was coming on his behalf. Because there was no doubt about it.

Once news of Nweke's death got out and coupled with Xandra not killing Duke Odili, Himba would be out for blood.

Xandra had to go and face her sponsor and keep Ebuka out of the line of fire. It was better that way.

Ebuka wouldn't want someone like her in his life permanently. He was too good a person.

She would only bring more trouble to his doorstep.

Sitting with him in the truck, knowing what lay ahead, proved more difficult than she'd realized. Throat sore, her chest ached, and her body went cold. This feeling, this sadness, was alien. Strange. Something she had never encountered before.

Was this grief?

How could she be grieving when the man sat next to her in the car?

Yet, it felt like he was already lost to her. As if this journey to the ranch was just the final step to their separation.

She had dealt with physical hurt before. But this emotional pain was almost debilitating. What was wrong with her?

She was Xandra. There wasn't anything she couldn't handle. Anyone she couldn't leave.

She just had to concentrate on getting Ebuka home. Period. She kept her gaze out of the windscreen.

The landscape provided an occasional escape from the gloomy thoughts. The scenery was breathtaking where the highway cut through thick emerald vegetation and swerved around the edge of the mountain roads.

Until she met Ebuka, she hadn't paid much attention to the scenery except for how it aided her work. Now she appreciated these things because they were simply there.

"Do you think I should call the ranch?" Ebuka asked.

The tension in her shoulders loosened on hearing his voice for the first time in an hour.

Damn. She was going to miss the quiet huskiness, the sexiness of his voice.

She glanced at him. "No. I don't think it's a good idea. Remember they don't know where you've been for months. It's just a few more minutes, and you'll see them."

From the landmarks, they weren't far.

"Yeah. You're right. It's just that I've been thinking about all the questions they'll ask, and I'm not sure I can answer them all."

"I know. It will be tough and a big shock for them to see you after all this time. But let's just take it one step at a time. They'll be pleased to see you alive and well." Considering he was supposed to be dead; his family's relief would be palpable.

"Yes, they'll be pleased."

At the archway announcing Njoku Ranch and Farms, she got off the highway onto the dusty road leading to the house. The tension in her body tightened. Ebuka would feel a double whammy of excitement and apprehension at what would happen once they arrived.

She was thrilled about seeing Ginika and the place again. She also had knots in her gut about what would come after the euphoria of the reunion had died down.

The stones on the road made the truck bounce as they approached the house. The place didn't look any different. The stone-wall house, the barns and paddock with the horses.

Ebuka watched everything as if taking in the details and checking for anything out of place.

A young woman in jeans and t-shirt stepped onto the stone porch of the house as the car rolled onto the gravel and stopped.

"Ginika," Ebuka whispered as he opened the door before she killed the engine and counted a few heartbeats before stepping out.

Ginika tilted her head to the side as she watched Ebuka approach. She looked at him as if he was a stranger. Granted, Ebuka had changed. His head had been shaved and only started growing back since he'd been with Xandra. His hooded top and leather boots were more appropriate for a biker than a ranch owner.

At the bottom of the stairs, he shoved the hood down and said, "Gigi, it's me."

"Ebuka?" she said in a low voice, a frown on her face.

He nodded. "It's me."

"Ebuka!" she screamed and leapt across the porch and down the stair, jumping into his arms.

"Is this really you?" she said as she pulled back to look at his face and then hugged him again. "Mama! Mama!"

Ebuka carried her up the steps. An older woman in a green dress and black headwrap came out of the house.

"What's going on?" the woman asked.

"Mama, it's me, Ebuka," he said as he put Ginika down.

The woman stepped back as if she'd seen an apparition. "Ebuka, nwa m?"

"Yes, Mama."

Tears flooded her eyes as she stood rigid for a few seconds then took a step towards him. "Oh, God. You're alive."

"Yes."

She clutched her arms around him so tight and wept. "We thought you were dead."

All three of them hugged.

Taking the bags out of the boot, Xandra stood on the gravel, watching them. The display of emotion and affection was more than she had ever witnessed. An inexplicable weird sensation passed through her.

On the one hand, she was pleased to see them reunited. On the other hand, she had to be prepared to let Ebuka go. These people needed him more than she did.

His mother stepped back, wiping her face. "Where have you been all this time?"

"Let's go inside, and I'll explain everything," Ebuka replied.

The women nodded, and his mother held onto his hand as if he would disappear if she didn't.

"Who's this?" Mama asked.

Ebuka turned. "This is Xandra. She helped to bring me home."

Her chest constricted and she puffed out a relieved breath. She had been worried about how he would introduce her to his family. He had chosen to paint her in a good light.

"I know you, don't I?" Ginika asked, her face furrowed in a frown.

"Yes, we met months ago when I came to work here." Xandra had worn long hair and makeup to disguise her face. But it seemed the woman had an eye for details.

"OMG! Allie." Ginika hugged her tight. "I thought I'd never see you again. Come in out of the sun."

Xandra followed them into the cool house. Seeing the cream walls and antique furniture held such familiarity almost like home. She left the bags in the hallway before entering the living room.

Ebuka was already sitting down next to his mother on a sofa. Xandra sat on the adjacent one by Ginika.

Mrs Njoku insisted Ebuka explain what had happened and he told them about what happened after they dropped Ginika to the airport, the night the assassins came to the house. He'd been shot in the process. He spoke about losing his memory, waking up in a strange place with men watching over him. He didn't go into details.

They listened, cried, hugged him and cried some more.

When everyone seemed less emotional, Ebuka asked about the ranch while Ginika served drinks and finger food.

Seeing Ebuka and his family happy again, Xandra decided it was time to put her plans into action.

"I'm going to head back into town now," she said and stood.

They all turned, and Ebuka met her gaze. He looked shocked. "You're going?"

"Yes, I'll stay in a hotel in town."

"No, you can't." He stood.

She raised a brow. "I don't want to intrude in your family time. You have a lot to catch up on."

She was a fool to think she could ever share in what they had. It was too good, too wholesome. She didn't want to taint it with her life. With blood.

"Nonsense." He gripped her hand. "You're staying here with us. You're not intruding. This is my home. Ginika and Mama don't mind having you here."

"No, we don't," Ginika chipped in. "Come on. I'll show you to your old room."

"Okay. Thank you."

Xandra followed her up the stairs and to the light and airy room she'd stayed in the first time she came to the ranch.

"Thanks again for letting me stay," she said, dumping the bag beside the bed.

"No. We owe you a lot of thanks for bringing back Ebuka to us. You don't know what you've done for us. We are totally in your debt. Thank you." There were tears in Ginika's eyes as she hugged Xandra.

A lump lodged in Xandra's throat and her chest constricted. Then Gigi stepped back.

"I'll leave you to settle in," she said with a smile before walking out of the room.

Xandra realized that the best thing she had ever done was keeping Ebuka alive and bringing him home to his family. She had done it for him. For Ginika. For his family.

And she was going to eliminate the threat to his family, permanently.

TWENTY-SEVEN

THAT NIGHT, Xandra packed her things, and then she wrote a note explaining where she'd gone and the reasons for what she was about to do.

She waited until she was sure everyone was asleep before pocketing the syringe with a dose of sedative and the letter, then walking across to Ebuka's room and knocking gently.

She heard footsteps before the door handle twisted and the wooden slab swung inwards.

"Are you okay?" he asked, looking concerned in the dim light from his nightstand.

"Yeah. Can I come in and speak to you?"

"Sure." He stepped aside.

She strode in, and he shut the door. Turning around, she stepped up to him until he leaned against the door, a slow grin spreading across his face.

She leaned in and kissed him slowly, brushing her lips against his. Aside from a soft gasp, he didn't take over. Just let her taste him the way she wanted. With her tongue, she traced the edges of his firm lips, enjoying the contours, inhaling his clean scent. It seemed he'd been in the shower recently.

She pressed against him, chest-to-chest, hips-to-hips, grinding gently. She moaned as she did, body getting inflamed. Her tongue probed his mouth, and he opened for her. She delved in, tasting fresh mint and man.

Groaning, one of his hands landed on her hip while the other fisted the hair at her nape and tugged.

"God, Xan. I don't think I can wait any longer to be inside you."

His words reminded her of what she needed to do, and she closed her eyes briefly. When she opened them, she met his gaze, schooling her expression.

"I'm sorry, Ebuka. I came to say goodbye."

"What?" His hand slackened in her hair, and she missed his grip.

Hand in her pocket, she unclipped the cap on the syringe and lifted it behind Ebuka. "I shouldn't be here."

He didn't see the syringe until it was too late, as she plunged it into the junction of his neck and shoulder. His eyes went wide for a couple of seconds before his lids closed, and his body sagged against hers.

She carried him across to the bed and laid him out on his stomach. She arranged the items from the leather kit pouch she needed on the bedside unit.

Then she cut through his t-shirt with a knife so she could see the caramel skin covering his vertebrae. She pressed on the ridges until she found what she needed.

With a scalpel, she cut a small incision into his skin. Blood welled up as she pulled out the little tracking chip embedded in his dermis. She cleaned out the cut, stitched it up and dressed it to allow it to start healing before he woke up. She stretched him out properly in bed and covered him up with the sheet. Then she packed up everything she'd used and tidied up.

Finally, she sat at the edge of the bed and pulled out the letter, placing it on the bedside table, using the base of the lamp to hold it in place so that it didn't get knocked over and missed.

She caressed the skin on Ebuka's cheek before pressing her mouth to it. She felt a pang of longing as she stood and walked out of his room. But she didn't look back. She couldn't. If she did, she might not leave.

She had to leave. Because trouble was coming from Himba and she didn't want Ebuka tangled in it. She would take the heat for him.

Returning to the room, she took her bag and walked out of the house as quietly as possible. She tossed the bag onto the seat and climbed into her car. Then she started the engine and drove out of the ranch, hoping that no one woke up and went to investigate. Even if they did, they wouldn't be able to wake Ebuka for a few hours. That would provide all the time she needed.

By the time the sun had risen, she was on the Jokogi region limits. Instead of feeling relief at the actions she'd taken, she felt restless.

Her chest felt hollow, and she was fatigued. Crushed under a weight. She needed penance.

She stopped the car at a petrol station and sent Osagie a message. He'd ended their arrangement, but he'd kept in touch, and hopefully, he would be open to renegotiating their terms.

Need to confess. Open to your terms.

She didn't get a response until she was a few streets from her house. She stopped in front of her house and checked the message.

Tomorrow. 8 pm.

She typed a quick reply. *Can't wait. Urgent.*

A response pinged back immediately. *Today. 2 pm.*

Exhaling in relief, she got out of the parked car and took her bag. She needed to grab somethings before heading for Lori Osa. No point parking the vehicle properly.

She typed another message. *Thank you.*

It wasn't until she punched the code to unlock the front door that she realized something was wrong. The clicking sound she heard was different from the one to open the door.

Something was wrong.

She ran down the path just as the house lit up with a big ka-boom, the blast lifting and smashing her right onto the tarmac.

Slightly dazed, she managed to duck as a second explosion went off and fire blazed.

TWENTY-EIGHT

EBUKA WOKE to a nasty headache and pain in his body. For a moment, he thought he was back in the hell of the slave house until he opened his eyes to bright sunlight and recognized the room.

Why was he lying on his stomach? He didn't usually sleep in this position. Had he been drinking last night? Nothing that required this level of a hangover.

He rolled over, and the pain in his back increased. He staggered off the bed, toward the mirror in the closet. Twisting to look, he saw the white surgical dressing taped to his back.

What the hell?

A wave of nausea rolled through him, and he returned to flop on the bed. After a few inhales and exhales, he felt better. He pushed off the bedside table, and his fingers brushed against the sheet of paper tucked under the lamp.

He recognized Xandra's handwriting and picked it up to read.

Ebuka,

There's no easy way to say this, so I'm just going to say it. By the time you wake up enough to read this, I will be on the way back to Jokogi.

I know you hate the fact that I'm a killer. But this is who I am. I can't change it any more than I can change the fact that I have feelings for you.

Spending time with you and Ginika on the ranch showed me another side to life, and I have no regrets for that.

You and your family gave me so much in the time I spent with you, and the least I can do is to give you back your freedom.

You had a tracker chip in your back which was placed when you were with Madaki. I was going to use it for hunting you if you ever betrayed me.

But you don't have to worry any more. I've removed the chip from you back, and you are free. You don't have to return to Laroca. You don't owe me anything.

You are free to be Ebuka Njoku, ranch owner again without fear from Nweke or Himba, now you're under Odili's protection.

Oh, and if anyone tries to paint Nweke as a nice person, there is a memory stick in the pill bottle stored in the pantry, which has evidence of his corruption. Use it as you see fit.

You are a good man, and you're better off without me staining your life with all my kills. I won't say goodbye because I know I'll see you again. Perhaps on the other side.

Obele

For a few seconds after reading the letter, Ebuka couldn't move, couldn't breathe.

The memories rushed at him. He remembered everything. Remembered Allie. Allie was Xandra.

A knock sounded on the door.

"Ebuka," his sister's muffled voice came through the panel.

"Hang on." Putting the paper down, he pulled on a shirt and a pair of jeans before walking across the room.

"Something terrible has happened. Ralph is dead," she said. "When? How do you know?"

"It's in the news on TV. He was assassinated along with Sabina, and his guards were killed too. They were both here only a few weeks ago."

"That's sad." His mother had told him about Ralph's visit. He'd offered money for the land. His mother had been considering taking the offer. Knowing the man had intended to rip his family off had alleviated Ebuka's remorse for killing him.

"Yes. It's terrible. Who could've done such a thing? I know Ralph was bad but..." She trailed off.

Pulling her into his arms, he hugged her. She'd had a crush on Nweke when they were younger. Ebuka hoped it was nothing more than a teenage crush. The man hadn't been good for her.

"Are you going to be okay?" he asked, pulling back.

She nodded. "Yes, I'm fine. It's just a shock, that's all. What about you?"

"Of course, I'm sad that they are both dead. I'm going to make a few phone calls," he changed the subject so she wouldn't see his guilt and headed towards the stairs.

"Okay. I'll see if Xandra wants some breakfast."

"Sorry. She left already. I'll explain later."

With an open mouth, she nodded. He had so much to explain. First, he had to make sure Xandra was okay.

The news would've reached Himba about Nweke's death. Coupled with the fact that Duke was still alive, Himba might want to punish Xandra again.

Ebuka couldn't let that happen.

In the office, he found his phone and dialled Duke's number.

"Mr O," he said when the man answered. "This is Ebuka. I need your help."

"What do you need?"

"I need men for a rescue mission in Jokogi. Can you help?"

"It can be arranged. Someone will contact you for details shortly." He hung up.

Ebuka paced the room as he waited, and two minutes later, Duke's right-hand man Mason called, confirming he was on a secure line.

Ebuka explained the situation and Mason agreed to meet him in Jokogi tonight with some men.

As soon as Ebuka hung up, he made travel arrangements and explained to Mama and Ginika that he had to go and help Xandra. He didn't explain the entire situation; that would have to wait until he got back. They were apprehensive, considering he had only just got home after six months.

A member of the Odili crew arrived in a car and drove him to Jokogi. True to his word, Mason was there to meet him at the designated point, along with Maddox and Bose.

They already had Xandra's home address. He didn't ask how they'd gotten it. When they arrived, the area was cordoned off with police tape, and the house was demolished, black char and rubble everywhere.

There were kids on bicycles standing across the street watching the house. Mason got out and strode to one of the boys. He returned a few minutes later.

"They say the owner of the house was outside when it exploded, and she had a fight with some men and got dragged into a van," he said.

"Shit," Ebuka blurted out, banging his hand against the back of the seat in front.

"She's still alive. So that's a good thing," Mason said. "If they'd wanted her dead, they would've killed her here."

"That doesn't reassure me," Ebuka said as his heart pounded. "The last time they got their hands on her, she ended up being set ablaze."

"Yes, we know. Norbert Gemade's handiwork. Head downtown. I think I know where they might be holding her."

Ebuka couldn't sit still, and his hands shook as the car raced across the city. They arrived at a warehouse. As they pulled up to the side of a building, another vehicle pulled up on the other side.

Men got out with guns drawn just as Mason and his men came out with their weapons.

"Mason Maduka, you're a long way from home," a man in a dark suit said.

"I could say the same thing about you, Osagie Peters. I'm here on a retrieval mission. One of ours."

"I'm here on business too. Doing a favour for a friend."

"Xandra?"

"Yes. I had a meeting with her, but she never showed. I have intel that she's being held here."

Who was this man, and why did Xandra arrange to meet him? The best thing was to get her out and then ask her.

"We're here to rescue her. You're welcome to stay as back up," Mason said before he pulled out a gun and handed it over to Ebuka. "Ready?"

"Yes," he replied.

"Stay low." He led the way, and Ebuka followed directly into a narrow passage.

Fluorescent light bulbs flickered harshly. The stained walls had peeling brown-blue paint.

Soon, gunshots exploded around him. He fired a couple of rounds and hit a man who'd been standing next to a window. Eventually, they got into the upper level of the building.

Xandra fought with another man, hand-to-hand. Her shirt was torn with bloodstains, and she had a cut on her head.

Where else was she injured?

Ebuka took a step towards her. Mason held his arm, shaking his head.

The man fighting her was a bulky muscleman, probably mid to late 30s. He looked like he could crush the lean, smaller Xandra.

Yet Ebuka had never seen Xandra like this.

She was vicious, displaying ferocity he hadn't witnessed this close. Her movements were graceful, whether she was kneeing the man in the groin, punching him with her elbow or grappling him as things crashed around them.

The man picked up a metal chair and swung it at Xandra's head.

Ebuka winced as Xan staggered back. Her opponent rushed at her, head down like a bull. Xan swivelled out of reach at the last moment, in a move that took Ebuka's breath away.

She gripped the guy in a headlock and slammed him into the wall. The man grunted, went limp and fell with a thud to the hard concrete floor.

Xandra lurched.

Ebuka couldn't hold back anymore. He hurried over and grabbed her in a hug.

"Ebuka?" She sounded shocked and leaned back.

"Yes. It's me. You didn't think you could leave like that. Did you think I wouldn't come after you?"

"I...I..." She seemed lost for words. Probably the first time he'd seen her this way.

Ebuka pulled her back in a hug and whispered in her ear. "Obele, I own you."

A gasp escaped her just as the man on the floor picked up a gun.

Ebuka pointed the one in his hand at him and emptied the rest of the magazine into him.

Xandra twisted, staring from the prone man to him with a raised brow. "You do realize you just shot Norbert Gemade, Himba's enforcer?"

Was he supposed to feel afraid for stepping into a mob war? Nah. The only fire in his vein was rage that the Gemade guy had intended to hurt Xan. His Xan.

"No one threatens what's mine and gets away with it. Come on. Let's get out of here."

He turned to find Mason and his men watching. The man he'd called Peters stood to one side.

"Osagie," Xandra said. "I'm sorry I missed our appointment."

"I can see something else came up," Osagie replied with a smile. "And it looks like you don't need me anyway."

"I hope we can reschedule the appointment," Xan said.

Osagie glanced at Ebuka before turning his gaze back to Xandra. "Of course. Send a message when you're ready."

He winked before turning and walking away.

"What appointment do you have with him?" Ebuka's voice came out low and gruff as his gut hardened at the notion that there was more between Xan and Osagie than just business.

"I'll explain later," she replied.

They headed outside. Xandra limped as she held his hand, and just before they got into the car, she said, "My things. My house. It's all gone."

"Don't worry about a thing. I'll take care of everything. You're coming home with me."

She beamed a huge smile, and for the first time in days, Ebuka knew everything would be alright.

TWENTY-NINE

"MY ADVICE is to get out of Jokogi immediately. There's no telling what Himba will do with Gemade dead. This is his city. No place is safe for you," Mason said in the car as they drove away from the warehouse.

The two men he'd arrived with were at the front of the seven-seater SUV, Mason in the middle row. Xan and Ebuka sat at the back.

"I know. I'm not planning on hanging around here," Xan said. "I just have a stopover to pick up something, and then I'm—" she glanced at Ebuka "—we're going to Lori Osa afterwards."

Ebuka raised a brow but didn't say anything.

"Oh? We're headed to Lori Osa too. You're welcome to ride with us." Xan looked at Ebuka again, and he nodded.

"That'll be good. Thank you," she replied.

"No problem. So where do you have to stopover?"

"Take the next right," Xan directed until the car pulled into the parking lot for a storage facility thirty minutes later.

Ebuka got out of the car with her. They strode across the darkened lot silently. Xan punched a code in the door to enter the unmanned entrance. Their footsteps echoed in the narrow corridor as the lights came on automatically. Then she stopped in front of a door, entered another code, and it popped open.

Next to a small table was a silver 4-wheel cabin case. She lifted it to the table and entered the code to open it. Inside were ID cards, passports and cash on top of clothes.

"Are those yours?" Ebuka asked. "I mean, I know they're yours. Why do you have them in a storage facility?"

She ripped off the torn blood-stained shirt. "As well as safe houses, I have items in storage in different locations, in case I need to get away at short notice."

Ebuka's throat constricted, and he nodded as she pulled on a clean top.

This life she lived, having to be always on the alert and moving, couldn't be easy.

He only had one home. The ranch. Most of his memories and belongings were there. He couldn't imagine leaving a piece of himself anywhere else.

Then again, a piece of him lived in Xandra, and wherever she went, she'd carry that piece of him.

"You're going to come and live at the ranch with Ginika and me and Mama. It is your home. Our home."

She gasped and turned to stare at him with mouth open. She scrubbed a hand over her head, mussing up the hair. "You want me to come and live with you at the ranch? After everything? Are you sure?"

He stepped up, crowding her into the corner. "Of course, I'm sure. We belong together. You are mine. My obele."

"I..." She scrubbed a hand over her face as if she struggled to form the words. This was a first. The Allie he'd met had been able to express herself freely.

"I remember you. I remember everything. I promised to take care of you." He curled a hand around her neck, using his thumb to tilt her chin so he would look her in the eyes. "You feel something for me, don't you? It's the reason you saved my life. It's the reason you put your life in danger for me."

She stiffened and tugged her head as if she wanted to wrench out of his grasp. Ebuka tightened his grip, refusing to let go.

"I don't know what I feel for you. But whatever it is, can't you see that it's going to destroy you if we stay together? I'm an assassin. I kill people for a living—"

"Every man on your list is a dead man," he cut her off, and her eyes narrowed. "But I'm alive and standing in front of you. You broke your rule for me. Not once. But twice."

"Yes, and you feel gratitude."

"Yes, I'm grateful that you didn't fulfil the contract. What I feel for you is so much more than gratitude. I know that I want to go to bed with you beside me. That I never want to wake and find you gone again. Remember what you said to me months ago. You said you wanted a relationship. You and me living together. Fucking exclusively. You're getting it. All of it."

The corner of her lips turned up. "You're serious."

"You bet I am."

"What about your family, your workers?"

He leaned forehead against her, stroking fingers on the smooth skin of her neck. "I told Mama and Ginika about us."

She pulled back, eyes wide, the corners of her lips tugging up. "You did? What did you say?"

A matching slow smile built up in him and curved his mouth. "Yes, I did. I told them I loved you and I had to find you and bring you home."

She blinked several times and sniffed. Her eyes misted over before she leaned in and kissed him.

The softness of her lips, the warmth of her body. He wanted to get lost in all of her. Instead, he tasted her briefly and pulled back, conscious of Mason and the rest of his team waiting for us.

"You're something else," Xan said.

"I could say the same about you," he replied, stepping away.

"We need to get to Lori Osa," she said as she tucked a gun into the holster and closed the case. "There's something you need to see."

"What is it?" Ebuka followed as she dragged the case out of the room and locked it.

"I need you to understand the person I am before we go back to the ranch. And the best way is to show you."

The warm night and cloudless sky seemed filled with promise as they returned to the parking lot. He stored the case in the trunk and joined Xandra in the back of the car.

"Everything okay?" Mason asked.

"Yes. Let's head to Lori Osa," Ebuka replied, leaning into the leather seat.

***

In Lori Osa, Ebuka and Xandra checked into a hotel Mason said was one of their safe places in the city, owned by the Odilis, same suite, adjoining bedrooms.

Afterwards, they hired a car and went shopping. Xandra bought a new phone and other items she needed.

Lori Osa was the biggest city Ebuka had been in—glass and metal skyscrapers, noisy, crowded pavements, exhaust fumes mixed with the smell of food from street vendors.

Back at the hotel, Xan spent most of the time, getting her new gadget up and running while Ebuka called home and spoke to his sister.

He finished the phone call and walked into Xan's room to find her still hunched over the gadget.

"What's up?" he asked, sitting on the bed beside her.

"I logged in to check if there are any new kill contracts out for you or me."

"And?"

"And nothing, which is strange. I was expecting a bounty on my head to go out immediately. But I've checked all the usual places, and there's nothing."

"Perhaps Himba is waiting until Gemade is buried before ordering anything. If I were him, I would wait until you've relaxed your guard and strike when you're least expecting it."

She nodded and stood. "I think you're right. He's going to know that I'd be expecting him to do something. I've got to think of what to do."

"No." Standing, Ebuka grabbed her arm. "We're going to think of what to do. You're not a lone wolf anymore. We're in this together. Plus, you now have the entire Odili crew as back up. Remember Mason and the rest of the guys dropped everything to come to your rescue. We need to talk to Duke. He'll know the best way to handle Himba."

"You're right." She puffed out a breath and smile. "Again."

"Of course, I am. So how about we take a shower and then you show me whatever it is you wanted to show me in Lori Osa."

"In that case, we're going to Arufin." A smile lit up her face.

"What is Arufin?"

"Oh, you'll see." She winked.

***

Hours later, Ebuka sat in an armchair in the blue room of Arufin and watched Xandra as she took her clothes off.

They had been getting dressed after showering when a knock had sounded on the door. It was the hotel concierge who'd delivered an envelope for Xandra. Inside had been a black glass card with Arufin embossed in gold cursive.

Xandra had explained the place as a club. But this was no ordinary club.

They had arrived through an impressive entrance at the side. The foyer and reception area appeared like one in a luxury hotel. A trip in the lift had taken them to this room.

He recognized some of the items in this space. The swing, the cross, the crops and whips and paddles on display. As a young man, he had discovered he had a darker side. A kinky side. He got a heady sensation from seeing someone submit to him, to his touch, to his restraint.

The moment Xandra has allowed him to subdue her at the cabin, he'd known she had complementing desires. But he hadn't expected this.

When she was naked and had put her clothes in the wardrobe, she walked to a dark, latticed box and sat on the bench, her head bent forward.

She has asked him to just watch and not say anything. Although he had questions running through his mind, he didn't voice any of them.

A single knock sounded on the door, and then it opened. A man walked in wearing the black flowing robe of a priest. What was a priest doing here?

He turned his head, and Ebuka recognized him as Osagie Peters. His black Chelsea boots thudded on the hard floor as he strode to the box and sat on the other side of the latticed partitioning.

"In the name of Arufin, I will hear your confession, child," Osagie said in a low voice.

The scene was familiar but out of place. Raised a Catholic, he'd been to confession enough times to recognize what was taking place, yet he just couldn't reconcile it to what he was seeing.

"Forgive me, Father, for I have sinned. It's been seven months since my last confession," Xandra said in a regretful voice. She sounded genuine. Without the visual, anyone would thing she spoke to a priest.

Ebuka listened to her listing all her sins, including the number of people she'd killed. Twenty-five. His stomach congealed. She'd taken so many lives. Some of those people were on his account.

Now Ebuka understood the burden she carried and the need to confess it. She couldn't say these things to a real priest, and this was a safe environment to unburden.

Jealousy burned across his chest that she was confessing it all to Osagie instead of him.

Although, by inviting him here today, he was included in the process.

Next time, Ebuka would be the only one with whom she shared her burdens.

"Child, is that all you have to confess?" Osagie had his head tilted and a frown on his face as if Xan had done something wrong.

"No, Father. I no longer have the sin of anger towards the nuns at the orphanage. I have a new family and people who love me." Xan looked up and met Ebuka's gaze.

In her eyes, she bared her soul to him. She had found a new family. Him.

Something clutched his heart as warmth spread through him. He nodded at her.

Osagie turned his head in Ebuka's direction and met his gaze too. He had a smile on his face. "That's good to know, child. Now say your act of contrition."

"I'm sorry for my sins. Please help me to do my penance and to do better," Xan replied. "I absolve you of your sins. Go and stand before the cross to begin your penance."

Xan met Ebuka's gaze again before walking over to stand before the St Andrew's cross. Osagie didn't move for several heartbeats. When he stood and pulled off his robe, Ebuka's eyes widened.

What exactly was he going to do to Xan? Ebuka didn't want him touching Xan and certainly not while she was naked.

Osagie turned and caught sight of Xan's naked body. He stiffened, and his breath hitched. "Xandra, are you sure you want to do this?"

He sounded shocked at the extent of Xan's burn scars.

Xan turned her head to the side but didn't look back. "Yes, I'm sure."

"You will receive thirty strokes of the cane for your penance."

Too much. What would be the impact of the cane on the damaged skin of her back?

"No. I expect more. Two for every person I killed," Xan said.

"Fifty? Hell no!" Standing up, Ebuka cut in before Osagie could reply.

Osagie's mouth closed, and a smirk curled his lips as if he knew something Ebuka didn't.

Xan turned. "I know it might seem a lot to you. But I can take it. Plus, I deserve it. If you can't watch, I'm sure Osagie will let you wait in the lounge."

"To Hell with that. I'm not going anywhere. And you don't decide what you deserve. I do. I say thirty is plenty enough." Ebuka crossed his arms over his chest.

Xan's lips tightened in displeasure. "I can take fifty."

"This isn't about what you can take. This is punishment, and from now on, I'm your confessor and your punisher. I alone decide your punishment."

She glared at him as if expecting him to back down.

Ebuka cocked his head and raised a brow, daring her to defy him. Their relationship depended on her ability to defer to him when it really mattered, like now.

Of course, she could refuse. Then they would have to sit and discuss it.

No matter what happened, Osagie wasn't going to touch her. He would rip the man's arm off first.

Xandra glanced at Osagie as if expecting the man's support but got nothing from the Edo man, who seemed amused by the whole situation.

"Fine," she said finally after huffing out a deep breath.

"I didn't think I'd live to see the day Xandra would give up control completely to someone else. But I'm glad I witnessed it because I know she's in great hands. And as it happens, my job here is done." Osagie turned and extended his hand.

Ebuka took his hand and shook it briefly. "Thank you for your help."

"You're welcome. Anytime you're in Lori Osa, feel free to visit Arufin. I'll make sure the blue room is available."

Ebuka nodded.

Osagie looked at Xandra again, his expression serious. "It's a good thing you killed Gemade already. Otherwise, I would've killed him myself. Take care."

Then he was gone.

For a few seconds after his departure, Xan and Ebuka just stared at each other, as if letting the air around them to settle and get used to the new dynamics.

Ebuka waited for Xan to reject his new position in her life. To say she didn't want him here playing the role Osagie used to play.

When she didn't say anything, Ebuka pulled the t-shirt over his head and tossed it on the chair.

Xan was probably still assessing him, trying to make sure that he could handle what was to come.

Pulling his belt out of the loops, he held the buckle and the other tip in his right hand.

Xan's chest rose and fell rapidly as she watched. She understood what the belt in his hand signified. This was him and her. They didn't need whips and chains. He could provide what she needed now that he understood her better.

"What is your safe word?" he asked.

"Blue," she said with a smile.

"Blue," he repeated, returning the smile. "Turn and hold onto the cross. Do I need to restrain you?"

"No. I'll be fine." She obeyed his command.

Warmth spread across his chest as he stepped close enough to whisper in her left ear, "I'll take care of you. Ready?"

She sucked in a sharp breath and nodded.

The constriction in his chest loosened. She was his indeed. His to punish. His to protect. His to love.

Moving back, he raised his right hand and flipped the strap across her backside.

THIRTY

THE INITIAL thud and sting of the belt quickly flared into a burning sensation that spread out all over Xandra's body. Emotions welled up inside her for the first time since she'd started the confession ritual. Pressure built up behind her eyeballs. She squeezed her eyes tight, not wanting the liquid to spill out.

What was going on with her? The pain from the belt didn't hurt as sharply as the sting of a cane. So, it couldn't be the ache causing her to feel this way.

It was something more. Something linked with Ebuka. Attached to the fact that she had finally submitted. Submitted to him, to anyone, for the first time in her life.

This wasn't an act or a game. This was real.

For some reason, she wanted to bawl her heart out. All the frustration she'd felt as a child welling up now and spilling through her lids.

She didn't know when the hits stopped. Only that Ebuka was beside her hooking arms under her legs and sweeping her into his arms when she would have slid to the floor.

She should fight. Tell him she could stand by herself.

Lacking the compulsion or the energy, she allowed him to carry her to the bed instead.

He laid her face down. After a few seconds, cold salve caressed the skin of her butt and thighs.

Another first.

She had never allowed Osagie to do this. Yet, she didn't protest.

When he finished, the bed sagged as he climbed onto it and settled beside her. Then he lifted her to lie beside him.

Sighing, she settled into the warmth of his body although he still wore his trousers. She must have drifted off to sleep because she woke with a jerk.

"Shhh... It's okay, I've got you." Warm breath whispered across her cheeks.

"Was I sleeping? I'm sorry." How could she have fallen asleep on him? She'd never done that before.

"It's okay. You were exhausted. You needed the snooze."

"I don't usually sleep here." She tried to get up, but he didn't let her. "I'm sure you want to fuck."

"Xandra, punishing you is not a source of pleasure for me. It's as distressing for you as it is for you. Don't you see? You suffer. I suffer."

She pulled out of his grasp, shuffling back on the bed. "You didn't have to do it if it's not your thing."

He sat up but didn't move towards her. "Taking care of you is my thing. And you needed the cleansing of confession and punishment. Otherwise, the burden would've been too much for you. I'm here to ease your worry, soothe your pain, and lighten your load."

She sighed. He understood exactly what she needed, and he'd been prepared to do whatever it took for her to be whole again.

"Thank you," she said.

"You're welcome, obele." He stood and tugged down his jeans before he reached out his hand. "I'd like to make love to you. Will you let me do that?"

"Yes," she said, throat thick with emotion as she shuffled across the bed to stand before him.

He gathered her in his arms and kissed her, fusing their mouths in passion. She sank into him, pleasure coursing through her, erasing her tiredness and filling her with arousal.

His hand stroked her skin, and she returned the gesture.

They fell onto the bed, writhing against each other.

Breaking the kiss, she came up for air.

"I need you," he whispered as he kissed a path along her collar.

Her body trembled, blood rushing loudly in her ears. "I can't wait either."

He settled between her legs and proceeded to eat her pussy like she was a delicious meal, and he was ravenous. He stroked in and out with fingers. She spread her thighs to give him better access, moaning while clutching his head against her. Soon a fever fired in her veins, and she called out his name in ecstasy.

Then he knelt, replacing his fingers with the broad head of his dick and slammed into her wet heat.

"I missed you so much," she whimpered, wrapping her legs around his hips, pulling him in deep, hands gripping the sheets.

The sting of the belt intensifying the experience. Her body burned as he pulled out and slammed in, again and again.

"Obele, I've missed you too." His dark eyes gleamed with desire and devotion.

Their warm breaths intermingled. The air was charged with energy like sizzling electricity.

She held her breath, pulse racing.

He kissed her.

His flavour in her mouth, his solidity deep inside her, surrounding her. She had never felt this good. This euphoric. Liquid heat flowed in her veins.

He hovered above her, arms braced each side of her chest, sliding out and thrusting in, making her feel amazing. His body glistened with sweat.

She writhed against him, her body flowing in rhythm with his. She didn't feel unsafe or worried. For the first time, she was with a man and not concerned about being ambushed or being vulnerable.

Even knowing that it had been months since they had fucked—no, this wasn't fucking. Not with the way he was looking at her. He was making love to her. She felt it in every nerve ending, and her heart constricted.

He grunted as he stroked backwards and forward, the sound of flesh smacking flesh mixing with the sound of groans. Her body arched, dancing to the tune he played.

She clenched her insides around his thickness, and he groaned, tilting his head back, the muscles of his arms and neck bulging and straining.

He looked amazing. Fucking sexy.

She remembered their time on the island and all those months apart. Now they were making up for all those lost times. She was going to make sure they got intimate whenever the opportunity came along. She wouldn't miss out on other chances to be with him like this.

He reached between their slick bodies, caressing her clit with his callused fingers. Another wave of heat sizzled along her nerve endings as a moan ripped from her throat.

He increased the speed, driving all the way to the hilt and sliding out, his balls hitting her ass.

"Obele, you're amazing," his voice came out raspy as he stroked harder into her.

Pleasure spiked, spreading out to her extremities.

"Boss...please," she begged, unable to hold on longer.

"Nye m ya," he ordered.

Euphoria ripped through her like a tidal wave. He kept stroking, drawing out her orgasm. Her body shook uncontrollably, and emotions welled through her, making her eyes water.

Ebuka's heat surrounded as he brushed his lips against hers.

"You are my everything. I love you," he whispered.

A lump wedged in her throat, preventing her from speaking. She didn't know what to say. Didn't know how she felt.

Then he was back on his knees, gripping her hips and fucking her like the boss he was. His expression was fierce as he slammed into her again and again.

"This is what you do to me, Xan. I can't get enough of you. I'm never going to let you go." He punctuated each sentence with ramming in and pulling out.

"Fuck! Xan." He growled the words and bowed his back as he filled her with his hot release. He jerked again and again; his face screwed up in a blissful expression. His chest rumbled with his grunts of pleasure.

Warmth spread through her as a smile curled her lips, knowing she'd done this to him. He was hers as she was his. This was the proof.

He slumped over her, dropping his head onto her shoulder as he gulped in a lungful of air.

This was the point of the evening where she would roll over and get into the shower to wash up and get dressed to leave.

Instead, she reached for his nape. He leaned forward as if sensing her need. Raising her head, she kissed him with everything inside of her.

She didn't want to be without him. She would kill anyone who ever looked at him or his family the wrong way.

This thing she felt. This fierce possessiveness. This band that wrapped around her heart. This emotional knot in her throat that wouldn't let her breathe properly. This overwhelming need to protect and be beside him for as long as she lived. This had to be love.

She broke the kiss, panting. Still holding onto the back of his neck, she stared into his dark eyes. "Ebuka, I love you."

He stilled as his eyes widened. "You don't have to say it."

"I do. I know I was afraid to admit it. But I don't want to miss the chance to tell you in case something happens."

"Nothing will happen."

She shook her head. "We have to be honest with each other. This life I dragged you into, it involves a lot of death. People die around me."

His eyes searched hers. "I know that. But you saved me from death."

"Yes. And I'll keep doing it for as long as I live."

"And I'll protect you every way that I can. I told you already to trust me on this."

She met his gaze and nodded. "I trust you."

Smiling, he leaned down and kissed her again.

EPILOGUE

EBUKA WAS a man of his word. Xandra's trust in him stayed valid.

After their night in Arufin, they remained in Lori Osa for another two weeks. They helped Duke Odili take down John Bull Owo, earning their places in the Odili crew.

She had been surprised at the ease with which Ebuka had taken on the role. He'd stayed and covered her during the shootout that ambushed The Baron when he'd gone to visit one of his girlfriends.

A few days later, they returned to Bakili. The welcome from Ebuka's sister and mother had been overwhelming. More than she had expected. Within days, Xandra was working on the ranch as if she had always been a part of it. It was now her home.

She worried about Himba and what actions he'd planned to take in retaliation for the death of his enforcer. She checked the listings regularly for any kill contracts, but none had her name or

Ebuka's. Still, she couldn't believe the man would be willing to let bygones be bygones.

Two months later, Ebuka and Xandra were in Opal City for the meeting of the heads of the regional cartel families. Xandra wouldn't usually attend such a gathering, but Duke had invited Ebuka and her along. She presumed he'd be making the official announcement that they were now part of his team.

Before the main meeting started, Duke introduced her to other members of his crew she hadn't met. She'd already met Mason and Maddox. But his other capos Rocha and Charles were new to her. Apparently, Rocha was Mason's brother. However, she disliked Rocha instantly. There was something in the way he looked at her with disapproval.

The person who drew her attention most, though, was Carla Owo, now Carla Odili. Intriguing. John Bull's daughter was now part of Duke's family.

After the meeting of heads concluded, Mason directed Xandra and Ebuka into a room where Don Tiye Himba sat along with Zoe.

Ebuka sat in a chair beside Duke and Xandra stood at the back of it. Mason sat in a chair the other side of Duke.

"What is this about?" Don Himba asked, not even bothering to acknowledge Xandra.

Only Zoe met her gaze briefly. But her expression stayed blank. Xandra hadn't spoken to her since they discussed the hit on Duke. Now they stood on opposing sides.

"I asked for this meeting so that we can discuss the matter of Gemade's death," Duke said.

Himba's jaw tightened. "There's nothing to discuss. Those responsible for Norbert's death will pay for it with their lives."

There it was. The threat Xandra had been expecting. Her body stiffened, and her hands balled into fists. She couldn't see Ebuka's face, but she was sure he felt the same way she did, although he didn't show it outwardly.

"I propose there be no further bloodshed on this matter unless you propose to start a war between the families," Duke said in a calm voice. "Then again, I suppose you declared war when you allowed one of your men to be used as a weapon by The Baron against me."

Himba's face went ashen, and some of his righteous anger seemed to dissipate.

Duke had him by the balls. Raising a finger against another member of the prominent five families amounted to sacrilege and the punishment was severe.

Because Xandra had worked for Himba when she had been sent to kill Duke, Himba was responsible, and Duke could call any forfeit he wanted. Or other members of the families could vote to expel Himba which would make him a crime boss without territory.

A generation ago, the families called a truce amongst themselves, choosing to collaborate and reap the rewards of a world at their mercy instead of fighting for turf. That truce had remained until now.

"So, while Gemade's death is unfortunate, I'd say it makes us even since you drew first blood," Duke continued.

"What are you saying? That I should let it go?" Himba seemed to have recovered some of his fury.

"That's exactly what I'm saying. The people you seek are now part of my family. They are under my protection. If anything happens to them or members of their family, I will take it as a declaration of war by you, and I won't hesitate to take you and your entire operation out. You know Don Sylvester supports me on this, and the other members of the Families will back me up. And I know the northern families will be interested to know about your involvement in Yahya's death."

Himba swallowed. Duke had him over a barrel.

Duke had just been declared the boss of Lori Osa which made him in charge of the largest territory available. The Baron's former operations were now under his control. He had significant influence, considering the landmass he controlled was equivalent to a small country.

Not to mention that if the northern cartels ever found out Himba had ordered Yahya's death, he'd have his hands full with a war with them.

There was only one option available for Himba. The alternative was death for him.

"You don't expect me to just accept those terms without any compensation for my loss," Himba bit out.

Duke tilted his head as if thinking about it. Himba was trying not to lose face by just giving in to Duke's demand. But Xandra couldn't see what Duke would offer that would assuage him.

"I'm willing to forgo the ten percent due to me from your operations in Jokogi. You keep total control, and you let this matter drop here and now." Duke straightened.

"You're willing to give up your share?" Himba looked sceptical.

Jokogi was under the Lori Osa territory, which meant anyone looking to do business in the area would pay Duke ten percent to trade peacefully. Xandra didn't know of any boss who would give up such an income, so she was as surprised as Himba.

"Yes. You can take it as my compensation to you for your loss."

"Then we're agreed." Himba stood and extended his hand.

Duke stood and took his hand.

Xandra exhaled in relief as she placed a hand on Ebuka's shoulder. He clasped his hand over hers.

Himba didn't stay after that and headed out. He didn't even spare her a glance. Zoe did, though, and there was a small smile on her lips.

As soon as they left the room, Ebuka stood and came around to pull Xandra into a hug. "I told you I'd get it sorted."

Xandra nodded as she clutched his shirt, and her throat clogged up. All her worry about keeping him alive dissipated.

He'd kept his word. He'd done what was needed to keep them alive.

When they pulled apart, Duke was the only one in the room. He had a smile on his face. "Go home. Spend time with your family. Take a few days. Do what you need to do. Setting up the Lori Osa operation is going to need a lot of hands-on-deck. I might need your help sooner rather than later."

"Of course, Duke," Ebuka replied. "We'll be there whenever you need us."

"Good. I'll see you soon," he said before walking out.

Xandra turned to Ebuka.

"Are you sure about doing this?" She waved a hand to encompass everything.

She was an assassin. A killer. She didn't deserve the kind of love Ebuka and his family had given her. Then again, she was a lucky woman. She shouldn't be alive after all the attempts on her life. Still, here she stood with a man who needed her as much as she needed him. She would make the most of each day with him.

He grinned. "I've never been surer of anything in my life. Come on, obele. Let's go home."

"Whatever you say, boss." She followed him.

His chuckle filled the air, spreading warmth through her.

She loved that sound as much as she loved the man and looked forward to hearing it every day for as long as she lived.

Thank you for reading Killer of Kings. If you enjoyed this story please leave a review at the site of purchase.

Want to read an epilogue? Scan the QR code to receive bonus content.

Visit www.kirutaye.com and sign up to Kiru's newsletter to receive book news via email. Join her forum for freebies and exclusive sneak peeks.

YADILI SERIES
Prince of Hearts
Killer of Kings
Bad Santa
Rough Diamond
Tough Alliance
More books coming soon.

Keep reading for a special sneak preview at ***Bad Santa, Yadili series #3*** by Kiru Taye

BLURB

Although Gina Badu is a good girl all-year-round, she knows her Christmas wish will never come true. Not with a recent divorce, late parents and a sister who courts trouble.

Then Santa abducts her in the middle of the night. Except this Santa is terrible—a silver fox of a tattooed fallen angel.

Osagie Peters is a ruthless, cartel boss whose dark soul threatens to consume her. He scares her as much as he fascinates her. It seems he's got her on the naughty list. Still, there's a chance she might have a Merry Christmas after all.

BAD SANTA – CHAPTER ONE

"SIR, THE PARTY PLANNER, for the Odilis' New Year's Eve dinner party, wants to know if you will have an escort. She is finalising numbers and seating arrangements. What should I tell her?"

It took two words to ruin Osagie Peters' day.

Party planner and dinner party. Actually, four damned words but hey, he could be excused for miscounting.

He didn't have a university degree, as some people liked to remind him. Polite society didn't want him. But they loved the taxes he paid, loved that he employed people, and loved that his businesses attracted visitors, contributing to local tourism and the economy.

Nicknamed the 'King of Clubs', Osagie owned the most popular party venue in the country and perhaps, the African continent. Club Arufin was the crown jewel in his nightclubs chain, and almost a million partygoers walked through the doors annually. He controlled one hundred franchisees and many more associates. Anyone who wanted to run a successful club in the region paid dues to him.

Yet, the word 'party' might as well be a trigger. Mention it in Osagie's presence and his stomach clenched hard, while his body temperature elevated.

He maintained outward calm at his assistant, Remi's question.

He had no problems with the upcoming event.

Duke Odili was the new boss in town. Almost a year ago he'd eliminated John Bull Owo and his son Marlon in a cartel war, married the Owo heiress, Carla and taken over the Owo operations in Lori Osa and surrounding regions. He'd ascended into the head of the Odili family's position in the megacity, a coveted rank in the Yadili network.

With Duke's promotion from 'Underboss' to 'Boss', he'd extended a hand of friendship to Osagie. They were working on an alliance that would protect their interests and expand their reaches.

To Osagie's knowledge, the party was Duke's way of cementing the new alliances. He would need them to survive in the shark-infested waters of doing business in Lori Osa.

Although Osagie was at least fifteen years older than Duke, he appreciated the invitation and respected the man. In this game, age meant jack all. What mattered was the clout, connections, and cash a person brought to a deal. Duke had all three, and as the son of a late statesman, he was also political nobility.

However, the event drew a twinge of discomfort, reminding Osagie of his one regret—he didn't have his family close. Or rather, what should have been his family.

More specifically, his son.

His ex-wife, though. She could burn in Hell, after what she did to him. She was lucky not to have become a late wife.

He had no illusions about the kind of person he was. He was not a nice man. He'd been on Santa's naughty list for too many years.

However, he could never live with himself if he'd hurt the mother of his child.

Not even after he'd caught her in bed with another man. She'd begged for her life. Her excuse had been that he wasn't educated and her family hadn't approved of him because of it. She'd felt under pressure and had succumbed to the affair with another man.

Educated ko, pressure ni, as his half-Yoruba business partner had said in disdain at the time.

What about his love for her, his willingness to do anything for her?

What about her loving him back, and telling her snobbish family to go to Blazes?

As an orphan, he'd wanted a family of his own so much. He would have done anything to provide for and protect them. He'd been young and stupid enough to believe that a woman from a different background would return his affection.

Instead of love, she'd betrayed him and taught him valuable lessons. He would never be good enough for polite society, so why bother trying to appease them.

Instead of slitting hers and her lover's throats, he'd walked out of the house and divorced her.

She'd remarried and had more children.

He would've loved to keep Odigie, his eighteen-month-old son, with him. Still, he'd accepted the boy had been too young to be without his mother at the time.

That had been twenty years ago.

In the early years of their separation, they'd rotated who had custody during the summer, Easter, and Christmas holidays. He never missed birthdays or special occasions if he could help it.

Now Odigie was old enough to choose where he wanted to spend his holidays. The boy hadn't mentioned if he would visit soon, although they communicated regularly via facetime.

Osagie wouldn't dictate or beg for a visit. If his son preferred to spend the festive season with his other family, so be it.

It didn't stop the hollowness in his chest or the fatigue descending on him. He didn't feel sociable or interested in parties.

As for female companionship, while there'd been sexual encounters, he hadn't entertained any candidates for the next Mrs Peters. He wouldn't give his heart away again.

Instead, he'd sunken his time and energy into running his businesses both legit and not-so-legit. He had neither the time nor the inclination to keep a steady lover.

"Sir?" Remi's tentative voice pulled him from his reverie.

"Tell her I'll have a companion." His contact list was full of options.

The sound of the opening door caught Osagie's attention.

Idehen Cruz walked in, his expression grim, and his voice gruff. "Remi, excuse us."

Osagie rubbed his hand on his temple. His friend's countenance didn't bode well, and Osagie wasn't in the mood for any bad news.

Remi shifted in the leather chair across the desk, eyes widened and alarmed. "Will that be all, sir?"

"Yes, thank you," he said, glad he'd already given out instructions before his friend's arrival. He lifted the bottle of water and poured into a glass, sipping the cold liquid before taking a deep calming breath.

The woman looked uncomfortable as she packed up the folder and retreated hastily.

Osagie stared at his oldest friend and business partner who marched to-and-fro, at risk of burning a path through the hard-wearing carpet.

Just like Osagie, Idehen had started greying and had trimmed white facial hair against umber skin. But unlike him, his friend had a completely shaved head while Osagie had a shock of salt and pepper hair he kept cut almost to the scalp. His eyes were whisky-brown compared to Osagie's midnight-black.

Idehen was a formidable figure, broad-shouldered and at over six feet. Yet, he was generally the more mellow of the two friends, the one who made silly jokes. One of the few people who could make Osagie laugh.

Osagie was the one often described as unapproachable, the cold, calculating one and people scurried away from him before he'd even spoken.

But Idehen's warm and jovial appearance could be deceptive. Like a hurricane, he had the power to cut down a mob of men in a fight.

And right now, Idehen moved like a tornado.

They had been homeless street boys who had fought and stolen for survival, for the food in their bellies, the clothes on their back, even the places they'd lain their heads. They had been each other's keepers. Even taken care of other vulnerable children around them.

Over the years, Osagie had learned to adapt and evolve with the times like a chameleon. The key to his survival and staying relevant in an ever-changing world. He couldn't remember stepping into a classroom. Everything he'd learned had been self-taught. He'd spent most of his youth at internet cafes, reading, learning and, of course, grifting.

Idehen had been by his side through it all. A combination of savvy brain and quick-footed brawn had kept them not entirely on the right side of polite society and yet not hardcore enough to be excluded totally.

Now, Osagie grabbed glasses and a cognac bottle. He strode through a door behind his desk. The soundproof private lounge provided a haven in the bustle of a busy enterprise.

He lowered the items on the dark wood low table, removed the tailor-made jacket of his charcoal suit, hung it over the arm of the sofa and sank into the worn leather sofa.

Idehen followed, the door slamming behind him.

"What's the bad news?" Osagie poured the dark-amber liquor into the tumblers.

His friend said nothing for a few seconds that stretched painfully.

"We've been hacked," Idehen said finally, his voice gruff as if he'd been shouting all day.

"Hacked?" Osagie lifted his eyebrow and tilted his head.

"Yes. Someone hacked into our system and wired money out of one of the accounts."

Osagie said nothing while he processed the information. This wasn't the first time someone had attempted to defraud them. It came with the territory. However, not many people were brave enough to try it in the first place because the consequences were dire.

Osagie did not forgive. He'd used up his forgiveness quota on his ex-wife.

Anyone who slighted him was punished heavily. Painfully.

"How much?" he asked, running his finger around the rim of the short glass. It helped to calm him and kept his head clear of emotions.

"Ten thousand dollars."

He didn't flinch. It wasn't the first time they'd lost money. Still, it was large enough to require a hefty penalty. He couldn't ignore it.

"How was this possible?"

Idehen balled his hand into fists. "The accounting and IT teams have felt my rage already. I think it was an internal job. One member of the team wasn't at work today."

Osagie could imagine that Idehen had blazed through the accounting team and the IT guys. Whatever the loophole would be fixed.

"Who?"

"Dani. Daniella Badu." Idehen pulled out a digital device from his pocket, tapped on the screen and slid it across the table.

Osagie picked it and stared at the photo of a woman posted on social media.

She was a software developer in the IT department. The shot was of her in a pouty selfie with heavy makeup and long hair extensions. She looked like she was performing for the camera, for an audience.

The consequence for stealing from him was severe. The staff knew him. Yet this one had dared to try. She wouldn't get away with it. If she did, others would think he had gone soft and try to steal more. And there would be those who would even attempt to take over his operations, which meant his death.

He took another sip of cognac and placed the glass on the table. His movement was precise and smooth, his expression blank.

"Find her." His voice was cold. He tapped the screen again, and another photo showed up. A different woman in a crop sports top and leggings stared at him from a reclined position on a yoga mat. Something fluttered in his chest. "Hang on. Who's this?"

He tapped on the screen to read the birthday post from earlier in the month.

This was Daniella's sister? And she'd recently turned forty years old?

The woman was stunning—oval face, brown eyes, cinnamon skin, toned abs, lean-fit body that didn't look a day over thirty. Even the long dark hair parted in the middle and packed into two low buns added a touch of cuteness.

Perfection.

Mouth moistening, he gaped at the photo, momentarily forgetting his anger at the missing money.

Idehen leaned across the table to look at the picture. "That's Dani's sister, Gina."

"Yes, I read the post," Osagie replied, annoyed at the effect the woman's image seemed to have on him.

The sisters probably colluded to defraud him and were out there, right now, spending his money and laughing at him.

His interest should be in recovering the funds and punishing the culprits. Not ogling one of the suspects, no matter how fine she was.

"The two live together down in Daware," Idehen said, lifting the drink to his lips.

"Then find both of them." Osagie pushed the phone across the table towards his friend.

***

"Tell me again why we're doing this instead of sending the boys to handle it?" Idehen asked, two days later, as he parked the SUV on a quiet residential street and killed the engine.

Good question.

Osagie sat in the front passenger seat. Still dark, they had driven about an hour across the city to this estate in the Daware suburb. Now, the sky was dawn grey, neither dark nor light.

They could have sent others. Their boys had investigated and reported that Daniella was nowhere to be found. Her sister, however, was here. The next step would have been to instruct the boys to take and secure the sibling until Daniella was located.

He'd imagined his men maltreating Georgina—apparently, that was Gina's full name which he preferred—and his blood had run cold.

He didn't want her injured in the process. Regardless of her status as Daniella's sister, he had no proof of her direct involvement.

The hacking and theft incidents weren't the end of the world. But it could mark the beginning of the end for Osagie. If he didn't catch and punish the culprits severely, many more thefts would follow. He had no doubt employees, and others were watching and waiting to see his response.

Mostly since there were women involved this time.

He wasn't in the business of harming the innocent. He'd sworn to adhere to certain principles no matter what—protect the weak, and touch not the innocent were two codes he stuck to amongst others.

Georgina wasn't weak. He'd watched some of her fitness videos on social media. The woman was physically and mentally strong, no doubt. However, until he could ascertain her involvement, he would treat her as an innocent—someone outside of his tainted world.

So, the only people he trusted with her welfare were in this car right now.

"Some jobs are best done yourself," Osagie rationalised.

"Mmhmm." His friend didn't sound convinced. "Is that the only reason?"

Osagie's face tingled. He stiffened, annoyed for feeling like the hungry boy caught trying to steal food. Perhaps he shouldn't be concerned about the woman's welfare. Still, he had no reason to feel embarrassed for trying to protect an innocent. Once Dani was found, he had no business sitting in the car outside the woman's house.

"What other reason is there? If they mess it up, we don't get our money back."

"Just saying." Idehen shook his head as a grin split his face. "We became big men, so others can do this kind of shit."

"Big men, huh?" His friend's humour made Osagie chuckle. "Seriously though, don't you miss this?"

"This?" His friend turned to look at him.

"Yes, this." Osagie waved his hand to indicate their current situation. "The thrill of the hustle.

Picking a mark, planning, and executing the score. Avoiding detection."

"Sometimes, I miss it. But we were struggling for survival in those days. This is not the same thing. This is a matter of respect and that Dani woman needs a serious lesson in respect. You don't spit in your fucking eating bowl."

His friend's outburst sparked questions in Osagie. Was there more going on than Idehen had revealed?

Before he could ask, movement across the street distracted him. His pulse rate spiked, and he leaned forward.

The metal pedestrian gate to Georgina's two-bedroom ground-floor apartment building cranked open.

"Here we go," Idehen muttered.

Georgina came out, dressed in another crop sports top and leggings combo with brightly coloured trainers, hair in a low bun. She pulled the barrier shut and jogged along the pavement of the hundred-residence Highgate Estate. Her running shoes pounded the tarmac as she headed across the road, squeezing between parked cars to go toward the field.

"Check out the apartment. See if there's anything that indicates where her sister's gone. I'll follow her and let you know when she heads back." Osagie reached for the door and stepped out.

"Right." Idehen exited the car, clicking the fob to lock it. "Happy hunting."

Osagie grinned at the old remark. They used to say that to each other when they were younger men hustling for pay-days. He tugged the hood of the black long-sleeved jersey over his head and entered the park.

Ahead, trees stood as unmoving sentries and bushes demarcated the adventure playground's shadows from the ghost mist hovering over the sizeable glittering pond. A chilly Harmattan breeze whipped dust and the leaves in the trees.

It was damned cold. His head-to-toe kit provided cover, and the run would warm him up. Still, he would rather jog on a treadmill than exercise with the sand in his eyes.

It seemed Georgina preferred the opposite. She co-owned a gymnasium not far from here. Yet, according to the report he'd received, she used the park at dawn daily, adding to the things about her that fascinated him.

Hence the reason he was braving the brisk weather on a December morning. He kept his distance from her, staying out of sight until he got the lay of the park. He expected more people, joggers, dog-walkers, or people just cutting-through to different destination.

However, after ten minutes, he spotted only one other person. Perhaps, the regular users had travelled for the festivities since it was less than a week until Christmas.

Keeping to the open space, Georgina completed two laps before she paused to stretch her warmed muscles. Then she continued her third lap. Her movement was fluid and entrancing, the strides of an athlete.

He took advantage of the deserted location and headed in her direction but maintained the gap.

As if she sensed his presence, she glanced back.

His drab black outfit would make him appear indistinguishable in the grey light and with the distance. He wore long-sleeves to hide his tattoos. Only his face and hands were visible.

Hopefully, if Idehen found her sister's location, he wouldn't have to contact Georgina.

And Osagie would be rid of this constant lust. From the moment he'd seen her photo on Idehen's phone, she'd lit a fire in his veins.

But Georgina looked too sweet and clean for his twisted life. And he didn't fuck around with lovely and naïve. So yes, he was keeping his distance.

He was only here because she may have colluded with her sister to steal from him. He had to keep his mind on the goal.

Georgina gave him a second curious look. Then she turned away, adjusted her earbuds, fiddled with the phone attached to a pack on her back and increased her running speed. She did another set of laps, avoiding the dark, dense foliage of trees.

She disappeared behind some shrubs, and he stayed back, not wanting to spook her. Or make her return home too early. Idehen needed time to search the house.

Someone should have warned her about wearing headsets while running in a secluded park before sunrise. She didn't know who could be lurking about like he was, even if this was supposed to be a secure neighbourhood.

After five more laps, she slowed down, pulled a water bottle from the pack's latch, and took a drink.

Watching her throat ripple as she drank made him thirst, for cool refreshing water, for the salty taste of her skin.

Damn, he had it bad.

Putting the bottle aside, she took a couple of steps and stumbled.

Unable to keep away, he sprinted towards her, discarding caution.

She spread her arms, righting herself. Then she froze and stared at him with genuine appreciation until he stopped beside her.

"Are you okay?" he asked, his voice unexpectedly husky. He searched her face, checking her over. He couldn't explain this need to be near her. To make sure she was unharmed.

Up close, her photos didn't convey her brilliance.

Although he was taller and worked out regularly at the gym, she outclassed him. Her ripped abs alone could put him to shame.

She was beautiful and knowledgeable. He'd discovered she was studying for a Master programme. He hadn't even finished secondary school.

Not to mention that he was older and she looked like she would look great with one of those younger celebrities hanging off her arm.

She was a goddess.

He was in awe and would die to worship at her altar even for one night.

Swallowing hard, she bobbed her head, as if unable to work saliva into her mouth. Sheens of sweat beaded her deep-arched brows and the top of her bow-shaped lips.

She opened her mouth and closed it, seeming to struggle with breathing. Her body swayed.

"You don't look well. Lean forward," he instructed and reached out, hand sliding over her shoulder gently. "Breathe deep."

She leaned in, gulping air.

"Have a drink." He stepped close, reached for her pack, and withdrew the bottle of water. In protective mode, his actions were without timidity or uneasiness.

"I'm all right." She took the bottle off him and drank. Then she looked up at his face, scrutinising him. "Do I know you?"

"No." His heart raced. He shouldn't have come this close. Now that she'd seen his face, she might be able to identify him later.

Footsteps made him turn.

A man in a Tee and shorts set slowed his jogging and marked time beside them.

"Gina, are you all right?" the stranger asked, staring at her and then at the Osagie.

Osagie's spine stiffened, and his jaw tightened. Who was the man?

"Hi, Bob. I'm okay," she replied after drawing in a shaky breath. She glanced at the Osagie and said, "I have to go."

His expression remained inscrutable, but he nodded at her.

She ran off with the Bob guy.

Osagie pulled his phone from his pocket and sent a message to Idehen.

She's heading home. One minute.

He jogged towards the car.

Idehen already sat at the driver's seat with a scowl on his face.

"What's up?" Osagie asked as he got in.

"Can you imagine? The woman is in Dubai, spending our money. I'm going to strangle her when I get my hands on her."

Osagie chuckled. He'd never seen his friend so frustrated, certainly not over any woman. "It sounds to me like you want to do more than strangle Daniella. Is there something going on between you two?"

Idehen jerked back, looking affronted. "Of course, there's nothing between that troublesome woman and me. The last time she came to me, batting her long lashes, asking for some time off. And then the money went missing the next day."

"And now you want to strangle her."

"Yes!"

"I didn't know you were into erotic asphyxiation."

"What?" Idehen did the backward jerk again, eyes bulging in a comical expression.

"Gotcha." Osagie laughed out loud. "You should see your face."

"Bastard." His friend shook his head, lips curving upwards.

"And they say I don't crack jokes." Osagie sobered when someone came out of Gina's building. "There's a complication. Georgina saw my face."

The plan had been simple.

Locate the culprits—Daniella and accomplices. Recover the cash. Mete out the punishment. Avoid collateral damage—Georgina, specifically.

Now it seemed they had an inadvertent casualty.

Idehen scrubbed a palm over his face and puffed out air. "We can't leave her. We don't want her warning Dani that we're onto her."

"I know." Osagie sighed. "This is turning into one big party."

Except they didn't laugh at the joke because it meant the one thing he'd wanted to avoid—taking a hostage. Taking Georgina.

Find out more and sign up for LAP book news:
www.loveafricapress.com/newsletter